"Cutter, we've waited too long! Give the command!"

"Woodlock, no . . . "

Woodlock snapped Redlance a glare. "They've killed more of us through the seasons than Madcoil ever did."

"All true." Redlance stepped away and released Woodlock's arms. "So do what you have to, my friend. But kill the young human first." He pointed at the child who still sniffled against its mother's leg. "I want to see if you can."

Woodlock twisted a look over his shoulder, hands tightening on the curve of his bow. There was an ice in his face that Cutter had never thought to see in this hot, infertile land. "All right . . . " Woodlock nodded slowly. "All right," he said again, more firmly.

Strongbow slipped an arrow from the quiver on his back and laid it soundlessly across Woodlock's palm. Woodlock took it without question, and fitted it against his own weapon's string. Cutter heard the stiff wood creak, dry and hard from seven summers without use, and Woodlock lifted the curve of polished wood to draw the sinew back to touch his cheek.

Prepared as he was, Cutter still jumped when the bow-string thrummed and the arrow whistled into flight. The strength of his sudden revulsion frightened him—he didn't want to watch, didn't want to see any child, not even a human's, pierced and bleeding from an elfin arrow.

He jerked forward to stop the killing . . .

The Elfquest *Series*
by Wendy and Richard Pini from Ace Books

JOURNEY TO SORROW'S END
THE QUEST BEGINS

ELFQUEST

THE QUEST BEGINS

WENDY AND RICHARD PINI

ACE BOOKS, NEW YORK

This book is an Ace original edition,
and has never been previously published.

ELFQUEST: THE QUEST BEGINS

An Ace Book / published by arrangement with
Warp Graphics, Inc.

PRINTING HISTORY
Ace edition / January 1996

ISBN: 0-441-00294-3

ACE®
Ace Books are published by The Berkley Publishing Group,
200 Madison Avenue, New York, NY 10016.
ACE and the "A" design are trademarks
belonging to Charter Communications, Inc.

10 9 8 7 6 5 4 3 2 1

THE QUEST BEGINS

CHAPTER ONE

CUTTER CROUCHED BE-side a tangle of dry branches, bow balanced across his knees, heels pressed flat to the sand as he studied each desert shadow with patience. His wide, upswept ears tracked the sounds of lizard feet across the sand, and his night-widened eyes flicked like silent moths toward the scrabble. Its spiny back bristling with some premonition of danger, the lizard skittered out of sight beneath a tumble of stones. Not that it mattered—Cutter had already deemed the little curly tail too small to be worth the bother.

Beside him, the tiny leaves of the sticker plant he'd chosen for his shelter clattered like cricket shells as his companion shook his head in irritation. Without turning to look, the elf reached over to grab the wolf's ear in one hand and pinch on it gently.

Hush, lazy-bones. He tried to send an image of Nightrunner moving his head out of the foliage if the branches tickled his ears. All he got in return was a wet wolf-snort against his wrist and a scrape of sandy claws on his back from Nightrunner's foot. The soft-edged swell of the wolf's boredom blossomed inside Cutter like a sigh.

Smiling, the elf leaned across his friend to trap Nightrunner's head beneath one elbow and roughly tousle the old wolf's mane. "What's the matter?" he asked, so softly that only he and Nightrunner could hear. "No patience for hunting when somebody else does it for you?" They weren't easy words. They made Cutter think about the two rabbits he'd caught already, and how Nightrunner probably wouldn't even finish those, no matter how long it had been since his last meal. The old wolf didn't understand the speaking, though, and Cutter suspected the whirl of thoughts connected with it were too strange for wolf-thinking to even notice. He knew he was right when Nightrunner's only reply was to toss his head and snatch a mouthful of Cutter's corn-silk hair in an invitation to play.

"Uh-uh." He nipped at the wolf's broad muzzle. "Not till we— Hey!"

Fur in his nose and the jolt of bony shoulder beneath his rib cage, and Cutter had to grab at Nightrunner's ruff to keep from tumbling over the wolf's rising back. **Do you want more food or don't you?**

Hind feet scrabbling in the dry dirt, Nightrunner cleared the sticker bush in a single awkward leap. Cutter hauled himself upright and grumbled. "I guess not."

He swung his leg across the wolf's back, and snatched the rabbits from their hanging place in the bush when Nightrunner capered past. They would be stringy, Cutter thought, sniffing at the still-warm limbs, and bitter tasting in the way everything from this desert seemed to be. He knew that wasn't what had made Nightrunner's hunger fade for the past few moons, but it helped to worry about the taste of the rabbits instead of the other things Nightrunner's narrowing frame might mean.

They headed back for the sleeping village without

Cutter consciously choosing the direction. It was still young in the evening—Mother Moon was barely half-way across the sky, with Child Moon just waking at the edge of the horizon. Cutter closed his eyes and listened to the steady *pad-pad* of Nightrunner's feet against the sand.

Time was, my friend, we could have traveled until morning at a near run the whole time. It had been barely an eyeblink of seasons since the wolf had carried Cutter to safety across this burning desert. Now, in only another eyeblink more, Cutter knew he would have to bid his friend good-bye when Nightrunner went to run with his ancestors. Who would cradle the old wolf's spirit when he finally passed on from this place of no trees and no branches? The thought bothered Cutter at times, but he never could think of an answer.

"Father! Father!"

Cutter knew the piping voice as well as he knew the dry, clean smell that brushed his nostrils ahead of it. Suntop waved from behind a pile of wind-smoothed rocks, bouncing a little with excitement before breaking into a run to join his father. Nightrunner grumbled softly, but slowed when Cutter asked him to.

"I waited for you." The young elf smiled with a brightness to match his sunny hair, squirming to seat himself across Nightrunner's back.

Cutter laced strong arms behind his son's back to hold him steady. "What's the matter, little cub? Couldn't sleep?"

Suntop shook his head with a serious, youthful sigh. "It's hard to sleep at night."

Cutter brushed a hand against his son's cheek and

smiled down into eyes as wide and blue as his own. "I know."

The scratch of sandals on the stone above them pricked his ears, but Cutter forced himself to keep looking at Suntop while he asked, "Where's your sister?"

A trill of laughter rippled down the rocks like forest water. "Here I am!" Ember landed on her father's shoulders with the force of a feisty tree cat.

Cutter made quite a show of crumpling beneath her attack. "Oh, what fearsome beast is this?" He reached around behind him to drag her on top of her brother. "Am I going to have to chew its ears off?"

The cubs tumbled together, squealing with delight at the threat. "Did I surprise you?" Ember struggled to sit up under her brother. "Did I *really* surprise you?"

Cutter laughed and nipped at her fingers. "You'll be a great hunter someday, Ember. But get down now." He swept her up on one arm and swung her to the ground. "Both of you," he went on, making a step for Suntop with his foot. "Nightrunner can't carry us all the way he used to."

The old wolf stretched and settled to the ground. Cutter sat beside him. Ember, flame-red hair disordered by her roughhousing, mimicked Nightrunner's stiff movements before flopping to lean against his side. The wolf grunted with weary annoyance, but made no attempt to discourage her.

A braid of ghostly voices floated down from the hills beyond the village. "Listen!" Ember twisted to look after the sound, and Nightrunner's ears flicked casually forward. "The wolves!"

"They've made a kill up there." Cutter rested his hand on Nightrunner's tail, sensing how the old wolf must feel at the sound of that song. "Probably some fat bristle-boar that wandered too far from its burrow."

Suntop cocked his head in that fearfully adult way Cutter saw in his son so much of the time. "Why doesn't Nightrunner lead the pack anymore?"

Cutter reached out to worm his fingers into Nightrunner's coarse, sandy fur. "He's too old. The younger wolves drove him away. If he tried to go back, they'd kill him."

Suntop's brows pulled tight above his nose. "That's cruel."

"No, Suntop, that's the Way." Cutter hated to hear his son talk like that. It reminded him of the Sun Folk, with their silly daylight values, and their pointless daylight ways. "And it's a good Way. Nightrunner understands. Besides . . ." He started working loose the leather lace binding the rabbits' feet to each other. "He has me to care for him now, as long as he might live."

"Which is just how it oughta be." Ember danced away from her brother, arms crossed with easy superiority. "I can't wait to have a wolf-friend of my own."

Spoken like a wolf chieftain's cub. Cutter turned to smile at her, then froze when he recognized the flicker of movement in the sand near her small sandal. "Hssst! Ember!"

She blinked, mouth open to question. Cutter silenced her with a wave of his hand. "Don't move . . . !"

Spidery legs feeling out a path across her sun-browned toes, the sting-tail climbed onto Ember's foot with mindless determination. Her hands twitched, just a little, when the deadly creature touched her, and Ember widened blue-green eyes to stare at the sting-tail with more fascination than fear. Cutter silently eased forward onto his knees, hand drawn back to strike. If he was careful, he could swat the sting-tail away and swing Ember to safety before it recovered. After all, a sting to him would have long minutes before it could prove fatal. But the same sting delivered to tiny Ember—

A flash of bright metal whispered past Cutter's shoulder, and a delicate knife clipped against the sting-tail's curling barb to toss the creature back onto the sand. Cutter felt his heart thump hard with surprise, but Ember only giggled and scampered off after the confused creature as it righted itself and scuttled away. "Thank you, Mother!"

Suntop darted off in her wake. "Ember! Wait up! I wanna see!"

Cutter sank back on his heels and tipped his head to smile up at his lifemate. "Fine throw." He plucked her knife out of the sand and turned it haft-first toward her.

"Fine teacher." Leetah wrapped brown fingers around her lifemate's hand and pulled him to his feet. "As usual, they insisted on waiting up for you."

"As usual." Cutter nuzzled her fingers before she released him to scabbard her dagger. "I'm glad you waited with them."

Leetah angled grass-green eyes at him and smiled slyly. "What else could I do?" she sighed with mock resignation. "Look at all this trouble you get my children into."

As if to demonstrate, the cubs came bounding back in a flurry of excitement. "Didya see?" Ember squealed, sliding headlong into her mother. "Scared right out of its skin! I've never seen a sting-tail move so fast!"

Suntop, forever thoughtful and more sedate, slipped

between his parents and took hold of a hand from each of them. "We should leave Nightrunner to eat, before his rabbits get too cold."

"That we should." Cutter laughed at the old wolf's impatient rumble. "Here you go." He dangled the rabbits in front of Nightrunner's nose, letting the wolf take his pick between them before dropping the other to the sand at his feet. Then he bent to nuzzle the top of Nightrunner's head. "Eat well, old friend."

Nightrunner interrupted his eating only long enough to lick the elf's closest ear. Cutter appreciated the gesture.

"Come on, cubs." He tugged Suntop between him and Leetah, leaving the wolf to his rabbits. "Time to go home."

Ember capered ahead of them on their way into the sleeping village. She chattered incessantly about something Wing had said that Newstar had done, or some other child business too arcane and complex for an adult like Cutter to understand. He smiled across at Leetah, who shrugged in equally hopeless ignorance. Suntop busied himself with the serious task of swinging his arms and his parents' in rhythm with their footsteps.

"Want to hear my song?" Suntop asked suddenly, not looking up from their moving feet.

Cutter raised his arm to lift Suntop over a squat, round cactus in their way. "Let's hear it."

"Oh, the tall plants grow with their sharp, sharp spines. Only Redlance knows how they twist and twine." He bobbed his head in time with his awkward singing, skipping ahead to pick their path through the tangle of spiny plants surrounding the village. "He makes them dance while they're standing still, in magic shapes bent all by his will!"

Ember, already waiting on the other side of the thicket, applauded with brisk approval. "You should sing that to Redlance," she informed him.

Suntop shrugged one shoulder, but Cutter could tell by his blush that he was pleased with the suggestion. "I think about Redlance every time I come through here," the little cub admitted. "These sticker plants make me feel funny, just like when Savah makes the light shine behind her chair."

Cutter had talked with his son about this "feeling" before, and had tried on more than one occasion to pry some explanation of it from the village's Mother of Memory, Savah. All the ancient elf would tell Cutter was that Suntop possessed a special gift. A gift brought down from Leetah, his healer mother, perhaps, or carried quietly through the Wolfrider blood until no one left in Cutter's lifetime could place it. Whatever his talent's source, the cub could tell when magic was going on around him, or when it had been done in a place long ago. Cutter had seen Suntop pick out tree-shaped objects first formed by Redlance's long-dead ancestors, and had even used Suntop to locate Redlance once when the tree-shaper was too busy to be found. So he knew his son's special talents to be real, for all that he was the least likely ever to understand them.

"Ah, Suntop," he sighed. The cub looked up at him seriously, and Cutter smiled. "I always thought any male cub of mine would take after old Bearclaw." Cutter's father would have been howling in frustration over such a pensive, enigmatic grandson. "But it's Ember who'll be chief of the Wolfriders someday." She was a cub much more to Bearclaw's liking. "And you, Suntop . . ."

The cub laced his hands atop his silky blond head and shrugged with no sign of concern. "I'll be what I'll be."

"You'll be *quiet*!" The beaded curtain on a nearby window flew apart with a great clatter, and a mass of auburn hair spilled down the painted wall as Shenshen thrust her head out to glare at them. "Thistles and prickle-pears, Leetah! Don't your children ever *sleep*?"

"Very little, dear sister." Leetah propped an elbow on her sister's windowsill and raised an eyebrow at the young fellow waiting inside. "The night is in their blood."

" 'The night . . .' " Shenshen *hmphed* like a zwoot with a nose full of sand. "It's all your Wolfrider's fault! Next thing you know, he'll have them running on all fours and howling at the moons!" The bead curtain collapsed in on itself, rattling like the tail of an angry sand snake behind her, as she disappeared back into the hut.

Cutter, biting his own tongue to hold back laughter, clapped a hand over each cub's mouth when the children would have burst into giggles. "Shenshen doesn't exactly think the world of me," he commented to Leetah, "does she?"

Leetah folded her hands behind her back and regarded her lifemate with a coyly upraised brow. "Not since you dimmed her light the day Suntop and Ember were born."

As though any self-respecting father wouldn't draw his sword on the midwife who tried to bar him from the birthing of his children.

"She has few opportunities as it is to display her skills

at midwifery; she didn't need you tromping the Wolf-rider Way all over her finest hour."

Cutter gathered the children up, one on each hip, and fell into step beside Leetah with both little hearts beating against him. "It's a good Way," he argued firmly.

"It's the best Way," Leetah assured him. And he knew from her smile as she drew her finger across his chin that she meant it. "I was happiest of all to have you with me when they came."

"We started together, we'll see it through to-gether." Cutter stopped to let Ember squirm free of his hold as they came within sight of the hut he shared with Leetah.

"Beat you in!" Ember cried, slapping at her brother's foot.

"Will not!" Suntop nearly pulled his father over scrambling down to chase his sister. "Wait!"

Cutter released them both with a sigh, shouting, "Be quiet, you two!" at their swiftly retreating figures.

Leetah cuffed him playfully on the shoulder. "You're as bad as they are."

"No." He caught her hand with easy speed and pulled her into his arms. "They're as bad as me."

Her eyes, as cool as the moon and as green as fresh young leaves, bore into his until he could feel the urgent flutter of her thoughts entwine with his. "Have I told you lately that I love you?" she whispered.

Cutter smiled and brought his hands up to trace the long sweep of her beautiful ears. "You tell me every day that you let me stay in your life." **My heart is yours.** The touch of her skin against his was warm and exciting.

In the hills above the village, the night grew bright

with the voices of wolves. It was a sound still fairly new
to this desert, but one Cutter could now accept as part
of the place's nature, like the slither of sand against sand,
or the hollow moan of wind through bare rocks. He had
brought the wolves to Sorrow's End barely seven turns
of the seasons ago, yet they'd learned to find a place
among its sticker plants and burning hills, just as their
riders had learned to live among the colorful daylight
elves who made this village. Then why did tonight's
wolfsong make his stomach clench with fear? He pushed
Leetah gently away, and stood stone-still to listen, and
remember.

"Cutter?"

A terror he'd almost forgotten turned over inside
him, reawakening a hatred and anger he'd thought he'd
never feel again. All around the village he could see pale
faces appear in the windows and doorways of their
homes. Not Sun Folk faces—Wolfriders. They turned
moon-bright eyes on Cutter, their worried thoughts bat-
tering him like moths' wings as they hurried into the
open. Of all the Sun Folk, only Leetah was awake to
hear the frightful music, and even she couldn't know of
what horrors the wolves now sang.

"Father?" Suntop reappeared in the doorway, Ember at his side. "Father, what's wrong?"

He couldn't ignore the wolves' calling, no matter
how much he wished for it not to be true. "Leetah . . ."
He pushed her toward the cubs, backing away to join
the others. "I have to go."

She wouldn't let him release her arms. "Beloved,
your hands are cold—"

"*Cutter!*"

He spun, heart kicking up into his throat, and

hissed Skywise into silence. "I know! Now keep quiet!" The other elf slipped in the sand, sliding into Cutter and grabbing at his chieftain's arms to keep himself standing. He'd run the whole way from wherever he'd been, Cutter realized—his blue-gray trousers were soiled and torn, his silver hair in tangled disarray. Cutter touched the stargazer's flushed cheek to reassure him, turning so that his orders were given to all the gathering Wolfriders and not just Skywise alone. "Call Moonshade and·Rainsong to gather the cubs and bring them here. The rest of you, come on. We'll let the Sun Folk sleep while we handle this." Because there was always the chance that the wolves were wrong, that the Sun Folk would never have to know.

"Cutter!" Leetah grabbed his arm when he would turn away. Her eyes were frightened, her fear for him making her sound angry when he knew she wasn't. "Tell me what is happening!"

"The unthinkable." He dragged her into a hug so fierce he feared breaking them both. "Guard our cubs, beloved," he breathed. "Guard them like a she-wolf! Because I don't know how, or why, but humans have come to Sorrow's End."

CHAPTER TWO

H OW CAN THEY DO THIS
to us?" Skywise moaned. "*Why?*" He padded beside
Cutter as silently as any wolf but for his verbal worrying.
He'd drawn his sword before they'd even left the village,
and Cutter could see it flashing in the moonlight as they
ran. "They already took our home and everything we
ever lived for—why do they have to follow us and take
our future, too?"

Cutter didn't have an answer. He knew Skywise
didn't expect one—that there possibly wasn't one to
be had—and so he concentrated on bringing his shivering under control before they reached the others at
the edge of the desert. He couldn't sense the humans.
He never could. Cutter's father, Bearclaw, had claimed
to be able to feel them out from half-a-day's distance,
but Cutter had always found their thoughts too murky
and opaque to probe. Or maybe it was his own distaste
of them that kept their touch away. Whatever the
cause, he was secretly glad for it now, when he could
barely adjust to the concept of seeing a human again,
much less feeling one.

As Cutter and the others neared the last ridge of
rocks before the desert, the confused anger of gathered
wolves swarmed over them. He turned to climb toward them, and was caught off guard by Strongbow's

powerful sending, always so much clearer and sharper than any other elf's words.

What are we waiting for? They must die!

It was an open sending, Cutter realized, not specifically meant for him. Someone nearby must have answered the archer verbally, because Cutter was nearly to the top of the rise before Strongbow's thoughts blazed through him again.

Will his word make a difference? I say we kill them now!

And this time Cutter was close enough to hear One-Eye shout, "No! We wait for Cutter!"

I'm here.

Those of the tribe he hadn't left in the village were here, their backs to him and their frightened thoughts thundering against his like storm winds. Strongbow stood in the middle, tallest of all, his bowstring drawn back to his cheekbone and his thin body thrumming with a hatred and anger that ran even deeper than Cutter's. Pike and One-Eye flanked him, with Strongbow's young son, Dart, standing timidly behind all three. Dart twisted the cord on his arrow whip around and around in his hand, staring at his silent father with uncomprehending eyes. He was too young to remember, Cutter knew. Too young to know why these hulking, five-fingered monsters meant so much pain for his elders. The young chief looked beyond his tribesfolk to the pitiful creatures cowering within the circle of snarling wolves.

Humans—burned the color of raw meat by the sun, the angles of their bones jutting against their brittle skins. They clung to one another like desperate weeds, too weak to support their own great height.

Two men, a miserable woman, and a child whose sex Cutter couldn't tell from so high above. They smelled as bad as the mangy riding beast they had brought with them, the man draped across the beast's shoulders worst of all, with the sour blood smell of death rushing up from him. Their voices clapped off the rocks around them, harsh and loud for all that they believed they spoke in whispers. Cutter clenched his hand around the wood of his bow, hating the fact that he recognized more and more of their guttural language with every word they uttered.

Say the word, Cutter, Strongbow's knife-edged sending interrupted his thoughts. **My bow is ready.**

"Why are we standing here?"

Cutter turned as Woodlock scrabbled up the rock face behind Redlance and Nightfall. His clothing, the bright, woven fabrics of the Sun Folk, fouled with his bow when he stepped through to string it. Neither that nor his violently shaking hands slowed him, though, as he slid the sinew into place. "I say kill the round-eared filth! Let them rot in the sun! Let their bones lie like jewels on the breast of the desert!" He slid down the stone to stand, trembling, beside Strongbow. He didn't even have any arrows. "Kill them!"

Cutter raised his hand for patience, ignoring the blaze of disbelief that colored Woodlock's normally gentle face. Forcing his gaze back to the captive intruders, Cutter searched his brain for the memories, baring his teeth around the shapes of the ugly words. "Before you die," he grated, spitting out the human language, "say if any more of you come this way."

The standing male, his hand locked around the woman's arm, shook his head slowly. "We are all that you see. No one follows."

"Please!" The woman hugged her child's face against her breast. "Please, let us go! What harm have we done you?"

Cutter laughed, a wild, angry sound. "What harm?" He jumped down a level to stare at them through slitted eyes. "We 'demons' have long memories, humans. For seasons without end, you have tried to destroy us with your traps and poisons, slings and fire. We thought we were finally rid of you when we crossed the Burning Waste, but even here you plague us!" He kicked a shower of sand into the night wind. "I would sooner let my cubs play with a wounded bear than let you go."

"You hold much against us, demons," the man shouted back at him. His bravery surprised Cutter. "But you have no right! It is *we* who are wronged—*we* who have suffered because of you!"

"Aro, no!" The woman fell against him, as though she meant to drag him to his knees. "Do not anger them further, I beg you!"

Something in her weary panic tugged at Cutter, startling him with the pain it awakened. He was suddenly unwilling to let them hurt him any longer. "Enough! Pike, Strongbow . . ." He looked around at the gathered tribesfolk, counting all the knives and swords. "We need one more."

"I'm ready!"

He frowned down at the elf who reached up to grab his ankle. "*You*, Woodlock?"

Woodlock's knuckles whitened on his bow, his

ears growing dark with emotion. "I can deal death as easily as any of you when there's good reason."

But the young father's bloodthirst tasted like bile in Cutter's mouth. "All right," he said, very softly. "Stand your place with them." There would nothing good come of any of this, Cutter could tell already. "Make ready—"

"Wait!" Redlance pushed between the archers, pulling Woodlock to one side and holding him there as if he were a child. "Cutter, I want to hear what the human has to say." He swung around, red braids flying, at the first tingle of Strongbow's protest. "I have that right!"

The right to what? the archer argued. **More of what they gave you at their Killing Grounds?** He thumped his bow on the rock, dark eyes fierce and hard. **You should be standing here with us, tree-shaper, bow in hand, not defending them.**

"I'm not defending them," Redlance insisted. He turned pleading eyes up toward Cutter. "Don't think it doesn't sicken me to look at them, to remember what their kind once did to me . . ." He rubbed at the sweep of his ribs as if remembering how human knives and human blows had left their mark in more than flesh. "I kept asking them *why*—why the need for such cruelty and hate? They wouldn't answer me then." He looked down at the trembling creatures below him. "Let them speak now."

"Hear me, wolf demons!"

Cutter scowled down at the whip-thin human male, stomach burning with anger at his intrusion. The pitiful creature couldn't know what the elves were saying—like a harried dog, it only knew that it had somehow gained a few more moments of life.

Aro crept to the foot of the rocks, ugly face angled upward. "We are enemies," he called to Cutter, "but I will speak true. This world is not yours! Gotara, the supreme spirit, made this land for *men* to rule. *My* people were meant to hunt in the forest and fish in the waters—we were always first in Gotara's eyes." He reached up to grasp helplessly at the rocks above his head. "But you demons were hiding behind the thunderclouds, and you envied the beautiful land Gotara had given us. One day, you came down from the sky to take it for yourselves! We fought you in those days, and we fight you now. But your evil magic is strong. You molded the land to your liking—twisted the trees and rocks to form dwellings of them, made monsters to prey upon us. You stole our children for sport! Our rightful game fell to your arrows and to the killing jaws of the shadow beasts you ride! Can you wonder now why we hate you?" Cutter smelled the sharp sting of blood when the human pounded his bony fist against the stone. "You do not belong here! Go back! Go back into the storm! *Gotara despises you!*"

"So that's it." Cutter slid down to stand among the archers. "I used to wonder why there was always at least one group of humans camped near the holt, just looking for trouble." He crouched at the edge of the rocks and leaned forward as far as he dared, to snarl down at the bitter, filthy humans. "The forest was big," he growled in their language. "It could have fed and sheltered us all—our paths never had to cross. But you had your sacred duty to kill us, didn't you? And we learned to give back as good as we got." He clenched his hand around the body of his bow, wanting to flail about him at everything in sight, but knowing it was pointless. "No wonder this feud has gone on for so long."

"It isn't a feud," Aro grunted hoarsely. "It's the will of Gotara."

"Is it?" Cutter pushed to his feet with a growl. "Wasn't it enough that you drove us from our homes with fire? Have you come all this way to finish us off?" He paced the narrow ledge, his bow gripped across his thighs. "Your almighty Gotara tricked you, humans." A sidelong stare made Aro stumble backward a step. "You're in our hands now."

"Yes . . ." The human on the listless riding beast laughed a thin, crackling laugh, not even opening his eyes from where he hung, half-conscious, over the beast's shoulders. "It's our final punishment," he wheezed, "for destroying the forest. Yes . . . That must be it . . . !"

"Be quiet, old creature," Woodlock moaned. But the human was too far from the living world to hear him.

"For days the flames burned high. We floated in the center of the wide lake, praying for rain . . . which Gotara finally sent us." The sick human jerked suddenly upright and his blind, dry eyes flew wide. "Black! Black and ashes and death! We are wanderers in the blackness, searching for a bit of green!"

The woman ran to catch at his flailing hands, and the human child broke into tearless whimpers. Aro, passion bleeding from his burned face, took the child's tiny hand but didn't try to approach the riding animal.

"We traveled far in the direction of Sun-Goes-

Down," Aro said at last. The woman couldn't quiet the other man, but she'd crossed her hands over his jabbering mouth, as though afraid of what words he'd spew. "One day, we found another tribe of men. They took us into their circle and made us welcome. All would have been well, but . . ." He turned to look up at Cutter again. This time, the elf found the human's eyes unreadable. "Evil spirits claimed my brother, Dro, making him say and do strange things. And because we four would not be parted, we were cast out. Since then, we have found no place to settle. Our wanderings brought us here, to this desolate place . . ." A thin smile pulled at his cracked lips. "And to you, our ancient enemies."

"We saw the smoke from your fires!" The woman's voice was more fragile than Aro's, the emotion in it more plain. "We thought to beg food, and water—"

"—from friendly humans?" Cutter finished for her. He tried to tell himself that the stirring he felt in his chest was something other than pity. "You didn't expect to find us instead, did you?"

She dropped her gaze, but didn't answer.

"Gotara willed that the land be cleansed . . . and we cleansed it . . ." Dro laughed against the riding beast's mane, fingers twitching. "Cleansed it down to its bare, black bones! The wolf demons are destroyed! Do you hear, Great Spirit? We obey you . . . ! We praise . . ." His words dissolved into a fit of coughing, until even his breathing sounded too painful to bear.

Aro moved slowly toward his brother. "He will be dead soon," he whispered to the woman, pulling her away. "He no longer sees us."

"You will *all* die soon!" Woodlock gripped Cutter's

arm in a hand that shook as much as his voice. "Cutter, we've waited too long! Give the command!"

"Woodlock, no . . ." Redlance took his shoulders and made him turn until they faced. Even then, Cutter saw Woodlock's gray eyes travel to a spot somewhere beyond the tree-shaper's elbow, unwilling to confront that gentle gaze. "What's happened to you, life bearer?" Redlance asked in a near whisper. "*Your* cubs were the first born to the tribe after the monster Madcoil's attack. Coming from you now, words of death are foul."

"I don't ask for anything but what's necessary." Woodlock snapped Redlance a glare filled with more anger than Cutter would have guessed the father possessed. "They've killed more of us through the seasons than Madcoil ever did."

"All true." Redlance stepped away and released Woodlock's arms. "So do what you have to, my friend. But kill the young human first." He pointed at the child who still sniffled against its mother's leg. "I want to see if you can."

Woodlock twisted a look over his shoulder, hands tightening on the curve of his bow. A wind so light Cutter barely felt it ghosted feathers of dark blond hair across the father's gray eyes, and there was an ice in his face that Cutter had never thought to see in this hot, infertile land. "All right . . ." Woodlock nodded slowly, turning, and reached a hand out to Strongbow without looking at the archer. "All right," he said again, more firmly.

Strongbow slipped an arrow from the quiver on his back and laid it soundlessly across Woodlock's palm. Black-fletched and flawless, it was too long, really, for anything but the archer's powerful longbow. Still, Woodlock took it without question, and fitted it against his own weapon's string. Cutter heard the stiff wood creak, dry and hard from seven summers without use, and Woodlock lifted the curve of polished wood to draw the sinew back to touch his cheek.

I don't know why you're doing this, Cutter told Redlance suddenly, not liking the deadly grace of Woodlock's resolve, **but I'm trusting you.**

The older elf stood with his back to the rock face, arms crossed and one hand held pensively to his mouth. ***I'm* trusting *him*.**

Prepared as he was, Cutter still jumped when the bowstring thrummed and the arrow whistled into flight. The strength of his sudden revulsion frightened him— he didn't want to watch, didn't want to see any child, not even a human's, pierced and bleeding from an elf-in arrow. He jerked forward to stop the killing, too late—

—and Woodlock's arrow traced a rooster tail of dust across the ground as it skimmed left of the child's face and skittered harmlessly off into the darkness.

The elf's arms dropped to his sides, then his hands uncurled as though lacking all warmth and strength, and the bow struck the rock at his feet with a clatter. "Oh, what's the use?" His voice was a broken moan. "I promised Rainsong that we'd never see humans again, that our cubs would grow up without knowing fear . . ." Redlance knelt beside him when he sank to the ground, face in hands. "But now . . . ," he whispered. "Now, all my promises mean nothing."

"No." Redlance bent his head to touch the top of Woodlock's hair. "Not nothing. Everything we do means something."

If that were true, Cutter thought, *there'd be some sense in what humans and elves do to each other.* All he could see was a long braid of pain that never brought them anywhere and always gained them nothing.

"Dro?"

The human woman's voice cut across the elf chieftain's reverie. On the animal below him, the old human's weathered body curled in on itself and slowly slid off the beast's bony shoulders. She cried his name again, lunging to catch him, but it was Aro who reached his brother first. Weakened by waterless days in the Waste, they lowered the twisted corpse as gently as possible to the churned-up sand. Cutter saw the woman's face pull together in a expression very much like elfin crying, but she didn't even have the water in her for tears.

"He's dead," Aro said needlessly. He closed his brother's eyes with shaking fingers and bent to kiss the breathless lips. "He's dead, and we will join him soon."

Kill them! Cutter's blood insisted. *It's the law of life—you didn't ask them to come here!* But all his night-bright eyes could see was a grief so like what he'd felt after his father's death, and a child just as frightened of him as any elf cubling had ever been of humans.

"Go."

Behind him, he heard his tribe draw in a single breath of angry shock. The humans below only stared up at him blankly, silent and unmoving.

"*Go!*" Cutter shouted at them, suddenly hot with passionate if bitter confusion. "Let the dead one lie there as a warning! If you or others like you ever come here again, we'll kill you on sight! Understand?" When they hesitated, half-standing over the stiffening body, he flung his arm out toward the desert as though throwing them to the wind. "Go, damn you! Before I think twice!"

The woman grabbed her child above the elbow and turned to run through the circle of wolves. Aro paused to gather up the riding animal's tattered lead, then hurried after his mate as quickly as the starving beast could stagger. The wolves drew away from them, snarling darkly as they watched the humans flee. Cutter found himself clenching his teeth against the frustration of knowing that he'd granted the humans nothing, really—they left with no food, and no water, and only their lives between them. It made him wonder if Redlance was right, if anything they ever did accomplished anything.

You . . . let . . . them . . . *go!*

Strongbow's sending burned like liquid metal inside Cutter's brain. He turned, fists clenched, and locked icy blue eyes on the archer's snarl.

We had them *helpless* at our feet! Strongbow slashed at the air between them with his longbow. **And *you* let them *go*! Bearclaw would have cut out their living hearts and fed them to the wolves!**

Cutter struck him backhanded, hard enough to throw the archer to the ground. **I am *not* Bearclaw! I am *Cutter*!** Strongbow halted halfway to his knees, wincing beneath the power of his chieftain's thoughts. **Do you dare defy *me*?** He knew the answer, even as he asked it.

Strongbow's wolf, Briersting, had driven Nightrunner out of the pack less than a season ago. From that moment, it was only a matter of time before the wolf's newfound dominance pushed his elf-friend to make his own challenge. His mind boiling with thoughts that had no words, Strongbow launched himself across the distance. Cutter met him shoulder-first, staggering only a single step against the force of the archer's charge. Knife-edged shards of disbelief and anger tore into his senses, and Cutter drew his own thoughts into a stubborn fist to beat the archer's sendings aside.

I am Cutter! the wolf heart in him growled. **_Cutter!_** The blood of ten elf chieftains pulsed in him, and his soul blazed with a love for his small tribe stronger than even Strongbow could understand. It was these that gave him strength to push the archer physically away, these that let him wrap his mind around the barbed edges of Strongbow's fiercest thoughts and smooth them into harmlessness.

And it was Strongbow's ancient wisdom that let him sniff the greater power behind both those actions, and turn his face away. His bared throat granted Cutter the submission that Strongbow would never consciously admit, even to himself.

Cutter released his grip on Strongbow's shoulders, and stepped back to grant the older elf as much dignity as that little distance could give him. "Listen, my friend," he said, keeping his voice calm but knowing Strongbow would despise him if he tried to gentle it. "I know you want revenge on all humans—I do, too! But no good can come of it. There are too many of them, scattered everywhere!" He turned his sorrowful gaze on the withered corpse below them. "You heard them. Do you want to spend the rest of your life perched on this rock, just waiting to pick off anyone who comes in sight?" He angled a look at Strongbow, not sure how to read what he saw in the elder's face. "Because they _will_ come, you know. These were only the first we've seen."

"Then it's hopeless." Woodlock looked up from where he still sat between Redlance and Nightfall, his face glistening with regretful tears. "There's no place we can call our own, not even Sorrow's End."

"Don't say that, Woodlock . . ." The father's simple pain pierced Cutter deeper than the arrow Woodlock had launched at the human child. "I know that there's an answer," Cutter promised, drawing his little tribe around him as if his heart and arms could shelter them all. "There has to be . . . There just *has* to be . . ."

CHAPTER THREE

A̲N ANSWER, MY WOOD-
land cousin?" Savah paced her spacious hut in a swirl of
milky green skirts, her dark face pensive beneath the
folds of her silken cowl. "Would that I had one." She
settled gracefully into her chair and studied Cutter with
an ageless gaze so deep and knowing it made his stomach hurt. "In the distant past, my family founded Sorrow's End, believing that we had escaped human hatred
and violence forever. From my mother and myself sprang
the first inhabitants of this village, and I have been
Mother of Memory of all our dear descendants ever
since. The names and histories of those that are gone
live on in me. But of the High Ones . . ." She folded
her delicate hands into a basket on her lap. "Of them, I
can tell you little," she admitted sadly, "for they existed
long before even *my* time."

Cutter clenched his hand within Leetah's, feeling
her strong fingers respond with a faithful squeeze. "I
can't forget what the human said—that we don't *belong*
here." He looked up into Savah's face, like a child into
the face of his mother, and knelt to touch gently the fall
of her robes. "Where did the High Ones come from,
Savah? Where did they go? Can they *all* be dead? And
what if there are *other* tribes of elves somewhere, children
of the High Ones that we don't even know about?" The

questions were all coming so fast, were all so huge and frightening. "If we've got to fight the humans for our place in the world," he said, "we'll stand a better chance if we're all together."

Savah brushed her fingers through his chieftain's crest. "I agree." He felt her hand come to rest on the top of his head, and her thoughtful sigh traveled through him like his own. "Since you Wolfriders came to us, I have, in my way, been reaching out, hoping to touch others of our kind who may be searching, too. But . . ." She lifted his chin with one finger and smiled at him lovingly. "Perhaps my way is not direct enough. Perhaps *you* might succeed where I have not."

It was a thing to think on. His sight drifted away from hers, to the tall, multicolored window that filled the wall behind Savah's chair. All the disparate pieces, somehow found and fitted together by a craftsperson from many lifetimes ago. It was a miracle, really, in its beauty, just as it was a miracle that the Wolfriders had ever succeeded in bringing the remnants of their tribe across the burning desert. Now, fitted into this tiny village, they made a pattern with the Sun Folk no less lovely than this window. Did anyone have the right to expect that kind of miracle again?

A feather-light touch on his arm broke through his thoughts. "Father . . . ?"

Cutter turned, and the full wisdom of Suntop's quiet gaze cut through him like a blade. "Father, are you going away?"

For the first time he could remember, Cutter could think of no answer. He gathered the little cub against him, his face against the sun-colored hair, and tried not to fear a future that was meant to hold the answers.

*   *   *

"Suntop, I'm the chieftess! If you don't do what I tell you to, I'll stick this arrow right into your tail!"

"Ember!" Dart snatched his arrow whip away from the younger girl, glaring down at her in youthful reproach. "This isn't a toy," he lectured, successfully ignoring her stubborn scowl. "You mustn't ever point it at people, or say that you'll hurt someone with it, even in fun."

Ember stamped one sandaled foot with a *hmph!* and spattered herself with sand. "You sound just like your father."

Yes, Cutter thought from his observation point in the healer's hut window, *he does.*

"My father's one of the eldest in the tribe." Dart tucked the arrow back into his small quiver, standing very straight, as though he'd aged a dozen seasons just this morning. "He knows everything that's important— even your father says so." He tossed his chin haughtily. "I'll bet my father could be chief of the tribe anytime he wanted to."

"Could not!"

"Could, too!"

"Could not!" Ember shoved at him with all the fierceness of the eleven chiefs before her. "And if you don't stop saying that, Dart, I'll stick an arrow into *your* tail!"

True to Strongbow's bloodlines, Dart glowered balefully from his greater age and height. Then, entirely unlike his taciturn father, he flicked the end of his arrow whip and stung Ember with the string. The young chieftess yelped in protest of this affront to her dignity, then both of them sprinted out of sight around the building, with Ember howling dire threats in response to Dart's laughter.

So like Strongbow, Cutter thought, listening to their young voices fade with distance, *so like someone I'll never even know.* Strongbow had been many times Bearclaw's senior long before Cutter was born. The thought of him as a cub had been impossible for most of Cutter's life, and even now the only images Cutter could pull up were of a scowling, silent child no different from the elf who'd scolded Cutter since childhood. There was no one left but Treestump old enough to remember Strongbow at such a tender age, and Treestump never talked about the archer in his youth.

Had he ever been like Dart? Open, curious, willing to risk being wrong in exchange for listening to others and learning? It was hard for Cutter to imagine. What might the older archer have been like, given the chance to grow up without human hurts and hatreds to carve his softer parts away? What would that same life do to Ember, with her cubling fierceness, or Suntop, with so little wolf in him that Cutter feared for his survival in that bigger, harder world? The scene of placid village and peaceful children blurred behind sudden tears, and Cutter wiped at his eyes carefully, afraid to rub his priceless reality away.

"There . . ." Inside the cool darkness of the hut, Leetah's voice rolled like honey as she finished treating the villager who'd limped into her home only a short while ago. "Remember those aches and pains the next time you try to lift *two* jars of clay at once."

"I will." The potter settled back on his heels and stretched gingerly. Cutter could smell his embarrassment even from the other side of the building. "Thank you, healer." He graced Cutter with a quick, bashful smile before showing himself to the door, leaving the hut to the Wolfrider and his mate.

Cutter curled his knees up to his chest, but kept his place in the window. The pillows lining the floor of Lee-tah's healing area retained the blurred imprint of the potter's body, the air above them heavy with the aroma of the oils she'd rubbed into his injured muscles. She seemed to find a sweet delight in that spicy smell. Hands as delicate as birds' wings teased the pillows back into shape while a voice as light and clear as a nighttime breeze hummed snatches of a tune too fragmented for Cutter to recognize. His heart thumped dully against his ribs for love of her.

How fast the things of the world could change. Only a cub's lifetime ago, he couldn't dream of holding such a weight of love as he lived with every day now. And only yesterday there were no humans in Sorrow's End, and every reason to believe his days here would be endless and without pain. He slid down off the windowsill to pad across the distance between them.

She looked up from gathering together her jewelry when he sank to his knees beside her. The last bracelet glided onto her slender wrist, and she reached out to touch his face with her hand. "Have you decided?" He knew she was trying to sound as though she didn't already know his answer.

"I can't." Cutter raised his own hands to press her palms against his face. The warmth of her touch was too real to abandon. "I can't leave you and the cubs."

She laughed gently, softly, and pulled her hands away to stand. "My Tam . . ." She brushed her fingers through his topknot like a mother through the hair of her son. "You are little more than a 'cub' yourself—your life has just begun." Disentangling from his hold, she stooped to collect the last of her oil and towels. "My years have mellowed me somewhat. Part of me has always been prepared for the idea of your leaving."

"You're being too understanding." He turned on one knee, following her progress across the hut with a suspicious frown. "It worries me."

She shrugged without turning to face him. "Beloved, the sun rose and set before you came to me. It will rise and set after you go."

"But . . ." He bit off the rest of his protest as she disappeared down the steps into the cellar. He bounced to his feet to hurry after her. "You could come with—" he began, but she cut him off before he could finish.

"No." The speed of her reply shocked him into silence. "I am the healer. My responsibilities lie with this village." She didn't look around when he trotted down the stairs to join her, only continuing with the business of reshelving her medicaments the way she did after every routine healing. "But I will not cling to you, or hold you here." For the very first time she hesitated, the jar in her hand poised above a shelf as though she couldn't remember where it was supposed to go. "Although your dream may lead you into danger, it is not a foolish dream." She placed the errant bottle with authority, but not where Cutter knew it was usually stored.

He slipped up gently behind her and rested his hands atop her warm, smooth shoulders. "I'll only be gone a little while," he whispered, brushing his cheek against hers. "You *know* I'll come back."

"Of course!" A teasing smile curled her lips. "You

have to." She lifted another bottle onto the waiting shelves. "Because you cannot live without me . . . remember?"

He saw the tremor in her hand and took the bottle from her with fingers only slightly more steady. Sliding it up among the others, he moved to twine his arms with hers, and instead met her embrace when she spun to throw her arms around his neck in fierce possession. "Oh, Tam! I trust the wolf in you! He is your strength and your will to survive." He returned her hug as tightly as he could, as the first of her tears fell against his cheek. "And I promise you—he is the *only* reason why I can let you go."

Her faith in him burned away his indecision, but left behind an aching void. "He won't disappoint you," Cutter whispered, a promise.

Leetah laughed shakily, but held him even harder. "He wouldn't dare."

"It's decided."

Only one moon peeped at the edge of the sky, but Cutter saw by its light as clearly as the Sun Folk could see by day. Standing with one hand entwined in Nightrunner's coat, he faced his tiny tribe with eyes hard and chin high. On this of all nights, he didn't want it to show that his stomach still churned with uncertainty, that his heart fluttered faintly on the brink of indecision.

"One turn of the seasons," he told them, his voice clear and strong, "what Leetah's folk call a year. That's all I'll give myself. Then I'll be back to tell you what I found." His hand tightened into a fist among Nightrunner's hair. "Or what I *didn't* find."

He had wanted Leetah to be with him here tonight. She'd sent the cubs, as always, but had stayed back in the village herself. There was a zwoot to load, she'd insisted, and other preparations to be made before she could send him on his way. In truth, Cutter feared, she still felt out of place in such intimate tribal gatherings. He'd tried to explain that her position as his mate gave her access to the tribe unlike that enjoyed by any other Sun Folk. And she claimed to understand. Still, Cutter knew it wasn't lost on the others that she rarely troubled them with her presence during important Councils or cubling passages. Considering the long, long year during which he might be away, he begrudged her absence now with a loneliness unrelated to the loving, close-knit tribe that surrounded him.

Treestump shook his head, bushy brows drawn into a fierce frown. "Sounds mighty risky to me, lad," he rumbled. "How will you know where to look? And even supposing you *do* find other elves, what if they don't like strangers?"

Cutter tipped his head in acknowledgment. "As you say, there's some risk. That's why I'm going alone." He touched each elf with his gaze. "Things are different for the Wolfriders now. The wolves wander free in the mountains. We seldom see them these days. Some of you, like Rainsong here, have almost become Sun Folk yourselves." She twisted her hands in the gauzy, patterned fabric of her skirt, and Cutter smiled gently to try and take the sting out of his words. "You don't need me to lead you the way I used to," he said, to her and to the others.

Moonshade planted hands on hips and sniffed with easy derision. "Cutter, you know that some of us have never been truly happy here," she complained. "Now that we know Sorrow's End isn't the human-free haven we thought it was, what's the difference if we stay or go back to the woods with you?"

"The difference," Cutter said, "is that I want all of you in one place for now. I'm not even sure where *I'm* going—I don't need the worry of herding a bunch of *you* through unknown territory. If I'm to fit the puzzle of the High Ones together, I have to know where all the pieces are."

Cutter felt the stirrings of a pointed sending from Strongbow, and Moonshade already had her mouth open to back him. The tribe's eldest elf silenced them both with a lift of his hand. "You've made your point, lad," Treestump told Cutter, not even sparing a glance toward the other two. "We'll stay put like you say. But remember—if you're gone too long, we'll come looking for you."

If the older elf had said otherwise, Cutter would have been disappointed. "Fair enough." He nodded, smiling fondly. "Speak for me in Council while I'm gone."

"Aye." Treestump swept his nephew into an embrace that spoke to Cutter more than any words. "Just don't be gone too long." Cutter nodded, the only promise he trusted just now.

As though prompted by Treestump's unconcealed affection, the others came forward to join their thoughts and wishes to his in a sparkle of gentle sending. Warmth pressed close all around Cutter, hands and hugs reinforcing Wolfrider farewells. Nightfall, trying valiantly not to cry, wrapped her arms around his neck and sighed into his hair. "Your father would never have let you go off like this," she told him.

Cutter reached back to stroke her cheek with his hand. "My father would never have led us here in the first place." There was a time when comparisons became pointless.

One year. Strongbow came dangerously close to an expression of approval as he clasped Cutter's hand. **That's all you have.**

I know.

The archer didn't believe in the quest, didn't think anything good could come of it—Cutter could feel his cool disapproval like a chill wind through the thoughts left open between them. But he respected the young chieftain's decision, and tempered his reservations with an honest hope for Cutter's safe return. The archer's trust heartened Cutter in a way he hadn't expected. **Thank you.**

Strongbow drew away, leaving the usual gap between them beyond what words or mind could cross— a gap that suddenly seemed more empty than before because of the loss of one particular voice.

"Skywise?" Cutter turned to scan the faces around him. He couldn't swallow his disappointment when he didn't see the familiar white mane among them. "Where's Skywise?"

Nightfall twined his fingers with her own. "Don't be angry," she said. "This is hard for him, too."

Yes, hard. Everything was suddenly hard again. Cutter squeezed her hand in thanks, then pulled away from the tribe with grim reluctance. "Come on, cubs." He took Suntop and Ember, one in each hand. "We've got to meet your mother, and I've a long way to ride yet this evening." He thought it would lessen the hurt to say it aloud, but he was wrong.

Even Ember had nothing to say as they climbed down from Howling Rock and made their way around the edges of Sorrow's End. Cutter felt the tiny bones in her hand with his fingers, comparing them to Suntop's on his other side, thinking of their mother with every movement of their bodies, every breathy little sigh. Nightrunner followed behind them, slow and silent. Only the whispered *click-click* of his claws on the sandy stone marked his passage through the desert night.

Cutter saw the loaded zwoot before he caught sight of Leetah. It stood with its head between its knees, hip-shot and sleepy, completely unperturbed by the weight of provisions on its tall, sloping back. Nightrunner recognized the stupid beast for what it was, and circled around behind it, growling sulkily.

"Oh, hush," Cutter laughed, amused at the old wolf's jealousy. "It's three days across this desert, old friend. By the time we reach the other side, you'll wish *you* were riding the zwoot instead of me."

Nightrunner's dry snort indicated that he wasn't so sure.

Leetah stepped beneath the zwoot's long neck, casually pushing the lazy creature aside. She looked exquisitely lovely in the cool moonlight. Cutter had always thought her most beautiful in the darkness. "I'm ready," he said, without really needing to.

She nodded and came to stand with the cubs. There was so much more he wanted to say, so much he wanted her to understand and know before he rode away, perhaps forever. He reached for her with his mind by instinct, and her primitive sending stirred ever so faintly in response to his touch. Love ghosted up between them like fragrance from gently handled blossoms.

Leetah smiled, and rested her hands on each of the twins' heads. "You will never be farther away from me than these two," she promised.

Cutter's eyes stung with unshed tears. "My beautiful cubs . . ." He sank to his knees between them, devouring them with his gaze, memorizing every detail of their priceless, perfect faces so that he could carry them with him every day of his travels. "Do you understand why I have to go?"

"Yes, Father." Ember reached out to hook one finger in the golden band at his throat. "To find other elves like us."

"Oh . . ." He crushed them both against him and breathed in their smell. "There are *none* like you."

It took every shred of his courage to release them again and rock back on his heels. They both looked at him very seriously. His heart grew huge with pride.

"Ember . . ." He flicked her gold earrings with his finger, and she grinned and tucked her shoulder to her ear. "Learn all you can about hunting from Strongbow while I'm gone. He's the best teacher a young chieftess could want." Then he turned to Suntop, cupping his son's tiny face in his hands. "Suntop . . ." The differences between them seemed so vast, the link he felt in their souls so perfect and complete. How could he have sired such a wonder?

"Suntop, Savah says that you have gifts worthy of her training. That's a great honor." He looked between them both, his heart torn by their beauty. "I wonder how you'll grow while I'm gone . . ." Suddenly, he knew he couldn't leave them after all—couldn't miss those days, those months, those moments. Even wolves knew that time past could never again be found.

A brave touch on his shoulder broke through his private anguish. "Go now, beloved." Leetah slipped her hand beneath his elbow to urge him gently to his feet. "The night is aging, and you are losing precious traveling time."

Precious time—that's what he was losing anyway, no matter what he did.

"Leetah . . ." He turned to wind his arms around her narrow waist. "Do you believe in this quest?"

Her green eyes poured into him like summer rain. "I believe the attempt alone is a triumph." Then she pulled him close and hugged him, deeply and thoroughly enough to last him his entire year. "Farewell," she whispered.

There was nothing more to say. He disentangled himself more painfully than if he'd cut loose his own arm, then turned to face the sleepy zwoot and its load of clothing, water, and food. Scrambling aboard the woven saddle, he dragged the beast's head up and reined it about without looking back at his lifemate and children. One look behind, he knew, would be his undoing. Just feeling them drawing farther and farther behind him was almost too much for him to stand.

He tried to focus on the zwoot's rocking gait for distraction. He hated riding the awkward monsters—it always felt as if he were clinging to an unstable tree branch in a storm. *Just like my life.* The thought came all unbidden, and he clenched his teeth around the anger it brought on.

Why can't I be like Nightrunner? he wondered. The old wolf didn't know what this journey was all about, didn't care about anything but the moment, Cutter's presence, and the interest of the things around him at the time. He hadn't been far from the village since Briersting drove him from the pack, so everything around him looked delightful and new. Cutter wished he could leave with such a clear conscience, but he couldn't help fearing for things he'd left unfinished, plans that should have been made before he set off. If he'd waited for all those things, though, he knew he would have waited forever. There was no way to guarantee that everything was prepared for, and every moment he delayed would only make it harder to leave. And he had to leave. Even Leetah had been certain of that.

Nightrunner snuffled curiously, catching at Cutter's thoughts with his own sudden interest. Cutter heaved back on the zwoot's reins until it lumbered to an uneven stop, then turned in the saddle to frown after Nightrunner as the old wolf bounded into the cactus garden at the edge of the village. "Nightrunner!" Another wolf yipped a greeting, and Cutter tested the air for some identifying scent.

The overwhelming musk of a second zwoot swarmed over him just as Nightrunner frolicked back into view with Starjumper galloping at his heels. Cutter sat back with his arms folded, waiting for Skywise to clear the cactus garden before yelling at him.

"Evening, my chief!" The stargazer's zwoot stumbled along behind him almost as sleepily as Cutter's. If Skywise had dragged any harder at the huge brute's reins, he would have pulled the whole animal over.

Cutter slipped his leg out of the way while Skywise maneuvered their zwoots side by side. "I missed you tonight." He stopped himself from commenting further.

He didn't want his last words with his friend to be a fight.

The stargazer shrugged. "I was busy packing." He scrambled up the side of his zwoot with a dramatic "Oof!" and flopped into his saddle. "Quite a chore to mount one of these things, isn't it?"

"Mm-hm." Cutter leaned sideways to lift an eyebrow at the bulging packs on either side of Skywise's mount. "And where do you think *you're* going?"

Skywise flashed him one of his standard infuriating grins. "Guess."

"No." When his friend's only reaction was to thump heels on his zwoot and start it plodding, Cutter had to kick his own zwoot in a frustrating attempt to follow after. "No! You heard what I said, Skywise—I go alone!"

"Sorry, my chief. I promised Leetah I'd keep an eye on you." He hooked a foot through Cutter's reins and urged the other zwoot a little faster. "And I'd rather argue with *you* than *her* any day!"

There are things I must do before I can let you go, she'd said. He should have known she wasn't talking about another bag of travel fodder. Cutter settled into the great beast's rocking saunter and growled.

"Besides, we both know you can't find your way around a *tree* without getting lost."

He suspected from Skywise's delighted chatter that his effort to look stern and disapproving had failed. "Thank you," he grumbled softly.

"My pleasure."

Sand sprayed around the zwoots' legs as the wolves shot past, enjoying the open spaces and sunless evening. Skywise laughed, shouting encouragement when Nightrunner cut back with surprising speed and bowled Star-jumper over into a pile. It was all so easy for them, Cutter reflected. They had their bond-friends, they had each other. They didn't have memories of loves and lives beyond the now, of a lifemate and cubs who mattered more to them than anything, and whom they very possibly might never see again. Try as he might to be as free and brave about the future as his wolf-friend, all Cutter could think about was Leetah, and the family he was leaving behind. He missed them desperately already.

CHAPTER FOUR

Are you *sure* you want to go by way of the Troll Caverns?"

Cutter squatted to grin at Skywise under the belly of his sand-caked zwoot. "What's the matter? Don't like the view?" He finished unhitching the woven saddle strap while Skywise stalked away from the tunnel entrance in a swirl of scarlet cloak.

"Don't like the company," the stargazer admitted. "We didn't exactly leave the trolls on the most friendly of terms."

Considering that the bug-grubbers had abandoned the elves to death in the alien desert, Cutter couldn't very well argue with the observation. At least someone had seen fit to clear the rockfall from the Tunnel of Golden Light in the years since the Wolfriders' passage.

Nothing else about the place had changed, though. The tunnel still glared, black and empty, from the foot of a cliff so long and tall and steep that it seemed to split the whole world in two. Not even bird droppings discolored the red sandstone expanse. The young chieftain had to admit that if *he'd* been a troll trying to rid himself of wily elves, he could think of few better places to do it.

Cutter smiled as he dragged his zwoot's saddle to the ground and reached up for the braided leather bri-

43

dle. It would almost be worth crossing the desert this second time just to see the look on Greymung's face when they marched into his throne chamber. If they neglected to mention the help they had from the zwoots on this journey, they might even get some groveling out of the trolls. "I thought we might pay our old friend King Greymung a visit."

Skywise snorted, tossing his own riding gear next to Cutter's. "Isn't it a little too late for revenge?" He slapped his zwoot on the rear, and it jerked its head up with a grunt.

"Is it ever too late?" Before his friend could answer, though, Cutter waved the comment off as not worth pursuing. His own zwoot, now bare of its burden of water and food, wandered the few steps necessary to snuffle Skywise's mount as though never having seen it before. "The trolls go back as far in time as we do. Maybe we can worm some clues about other elves out of them."

This time Skywise laughed aloud. "Trusting sort, aren't you?"

No, but he was practical in a fashion Cutter sometimes wasn't sure Skywise could appreciate. Calling back Nightrunner from the marginal shadow he and Starjumper shared, he swept up the single pack he would carry from here.

"I just hope the trolls' tastes haven't run toward elf pot pie since the last time we came calling."

He looked aside at Skywise when the stargazer joined him at the tunnel. "Can you fly?" He tugged on the back of Skywise's hood to make him crane his gaze upward.

Confronted with the sheer rock face, the stargazer colored slightly. "Uh . . . no."

Cutter smothered his own grin. "Then we go this way." He stepped into the darkness without looking behind.

The interior of the passage was so instantly cool and damp after the desert outside, Cutter felt a shiver on his skin like ripples on the surface of still water. His eyes widened in search of some slight light. It was there, ghost patterns in the folds of rock that were the walls—the pale, glowing fungus that made the only light trolls could stand against their moist green skins and beady maggot eyes. Dry desert air had killed off the pads of it closest to the entrance, but the slimy plant grew thicker and more luminous the deeper into the tunnel it spread. Remembering what a distance they'd walked underground when first brought to this exit by the trolls, Cutter was relieved to see he and Skywise wouldn't have to retrace the route in total darkness.

A warm body bumped him lightly from behind, and Cutter heard Skywise swear softly in surprise. He reached back to draw his friend up next to him. "Will the lodestone guide us all the way back to the forest from here?" The wolves gathered against his hips, suspiciously testing the air.

"I wouldn't count on it." Skywise touched the stone on its string around his neck, but made no effort to lift it free of his cloak and vest. "It points out the way to the Hub Star," he reminded Cutter, "not just anywhere we want it to. Near as I can recall, these tunnels went all over the place." He shuffled a few feet forward to look deeper into the cave. "Mostly down. Just following the lodestone isn't going to lead us to the surface."

His eyes as adjusted to the fungal glow as they were likely to get, Cutter followed Skywise's lead. "Then what *is* going to lead us through here?"

The stargazer flashed him a smug, crooked grin. "Why, *I* am, of course." He started down the winding passageway with a sort of manic confidence.

Cutter hurried after. "Do you actually remember the route after all this time?"

"I think so." Skywise shrugged. "I tried to pay attention when Picknose brought us here." He paused at the first branching, though, and drummed his fingers on Starjumper's skull for a few agonizing heartbeats before choosing a tunnel. "What are you worried about? This is why you brought me, isn't it?"

Cutter decided it would just please Skywise too much to know how easily he could pluck his chief's annoyance. "Just try not to backtrack too many times," he grumbled. "We only gave ourselves a year."

Cutter jerked awake with his teeth clenched and his throat too tight to gasp. His elbows hit on clammy stone beneath him, and soil-thick darkness on all sides twisted his awareness of up and down until his head spun. Locking his body into stillness, he carefully traced out the positions of his limbs in his mind, noting each bend of joint, each texture, each weight. A long minute passed before he was sure again exactly how he sat. By then he'd even remembered where he was, and why.

He and Skywise had been tracking through the trolls' caverns for days. At least, Cutter was fairly sure it had been days. With no sun, and no moons or stars to chart their progress, he just had to trust in Skywise's memory and his own brutal instincts. They ate when they were hungry, slept when they could no longer travel, and alternated between riding their wolves and walking just for the sake of change. Two sleeps ago they'd started scraping the glowing fungus off the walls to carry with them in a gourd when Cutter noticed it no longer draped the rock in its earlier profusion. This improvised lantern cast only a pitiful illumination barely an arm's length ahead of their travel. It was better than no light at all, but it bothered Cutter that he didn't remember any such lightless passages on their journey out through the Tunnel of Golden Light. He hoped the dying fungus they'd been finding now didn't mean Sky-wise had lost them beyond recall.

He gasped a little when a cold, wet nose pressed into his armpit. "Nightrunner . . ." The old wolf butted his head beneath Cutter's arm, radiating confused worry. Cutter rubbed his cheek against his friend's grizzled fur. "It's all right, old friend," he whispered. "Just bad food, I guess."

Cutter?

He felt Skywise's mind brush his, heard the other elf sit upright on the other side of the darkness. **Go to sleep, Skywise. I didn't mean to wake you.**

I was ready to get up anyway. The soft shush of leather over stone marked the stargazer's movements, finally ending with the awkward clatter of their darkened fungus gourd. **Puckernuts. I think our fungus all died.** Sending didn't let Skywise hide his annoyance.

Cutter smiled. It was nice not to be the only one irritated for a change. Especially with Strongbow left at home. **We could try to start a fire.** It was a skill

Leetah had tried to teach him, and one to which he wished now he'd paid more attention.

No. Skywise's distracted thoughts were like a sigh. **The trolls are more likely to smell fire coming than they are to hear us talking.**

They'd given up speech what seemed like ages ago for just that reason.

There was still some fungus on the walls just a little ways back. I'll go scrape a bowl full and be right back.

Cutter made an abortive reach for his friend, then stopped himself when he met only darkness between them. "Are you sure you can find your way back here?" He forgot about silence in his concern.

I'll leave Starjumper, if that'll make you feel better. Skywise's emotions still tasted mostly of irritation for time lost, and impatience. He obviously wasn't lying to Cutter about not being worried. **I'm not going back far enough to forget the turns and steps—I could find my way back here with my eyes closed.** That final addition of the stargazer's characteristic humor made Cutter smile.

Go on, then. I'll pack up here.

By the time Skywise returned—cursing internally (but loud enough to overhear) about the knee-high rocks in his way—Cutter already had their meager belongings rolled together with the travel cloaks they now used only for sleeping. Feeling out their food and water against the cold flowstone floor had taken the longest; dividing their belongings by smell Cutter did almost without thought. As it was, Starjumper had most of Skywise's gear snuggled around him while he sulked in wait of his elf-friend's return.

The gourd's thin light was even more pale than before. Cutter squinted up into Skywise's green-lit face and twisted his lips into a skeptical frown. **Is that going to last us the rest of the way?**

I think so. Skywise scooped up his few remaining water bottles, pausing to reward Starjumper's vigilance with a scrub of his chin on the wolf's muzzle. **We ought to reach the outside today.**

The news bounced Cutter to his feet with renewed energy. **Good! I don't like the way this place feels.**

As if the trolls' caverns ever felt very homey.

Cutter fell into step beside his friend and shook his head thoughtfully. **I'm serious,** he sent. **Haven't you noticed? It doesn't smell like anyone's been through these tunnels in a long time.** In fact, the lack of any strong scent but their own and the wolves' had made this underground world seem vaguely unreal.

Skywise lifted his head alertly, and Cutter saw his nostrils flare as he tested the air. **I did expect to feel troll eyes on us long before now,** he admitted, scrubbing uneasily at Starjumper's ruff where the wolf paced beside him.

Maybe there never were that many trolls to begin with. Greymung said they never used the Tunnel of Golden Light.

Skywise snorted aloud. **Greymung lied about a lot of things he told us.**

True. **But you can't deny there are no trolls anywhere near here,** Cutter pressed. He caught himself glancing left and right whenever their footsteps ceased to echo, announcing a side passage that the dim light wouldn't let them see. **Maybe they, I don't know— moved, or something. Maybe they're just in some other part of the tunnels, and don't know we're here.**

And maybe we'd better start paying attention to what's around us. Skywise lifted his elbow to stop Cutter from passing him, and aimed a nod at a pool of darkness pouring into the wall directly to Skywise's right. **Up there should be Greymung's throne chamber.**

Cutter slipped his sword slowly from its scabbard. **Careful . . . ** His thoughts were so thin as to be a whisper. Skywise nodded.

The smoothly honed doorway bulged as wide as the elves stood tall. As light from their fungus lamp crept over the grotesque forms and faces carved into the jambs, Cutter saw the first step of many jutting out from the milky flowstone walls. Skywise held out the lamp at arm's length, and they both strained forward to peer into the darkness stretching up the flight ahead of them.

As I recall, Skywise remarked, shoving his scabbard back on his belt to make room to hang the lantern, **this is a *loooong* walk.**

And there should have been at least two guards at this entrance. Cutter motioned the wolves to follow silently as they mounted the troll-made climb.

True to trollish stone skills, each slab was flat and square and perfect—but too tall in the step and too deep in the run, carved as they were to match trollish feet and trollish strides. Around outsized corners, up steep, ladderlike runs, higher and higher into the darkness they climbed while shadow-faces scowled from the ornate walls, hinted at by clever troll hammers from who knew how long ago. Cutter found himself reaching for handholds among noses, teeth, and tongues when his legs began to burn with the stepping. He finally stopped to catch his wind when he noticed Skywise's own quick breathing sounding louder than his own beside him.

Too long without trees to climb, Cutter remarked, trying for levity. He was glad he didn't need to gasp around his words to talk.

Skywise straightened from rubbing at his legs and clapped Cutter on the shoulder. **Not like tree climbing, anyway,** he sent. **Face it, Cutter—we're just not trolls.**

And thank the High Ones for that.

They finished the climb in silence. Fungus reappeared so gradually on the glossy walls that Cutter barely realized it had returned until he looked up and saw the elaborate doorway towering over them a stone's throw farther up the stairs. Then he caught at Skywise's wrist and earned an impatient nod at the nudge of his wordless question. They stood motionless in the green half-dark, waiting for the wolves to cease their panting and for their own heartbeats to slow before creeping up the last few steps and leaning their shoulders to the heavy door.

Iron hinges squealed in a shower of crumbling rust, and Cutter's ruff prickled upright at the hideous sound. The stone door groaned inward slowly, and Skywise was through the tiny gap, sword drawn, before Cutter could think to stop him. **Skywise!** He heaved all the harder at the massive slab, expecting the bellow of murderous trolls and the clash of warring metal. Instead, there was only the crunch of trod-upon dust, and Skywise's startled exclamation.

"It's deserted!"

Cutter stopped pushing, but the door drifted onward as if in a dream, thumping against the wall behind it. Greymung's throne chamber lay empty. Dried, unidentifiable food made a pile on the floor between the

cracked halves of a stone table. Weapons lay, rusted and
bent, atop mildewed rugs that might have once been
made from golden thread and the finest moss. Even the
careless pillows about the foot of Greymung's throne
sprouted only pale, bald mushrooms in place of the
warty trollish beauties who used to lounge there. Cutter
stepped gingerly through the stones and rodent bones
around the dais, and sniffed at the throne's well-worn
seat.

"Long deserted, by the smell of it." He slipped his
sword New Moon into its scabbard and turned to shrug
at Skywise. Eyebrows raised in a question, Skywise threw
his hands up in reply. "All right," Cutter sighed. "Let's
have a look around."

But all throughout the trolls' kingdom, they found
the same. Once roaring forges now sat cold and ash-
filled. Cobwebs draped trollish sculptures until the features of those stone creations couldn't be found through
the gauzy haze. Food in the larders had welded itself
together with mold, and the crusty droppings of bats
layered troll beds too deeply to be recent. Righting a
disturbed table for no reason except that it looked so
pitiful with its legs reaching up into the air, Cutter commented, "Well, this explains why we didn't get met on
the way in."

"And why the fungus all died." Skywise followed
his chief's example and neatly stacked the table's dish-
ware without seeming to realize he did it. "I wonder
what happened."

"Who knows?" Cutter backed out of the room, ignoring the ghost of troll voices in his memory. "Who
cares? They left us for dead, and they got what was coming to them." He turned around with purpose and

headed up the one tunnel he still knew fairly well. "We've got plenty else to worry about without them. Let's have a look outside."

The Tunnel of the Green Wood was the only troll tunnel Cutter had known about for all his lifetime at the holt. It went the short distance from forest to Greymung's throne room. The Wolfriders had known it as the entrance to the troll caverns since before Cutter was even born, and during his reign as chief it had been the only route by which elves and trolls traded goods in their useful but unfriendly alliance. They always met in the forest night outside, and the trolls didn't think any elf had ever crept inside that precious entrance without their doorkeeper's knowledge. In truth, Bearclaw had shown more than one feisty youth how to access the filthy place, Cutter included. Cutter had never had enough of his father's sense of mischief to make use of the knowledge, but it had always been there. And it had served them well on the night their holt burned down.

A warm, rich flow of light met them just ahead of the tunnel entrance. After days of endless darkness, the touch of the sun burned Cutter's eyes. He wiped at the tears on his lashes, feeling for the edges of the door through his painful blindness. Sunlight prickled like fever on his cheeks as he stepped past the portal and into a world he hadn't seen since before his cubs were born.

"Oh . . . Oh, Skywise . . ." It wasn't just coming from the caverns' darkness that made the land so wide and bright—it was the openness, the emptiness, the lack of anything at all with which to block the sun.

Where once trees had stretched their ancient arms to lace a canopy of green and fragrance, only grasses and twiggy brush remained. Young saplings, their tops dusted with only a handful of leaves, strained valiantly to reach above the scrubby growth. Over it all, the broken, blackened skeletons of trees dotted the landscape like giant, rotted teeth. "It's as bad as the humans said . . . !"

"No . . ." Skywise sank to his knees at the edge of the grass and lifted a shard of burned wood to his lips. "It's worse . . . Much worse . . ."

CHAPTER FIVE

CUTTER KNELT BESIDE Skywise to dig his fingers into the brittle, crumbling soil. It didn't even smell like dirt. The spindly plants growing out of it clung to life with roots too white and fragile to seem real. When he dug down even a finger's length, he found chunks of cold charcoal that still held the shape of the wood they used to be. They turned to silky soot in his hands.

"It's so strange . . ." He wrapped his arm beneath Nightrunner's neck to take comfort in the wolf's strong presence. "The forest—gone! Just like that." A bird he didn't recognize flittered past, scolding them for lingering. "I never dreamed it would look this bad, so empty."

"Those crazy humans." Skywise pushed to his feet with a weary shake of his head. "I can't even hate them for doing this," he sighed, looking out across the treeless hills. "How could they—how could *anyone* have known that the fire would destroy *everything*?"

Even if someone had said as much to Cutter, he still wouldn't have realized exactly what it would mean—that the devastation could go so far. Standing, he moved away from the tunnel entrance in slow, uncertain steps. "Even standing here now, I keep seeing it the way it was the night we left." Thick with the smell of leaves and hot sap, distant tree trunks lit by more than that evening's moonslight. "These trees were *old*, Skywise! Older than the very first Wolfrider." He blinked the long dead images from his eyes, and walked in silence wherever his instincts led him.

Nightrunner and Starjumper trotted ahead with tails waving and ears high. They didn't recognize the place, Cutter realized. It was just some new interesting adventure, more suitable to them than desert rocks and lizards, but nothing that could reach past their wolfen present to remind them of a now lost home. Slowing, Nightrunner flicked his ears to the sound of gentle splashing, and angled away to sniff out the source. Starjumper bounded ahead of him, obviously excited by the smell that had only just drifted back to Cutter on the breeze.

Fresh water—the first they had seen in days. Cutter ran a hand up Nightrunner's back as he sank to one knee beside the wolf. The grizzled male touched the elf with a fleeting thought of greeting, but didn't lift his muzzle out of the quick flowing stream. When Cutter ducked his own face under the surface, the water tasted bright and faintly metallic—good in a way only something remembered from childhood could be.

He pulled his head up to the sound of Skywise filling their water flasks nearby. "This is our stream," he said.

Skywise glanced over at him, one eyebrow raised. "What's that?"

"This stream," Cutter said, more clearly. "This is the stream that used to run near the holt." He wiped at the water still dripping from his chin and climbed to his feet. "I think I know where we are."

For just an instant, things snapped into place, only to fall out again when Cutter looked too hard at the way the world around him really was. Ghostly trees shimmered in front of grassy knolls, as though the past overshadowed the present. Cutter trotted between those distant images as quickly as he dared, searching for the shadow of a particular tree, of the one place he half believed still stood despite this brutal destruction.

When he found it, it was only a waist-high ring of blackened timber, burned clear through to its hollow heart.

Skywise slowed to a stop beside him, gray eyes solemn. "The holt."

Cutter could only nod in answer.

The great Father Tree, the tree where Cutter had been born, once rose taller than the Wolfriders could reach if they all stood on one another's shoulders. Chief Goodtree, his ancestor, had shaped gentle hollows in the tree's living body, and Cutter had passed many mornings before sleep trying to imagine the lithe, ancient bodies of past elves circling his home in a tree-shaping dance. Now he crept, on the edges of his feet into the circle of the Father Tree's ruin, loathe to disturb the sleeping spirit so many seasons after it had died.

For so many turns of the seasons, Wolfriders had taken their shelter here—two chiefdoms of elves had chosen their mates and raised their cubs within the slow embrace of the Father Tree's arms. Cutter's mother had always claimed that the old tree cradled the spirits of those dead Wolfriders in its branches. Thinking now of Joyleaf, and Bearclaw, and all the other elves who had passed over before them, Cutter felt the sting of tears in his eyes as he wondered where the dead now rested without this home to come to.

Skywise approached from behind him, talking aloud to Starjumper as he came. "I found some arrowheads," he called before he'd even reached the edge of the tree's burned-out bole. "And what looks like Nightfall's metal candle bowl. It's all blistered and melted." Cutter knew he was only announcing his presence so as not to intrude on his chief's private thoughts, but Cutter appreciated the gesture. "What have you found?"

Cutter sat back on his heels, cradling a scrap of metal in both hands as Skywise came to join him. "Bearclaw's wolf-head necklace, I think." He tried to remember how big the necklace should have been, but could only remember it feeling huge and heavy in his cubling hands. "Parts of it, anyway."

Skywise knelt beside him and brushed the twisted metal with a fingertip. "I didn't know you kept it after he died."

Cutter nodded. He kept wanting to press the lump back into shape with his thumbs, but it stubbornly resisted manipulation. "The fire spread so fast, I didn't have time to take it with me." He'd carried the memory, though, dearly enough to describe it to Shenshen for stitching onto Ember's tunic. "Oh, well . . ." He dropped it among the other detritus in the bowels of the tree. At least it could rest here in memory of the elves who had once lived. "It's ruined now. Just like the holt." He turned away with all the finality he could muster, even though he had no idea where else they could go.

Skywise trotted a few steps to catch up with him.

"It'll be a long time before the forest comes back."

"I know." Cutter brushed his hand through the leaves of a young bush, flicked a bee off a clump of meadow flowers. "Leetah and the cubs will never know it as I did. When Suntop and Ember are grown"—he fondled the trunk of a tree no taller than the cubs themselves—"this sapling will still be too tender to bear their weight." It was all so pointless, so unfair.

Untroubled by changes he could neither stop nor explain, Nightrunner butted his muzzle underneath Cutter's hand. A few sloppy licks were all he granted the tree's tender leaves, then he grumbled at Cutter with a sharp pang of shared discomfort.

The elf couldn't help smiling as he bent to nestle his face against the big wolf's shoulders. "Hungry, old friend?" Nightrunner whined, and Cutter felt his own stomach pinch. "So am I."

"We should have killed one of the zwoots," Skywise complained. "Saved the meat instead of letting them go into the desert."

"It's always easy to see what we *should* have done." Turning his attention to the ground, Cutter kicked gently at the bushy growth around them, seeking some sign of roots. "We *should* have stopped the humans from burning down the forest," he said, moving forward as he searched. "We *should* have known Greymung was lying when he said he wanted to help us. We *should* have—"

"—known better than to trust we could steal food from the troll's store holes." Skywise waved him over to where he'd scuffed clear the base of a clump of maiden's lace. "There's nothing left to eat down there unless you like bat meat or raw cave slugs."

Cutter wrinkled his nose at the thought. "No, thanks." Whisking New Moon from its scabbard, he scraped at the sooty ground beneath the foliage. "We can dig up enough roots to tide us over. The wolves might even get lucky and spot a squirrel or something." The pale root he wiggled loose smelled bland, but better than nothing. He tossed the dirty tuber up to Skywise. "After we've had something to eat, we'll figure out where to go from here."

Skywise wiped off the root with his fingers. "It's an awfully big world," he said dubiously.

"I know, Skywise." Knowing how big still made Cutter's insides knot when he thought about trying to cover it all. "I know . . ."

The grass in front of him dipped shyly, bending away with the shift of the wind. The muddy smell of cesspools tingled Cutter's nose, but Starjumper surged to his feet with a growl before Cutter could identify the source.

"What is it?" Skywise asked his wolf. And his answer was a rumbling of coarse language that Cutter hadn't heard since fleeing the woods:

"Aim true, old one! We won't get a second chance!"

Jerking New Moon from the dirt, Cutter leapt up, turning, just as something soft and rotten slapped to the ground nearby. A cloud of rancid powder swelled up like smoke around them, and Cutter coughed violently against the smell. Skywise toppled, his arm across his mouth, and Cutter felt his own world flip crazily sideways as the ground whirled out from under him and dropped him atop his friend. He had only a moment in which to glimpse two hulking figures, swathed in sacks and furs against the sun, lumbering down the hillside toward them.

"I can't believe it, old Maggoty!" the largest one roared. "Your sleep powders worked!"

And Cutter's heart knew he recognized that pestilent voice, even though darkness took him before he could whisper the name to his brain.

CHAPTER SIX

AND THE LITTLE FERRET was using it to scrounge up *roots*, of all things! The fool!"

"He didn't realize what he held in his hands. And just as well, too."

The voices tromped all around Cutter like a herd of rutting zwoots: thundering, rumbling words and noises from the distant past that could only be from dreams, choking, dust-induced nightmares that smelled like dung and fungus and the dank undersides of trollish feet. Cutter tried to gather his arms under him, to push his face up away from the boards on which he was sprawled. All he did was thump the body beside him with an elbow and earn a nauseated grunt for his efforts.

Skywise?

The sending exploded as silent agony inside his head, ricocheting around his skull in search of a clean exit. Cutter managed to blearily clap one hand to his crown as he struggled to swallow and wet his tongue.

"Skywise . . . ?"

A rough whisper, but hearable.

His companion's response was less distinct. "Mmmmzz?"

"Can you sit up?"

Cutter felt a squirm of awkward movement beside

him, and thought at first Skywise had at least succeeded in getting up to all fours. Then the dull thump of a skull hitting wood punctuated Skywise's weary groan. "No," Skywise said at last.

Cutter grunted. "Me, either."

He couldn't roll over, either. At least, not completely. He managed to heave himself all the way over onto one hip before noticing that his legs weren't moving with him. Planting an elbow on Skywise's back, he squinted down the length of his body in search of his feet. He found them where they ought to be, in a tumble next to Skywise's, bound together by leg irons and a length of weighty chain. "Where *are* we?"

"There it is!" The nightmare voice belched out a boom of laughter from behind Cutter, and the elf jerked about in horrified surprise. "Just like Two-Edge promised, that crafty old roamer!"

Barely adjusted to the remnants of the woodland, Cutter hadn't expected another drastic change of scenery quite so quickly. They were inside a dark and smelly hovel, the walls smeared with soot and mud, the roof an awkward patchwork of sod, grass, and sticks. Cutter and Skywise had been tossed atop a wide shelf, along with a tatter of mildewed furs and some piles of crumbled mushroom. Below them, hunched over a crude wooden table, a troll nearly as broad and coarse as the hut itself chortled quietly while a warty, rheumy-eyed female rubbed her face all up and down his scaly arm.

"Oooo!" The troll maid's adoring voice sounded more like a death rattle than a coo to Cutter. "I'm so *excited*!"

"You should be, Oddbit." That hoarse bark jerked Cutter's attention to the hut's only window, where a fat, older troll busied herself stuffing grass and bits of hair into the cracks around the shutters as though to ward off any light. "Maybe *now* that oofless, lovesick Picknose of yours will amount to something." She turned and waddled back toward the table, pendulous breasts slapping against her knees. "Wouldn't that be a surprise?"

Skywise's head came up, even though his eyes were still cloudy and without focus. "Picknose?" he asked, as though not sure he'd heard correctly.

Remembering the smug, strutting troll guardsman who'd abandoned them to death in the desert, Cutter tightened his hands on the edge of the shelf, wishing it were Picknose's neck.

Picknose spat a great wad of phlegm at the old troll's feet. "Laugh at me now, Maggoty," he rumbled, curly black hair bobbing. "Because soon I'll be a king, and you won't be fit to lick my toenails then!" Hand fisted around the handle of a curving, bright sword, he thumped the pommel soundly against the tabletop between them. "I'm rich, I tell you! Rich!"

Cutter jerked as though stabbed through the heart. "New Moon!" He scrabbled to the edge of the shelf, focused on his father's sword through a haze of panic for what Picknose might do to the precious weapon. "Skywise, they've got New Moon!"

"Cutter! Wait!"

He tumbled off the shelf, still clumsy from sleep dust, and thumped his chin on the dirt floor when he didn't get his hands moving fast enough to break his fall. He didn't fall any farther, though. Jerking his body forward as hard as he could, he aimed himself at Picknose when the troll jumped to his feet. Still, Cutter didn't realize he'd caught his leg irons on the corner of

the shelf until all his struggles only gained him a rhythmic *clank-clank*ing from behind and an avalanche of
trollish laughter.

"Picknose!" He pushed up on his hands to snarl at
the troll's twisted green face. "You dirty, deceiving son
of a sick human! Give me back my sword!"

Picknose sauntered heavily across the crowded
hovel, floor-length beard puckered around an insincere
frown. "Now, now . . ."

"*Give it back!*" Cutter shouted. "I'm warning
you . . . !"

"Do tell." Even squatting, Picknose towered over
Cutter, his bulbous head almost as wide as his backside.
"Then I'd just better do as you say, hadn't I?" The polished pommel looked impossibly tiny between his thumb
and finger when he suspended the sword before Cutter's
eyes. "Here it is, little chieftain. Yours for the taking."

Cutter knew it was useless, but his blood burned
with a fury far outstretching the simple theft of his father's sword. He swiped clumsily at New Moon with one
hand, trying to balance on the other, and howled with
frustration when Picknose merely lifted the slim blade
out of his reach. When he got the sword in his hands
again, he was going to use it to carve off Picknose's
namesake and feed it to the slugs.

For now, though, he had to content himself with
biting the heel that was closest to him hard enough to
earn a mouthful of bitter trollish blood.

Picknose wailed like a rabbit and leapt away, leaving
Cutter with a mouthful of green skin. Cutter spat the
remnant onto the floor with some disgust. He was sure
his mouth would never taste decent again.

"You flea-ridden, milk-toothed whelp!" A hard

green hand knotted in the front of Cutter's shirt and jerked the elf up to troll eye level. "You want to chew on something?" Picknose growled, brandishing the sword over his meaty shoulder. "*I'll* give you something to bite!"

"Ooo! Picky!"

The troll twisted to scowl back at his maiden, and Cutter narrowed his eyes on the sinews in Picknose's wrist, considering another bite.

"Picky!" Oddbit squealed when she had her consort's attention. "It's those dreadful wolves! They'll break in!"

Cutter flashed his attention toward her, hearing Skywise gasp from up on the shelf. Beyond Oddbit's squat, lumpy outline, the hovel's lone window rattled softly, knocked about by the scratching of frantic wolf paws. Maggoty plucked a tuft of grass from the cracks to peer outside while Oddbit flapped her hands in distress. "*Do* something!"

Picknose grumbled, then dropped Cutter without the slightest warning. "It's always something . . ." The elf got his arms in place this time, not to mention scuffed on the floor through the sleeves of his tunic.

"Here—" Maggoty waddled forward to meet Picknose halfway to the outside door. "Unbar the door and give 'em another dose of dust." She pressed a bulging burlap pouch into his hand. "When they're out, you can skin 'em easy. But be careful!" This she punctuated with a sharp slap to the side of Picknose's head. "This is my last pouch."

Cutter!

As though not clear on where the blow had come

from, Picknose scrubbed at his scabby hairline while he nodded and reached for the door.

Cutter! Skywise's sending stumbled almost as much as his body as he dragged himself to the edge of the shelf. **We can't let him!**

I know!

Closing his eyes, Cutter bowed his head onto his hands and felt through his mind for some piece of steady thinking. Close by, he could feel Skywise's brightness stagger slowly into focus as they both reached out in search of a common goal.

Scattered, worried, always sniffing, the wolves' minds weren't much clearer than the elves'. *Wake up, gone gone, troll smell and fear much fear.* They'd tasted Maggoty's sleep dust, too, then, and had no idea what had become of their friends in the meantime. Picknose's hand fell on the door handle, and Cutter sharpened his thoughts with as much fear and urgency as he could summon. The contact rippled through the surface of Nightrunner's instincts, awakening the need to run, to save this danger until some other time. The big wolf hesitated, though, willing Cutter to reassure him that fleeing would not leave his friend all alone.

Go!

Picknose slammed the door open with a thunderous crash. "Try a whiff of *this,* you mangy beasts!" Cutter held his breath when Picknose froze in the doorway, then sighed in huge relief when the troll bawled, "Maggoty, they're running!" He turned to narrow brutal pebble eyes at the elves. "Almost as if they knew what I meant to do."

"Oh, what does it matter, my sweet?" Oddbit snuggled her face in his neck, fitting her corpulent body against his like a slug to a stone. "Just as long as they're gone."

Cutter defiantly returned Picknose's glare as Skywise fumbled to untangle the chains on his chieftain's feet from the shelf bracket. It seemed an uneven victory when Cutter finally fell free, and Picknose turned away from him to jam light-blocking material back into the cracks around the door.

"I have a *wonderful* idea!" Oddbit purred, prancing back to the table. "Let's have a party, to celebrate Picky finding the sword."

Picknose grunted, but smelled suddenly warmer, as though pleased by Oddbit's attentions. He turned New Moon over and over in his hands, scowling down at the elves. "What do we do with *them*?" he asked at last.

Cutter looked up from rubbing his ankles. "How about let us go?"

"Uppity creatures!" It was Maggoty who flung a handful of dung at them from the other side of the room. "You think you're so smart. You think you're better'n us." She shuffled across to display broken teeth in a grisly sneer. "Look at you! Ugly little snouts!" She poked a finger against Cutter's nose. "Ridiculous big eyes!" Skywise ducked away from her jab at his face. "Why, you haven't got a smidgin of character between you!"

"Oh, I don't know." Oddbit crouched so low her mossy bosom nearly overflowed the confines of her tattered gown. "I think this one's rather cute." She wiggled her tongue companionably at Skywise. "At least his nose turns down. Can I keep him, Grandmama?"

Maggoty slapped Oddbit's shoulder in a signal to stand up straight again. "I've got a better idea. Picknose!" She clamped a hand on each elf's arm and hauled them to their feet as though they were no more than sacks of dried grass. "They'll be your servants from now on. You'll be a troll of means very soon, and a wealthy troll should have attendants."

"Attendants . . ." Picknose strutted up to them and proudly fitted New Moon onto his belt as though he planned to keep it there. "Elfin attendants for a wealthy troll king . . ." The roar of laughter that shook his mighty frame made Cutter feel sick to the core.

CHAPTER SEVEN

WHEN ARE WE GOING TO escape?**

Cutter looked up at Skywise's sending, burning his hand on the edge of the heavy cauldron as they eased it from the fire. **Not yet!** he returned, sucking on his fingers.

Skywise thrust out his lower lip in obvious imitation of Cutter's daughter, but didn't distract his chief again from unhinging the iron pot.

"Mmmm! That smells *good*!" Picknose rumbled like a snoring hog as he dragged a great suck of air through his nostrils. "Stewed chipmunk and wormroot seasoned with herbs from Maggoty's garden. What a feast!" The table's few mugs and utensils jumped at the slam of his fist. "Bring it on, little slaves! Your masters are hungry!"

Skywise rolled his eyes, and Cutter flashed him a narrow frown as he hefted the pot between them. It scraped the floor despite their best efforts, leaving a torn-up trail through the hard-packed dirt. If the damage to their abode bothered the trolls, they didn't show it—the steaming chunks of stew barely had a chance to wet their plates before green lips and warty tongues sucked them away. Their sloppy fervor reminded Cutter of greedy buzzards, quarreling over the rotted remains of someone else's kill. He tried not to watch them while he and Skywise withdrew with the empty kettle.

These clumsy ankle chains are loose, Cutter. The stargazer's timing was better, although his sending was no less edged. **They're supposed to hold trolls, not us. Let's slip them and get out of here.**

Cutter shook his head and pushed the kettle against the back of the hearth with one foot. **I want to find out what became of all the other trolls first.**

Skywise nearly groaned aloud. **Why?**

Because. As soon as he sent it, Cutter thought it an unnecessarily petulant answer. Still, nothing better came immediately to mind, and that bothered him a little, too. **Curiosity,** he finally decided. **And because a lot of things have happened since we left the woods. Maybe what Picknose and his friends have to tell us might be important.**

He felt the first stirring of Skywise's answer, only to be startled out of contact by a wet, grotesque belch from the table behind them. Turning, Cutter made no effort to hide his disgust while Maggoty stabbed the last squirming morsels on her plate with a long, cracked fingernail.

"Ah, that was fine," she sighed. Even from across the hovel, her breath smelled like mildew. "I've a taste for some of that rare brew of mine. And I'd say the occasion warrants it." Her chair creaked from the strain of her turning to jab a hand toward Skywise. "Listen, elf—fetch me the big clay jug in the cupboard there. And be quick about it. And *you*!" She spat in Cutter's direction as Skywise trudged to obey. "Clear this table. Hop!"

His first instinct was to bare his teeth at her foul manners, but Cutter knew that would gain him nothing—and it certainly wouldn't get him New Moon back. Glancing wistfully at where Picknose toyed with the lovely blade against the edge of the tabletop, the young chief reminded himself that he still hoped to gain more than information by delaying their escape. He growled silently to himself and came to do as Maggoty ordered.

The dishes stank of troll tongues and troll handling. Cutter tried to pick them up suspended between both palms so that he only had to touch the edges, but gave up by the third plate, when the stack became too tall to manage. He decided not to sweep the food remnants off the table unless the trolls demanded it. They didn't, so he turned away from the table with his armload of filth and started back toward the fire.

Skywise still struggled by the open cupboard, his arms wrapped around the heavy jug now sitting on the floor outside the cabinet, his feet splayed wide for purchase. Cutter dumped the dishes in the same corner where they'd thrown the bones and trimmings from dinner, and hurried over to aid his friend before the trolls could start grumping again.

Whatever it is, Skywise grumbled mentally, **it sure is heavy.**

And liquid. The contents sloshed with every step, knocking them this way and that as they hauled the jug between them toward the table. Cutter had to squat to put his shoulder under the bottom and lift it to table height. It was still more than he could stand while he waited for Skywise to guide the spout on the jug to the mouth of each troll's mug.

The purple fluid poured like water, sloppy and light, and reeked of the sharp smell of rotten berries. Cutter heard Skywise snort at the billow of smell, and the chief wrinkled his own nose against it, not sure if he liked or loathed the concoction.

By the time they'd staggered around the table, filling each mug, the jug was considerably lighter and the trolls were grinning with obvious delight. Maggoty moved first, sweeping up her mug and spilling half its contents into a fragrant splash near the center of the table.

"To Picknose!" she crowed, and the others raised their own tankards, cheering. "Former guardsman of Greymung the Shiftless! To your health and forthcoming fortune." She leaned forward, dragging her bosom through the spilled liquid. "And to your wedding night, when you'll finally have earned my granddaughter's"— she cackled wickedly, eyes squinting small—"hand."

Oddbit fell on Picknose's neck, sighing, and the big troll rumbled happily. "Now *that's* something to drink to." He tossed back his head and upended his mug without even appearing to swallow. Cutter was impressed to see that not a drop of the purple fluid overran his cheeks or chin. The female trolls followed no more gracefully, Oddbit hiccuping daintily with each sloppy suck.

When Picknose's mug hit the table again, it was followed by a belch wet and loud enough to summon a summer storm. "*More,* slaves! I barely wet my lips on that first one."

Cutter stooped to upend the jug again while Skywise pulled the mug across the table. "What *is* this stuff?" the stargazer asked. Purple liquid splashed into the tankard, and Skywise scowled with disapproval. "It smells like dreamberries."

Picknose and Maggoty burst into roils of laughter

while Oddbit burped with startling violence into her hand.

"It *is* dreamberries, boy," Maggoty said. She thrust out her own mug for refilling. "They still grow around here. Maggoty knows a secret way to brew the juice from those little squishers. Makes mighty fine drinkin' if you've got the belly for it." She poked Skywise in the belt to make her point, cackling when he jerked away and nearly dropped the jug in her lap.

"You know, elf . . ."

A rough hand yanked on Cutter's hair, and the young chief stumbled upright from settling the jug on the floor, only to land disgustingly close to Picknose's armpit.

The troll smelled of dreamberries and sudden sentiment. "Your old sire, Bearclaw, had quite a taste for dreamberry wine."

"Wine?" Cutter struggled out from under Picknose's hold. "What's wine? Bearclaw never told me about it."

Picknose raked fingers through his curly beard, laughing. "Of course not!" He stood suddenly, swaying, and turned to lumber toward the cupboard. "There's a lot he didn't tell you. Right, Maggoty?"

"Oh, that one . . . !" Cutter was surprised by the fondness in the old crone's voice, and she sighed into her empty mug. "He was the only elf I ever came close to liking in all my days." She took the jug from Skywise and upended the last of its contents into her tankard. "What a hotburr he was."

"Well, let's see if his son is made of the same stuff." Picknose clumped back to the table, two jugs just like the first gripped under each thick arm. He thumped one onto the tabletop, then pulled a mug to the edge of the table and yanked the cork out of one of the jugs with his teeth. "Here, elf . . ." He spat the cork toward the fireplace and poured a healthy dose of the pungent wine. "Drink up! Your dad could do it all in one gulp."

Cutter scowled down at the tankard. His own reflection scowled back up at him, purple and wavery. "Picknose . . ."

"What's the matter? You carry his sword, but not his guts?"

Resentment flared in Cutter like flames through dry leaves, and he caught the mug in both hands and raised it to his nose. The sharp smell still stung his nostrils, but he had to admit it wasn't quite so foul as he'd thought when they first uncorked the jug. Knowing to connect the smell to familiar dreamberries also helped him understand it a little better. How hard could it be to swallow? If Bearclaw could do it—and like it—then what did he have to fear? Besides humiliating himself in front of three trolls and someone from his own tribe. At least he could swear Skywise to secrecy if he made too much of a fool of himself.

Tipping the mug, he took the wine in a single swig. It felt hot at first when it hit his tongue, more like nettle burrs than fire. His throat clamped, gagging in protest, but Cutter only squeezed his eyes shut and willed himself to swallow. The liquid went down in a rush of wild warmth, and he was left with a strong but not unpleasant taste sitting on the back of his tongue. Almost immediately, a thrill of lightness raced through his body and into his head. He felt as though he'd suddenly floated half his own height off the ground. Instead, all he did was flop straight down onto his behind, the mug still cradled in both hands between his knees.

"It's . . ." He tried to think of some truly appropriate word, but could only come up with "*good!*"

Above him, Picknose nodded with slow approval, like Strongbow after a satisfactory lesson. "Not bad," the troll allowed congenially. "Not bad at all for a puppy like you." Cutter felt a meaty hand catch the neck of his shirt, and he was suddenly off the ground again, suspended above a chair. "Siddown!" Picknose backed up his suggestion by dropping Cutter into the seat. "Have another! After all, you're the reason we're celebrating."

Yes, Cutter thought. *We're celebrating. How nice.*

"You, too, dearie."

He blinked several times, trying to focus on the other side of the table as Maggoty slid a mug in front of Skywise. "Pull up a stool and give it a try."

Skywise curled his mouth into a skeptical frown, but reached behind him with one foot to hook a chair and pull it underneath him. "Might as well . . ." He sighed and sat down.

Skywise sipped his wine a bit more judiciously than Cutter's all-out gulp. Then he paused, and took a slightly deeper swallow. *What an interesting shade of pink Skywise's cheeks turn,* Cutter mused, fascinated. *And what a ridiculous smile he's wearing.* Well, at least if they both made fools of themselves, neither one could tell tales about the other without facing similar ridicule. The thought warmed Cutter somewhat.

"Here!" Picknose leaned down to heft the open jug again, and Cutter caught sight of the delicate sword thrust into the troll's belt. He thrust his lip out, remembering why they were here and what he wanted, and nearly refused the new mug of wine Picknose clunked down in front of him.

"What?" the troll grumbled, affronted. "Why the long face?"

Cutter collapsed forward onto the table, head in hands. "Want my sword back. Father gave it t'me."

Picknose snorted into his mug, spewing wine onto the table. "That's all *you* know of its value," he scoffed. Jerking the sword from his belt, he lifted one foot to hold Cutter at bay as he fumbled with the pommel. "Let me show you something, wolf chief."

He picked at the leather bindings on the hilt with one clumsy finger until a flap came loose. Letting the bindings spiral open, he shoved his thumbnail under the head of a bright pin just underneath the pommel's ball, and popped it out into his palm. Then he took hold of the pommel with infinite care and wiggled it free of the hilt. It came away with a flat, irregular length of metal protruding out the end that had connected it with the sword.

Cutter reached for it in wonderment, but Picknose lifted it with easy greed above the elf's reach. "What is it?" It looked like a tiny metal jaw, all filled with broken teeth.

Picknose smiled at the tiny object, holding it above his head until it glowed like gold in the light from the cooking fire. "This, little chieftain," he purred, turning it over and over in his hands, "is called—a key."

CHAPTER EIGHT

A KEY?" CUTTER BLINKED at the little metal scrap, trying out the shape of the word on his wine-numbed tongue. "What's a key?"

Picknose rumbled. A kind of laughter, Cutter thought, although it wasn't all that easy to tell. "It opens things. *Wonderful* things." He drew the key very close to his nose and leered around its edges. "And it's going to make *me* the world's richest troll."

"Oooooo, Picky!" Oddbit shivered with delight. "I just *love* it when you say that!"

"But . . ." Cutter circled from shoulder to shoulder behind Picknose's back, trying to get a better look at the key while the troll held it out of his reach above the table. "But Bearclaw never showed the key to *me*!"

"That's because he never knew about it," Picknose told him. "No one did, except for the one who made the sword." He polished the golden ball against the front of his grimy tunic. "Old King Greymung let it all slip through his fingers—sword, key, treasure, and all." Obviously not intending to let the same thing happen to him, he tucked the key into his belt and gave it a protective pat.

"Treasure?" Skywise prompted. He had his head propped on one unsteady hand, but looked at least a little more attentive than before.

Maggoty jerked her head up in surprise and nearly drowned Skywise pushing his head closer to his mug. "Eh, have some more, dearie!" she offered loudly. Then she scowled at Picknose and hissed in what was apparently a trollish whisper, "Shut your blathering mouth, fool! Are you going to tell them everything?"

Whether Picknose knew that the elves' sensitive ears could hear their talk, Cutter couldn't tell. But the big troll was obviously not impressed by Maggoty or her paranoia. "Why not?" he countered in a troll's normal bellow. "They're not going anywhere."

Cutter tried to wave her fears aside, but only succeeded in knocking over his mug. "I don't care about any treasure," he complained, righting the empty container. "I just want to know where the rest of your folk are. We came back through the caverns and there was no one there."

Maggoty sniffed and rubbed her knuckles into one beady eye. "Oh, they're gone, elf . . ." She sighed. "Long gone . . ."

She didn't even try to smile when Oddbit reached across to pat her hand. "There, there, Grandmama."

Instead, she pulled away from the other troll and waddled over to the fire, sniffling loudly as she poked a stick at the flames. "They was dragged away to the mining pits up in the white cold land, where we'll never see them again."

"What happened?" Skywise asked.

"Troll warriors from the frozen mountains surprised us," Picknose replied. His voice cracked against the walls of the hovel, as angry and hard as thrown stones. "They broke into our living chambers through a tunnel that had been sealed off so long we'd forgotten it."

Cutter felt a little surge of excitement and reached out a thought to his friend. **Skywise! Hear that?** He seemed to connect with something, but wasn't sure exactly what. Leaning back, he tried to find Skywise's gaze behind Picknose's broad figure in the hopes eye contact would help, as it did when sending with wolves. All he found for sure was that his balance wasn't as good as he remembered. He had to grab the edge of the table to keep from toppling over. **There's other trolls! The world is just *full* of trolls and elves!**

Maybe. Skywise's thoughts were uncharacteristically practical. The wine no doubt brought out the best in him. **We don't know how much of this is truth and how much is dreamberry talk.** He frowned suddenly, peering at Cutter through narrowed eyes. **Is my sending as fuzzy as yours?**

It was. But before Cutter could frame a clear mental response, a hard swat between the shoulders knocked him upright and breathless.

"You paying attention, elf?" Picknose snarled.

Cutter fumbled to redirect his attention. "Huh?"

"Huh?" Picknose echoed in a mockingly high falsetto. Then he laughed. "The great chief of the Wolfriders! You elves thought you owned the forest, didn't you? Always bragging about your fancy ancestors, the High Ones. Well, we trolls have a noble heritage, too."

Picknose stood, thumbs hooked in his wide belt, and paced the hovel with warty nose held high. "*Our* forefathers were clever and strong," he announced, implying that the elves' had not been. "They lived way up at the top of the land, where it's always snowing. The mountains were their domain, and no creature, big or small, escaped their hidden traps.''

If they were really all that clever, Skywise noted, **they would have hunted out in the open like everybody else.**

Shhh!

"But a time came when big, heavy sheets of ice started crunching down around the mountains, filling up the crevices and valleys, and shaking up the tunnels something fierce.'' Picknose frowned, shuddering as though he could remember those times himself. "As it got colder and colder, and the ice got thicker and thicker around them, my ancestors decided to dig their way to a warmer place. It took a long time, and the cold seemed to follow them downland. But, finally, their tunnel ended here, under the warm ground where the woods you elves used to call the holt stood. Course, this was well before you Wolfriders settled here,'' he added with a dismissive wave.

Recrossing the small room, Picknose stopped by the fire to stare furiously into the flames. "A lot more time passed.'' He'd gotten to history he could almost remember, Cutter realized, watching the play of shadow memories in the troll's dark eyes. "Time well spent in learning the ways of metalworking and cavern gardening. Then one day, King Guttlekraw up and decided he wanted all his subjects to return with him to the frozen mountains. Greymung—who was only a young mump then—and many other trolls refused. There was a rebellion and a big battle, and when it was all over, Greymung's side had won! Greymung drove Guttlekraw and his followers back through the tunnel and sealed it off for good.'' He turned back to them, but there was little triumph on his face. "And so Greymung became king of his own group of trolls."

"And got fat and lazy!" Maggoty thumped her fist against her leg, scowling. "Why, I wiped Greymung's nose and fed him his moss mush when he was only a tot." Then her expression softened somewhat as other memories surfaced behind those. "You're *all* just babies next to me," she chuckled, "you know that?"

Cutter had guessed it, but didn't admit as much now.

"We trolls knew it when the first Wolfriders came to the woods," Maggoty told him, focused very seriously now on his young face. "But we made sure you never, ever found out about us. I'll bet you elves always wondered who kept picking your dreamberry bushes clean without leaving a clue."

It was Cutter's history they tread on now, and he felt a swell of pride remembering stories he'd heard for as long as he could recall. "But Bearclaw finally caught you, didn't he?"

"That he did, the wicked scamp." She sighed with that surprising softness again, and settled back in her seat with hands across her breasts. "I never picked the same bush twice in a row. Had my own foolproof method, too—I dug holes under every one of them bushes, and had clever little plugs to cover 'em so even you Wolfriders couldn't see." She shook her head. "But that young rascal Bearclaw sat through a full change of the Mother Moon, just waiting for me to come round to that most particular bush."

Skywise's laughter surprised Cutter. "Only Bearclaw cared enough about dreamberries to go to all that trouble." It was hard sometimes to remember that Skywise was old enough to have known his father back then.

Picknose blew a disgusted snort. "Snoopingest elf that ever lived."

"Oh, you trolls never had reason to be sorry Bear-claw discovered you." Cutter tugged at Picknose's belt, but got his hand slapped just short of reaching the key. "You really *liked* the furs and leathers and good red meat we traded you for your metalwork."

To Cutter's surprise, Picknose exploded to his feet, face growing hot and green with anger. "That's just the point! Our lives got too soft, all because of you! We weren't prepared to fend off Guttlekraw's warriors when they came again. Greymung wasn't fit to lead us in battle anymore." He spun away from the table and clenched his fists on empty air. "It was horrible! They made prisoners of all those they didn't kill. And what they did with the dead, even with Greymung . . ." A sudden thickness came into his voice, and he stalked to the boarded window to push it open onto the fading sun. "I don't even like to think about it." Cutter had to admit he could almost feel sorry for the troll. "They've changed, those trolls from the frozen mountains."

Silence clogged the little hovel for what seemed a very long time. Then Cutter stood and shuffled, leg irons and all, to stand near Picknose at the window. "So you got yours right after you snooked us through the Tunnel of Golden Light." The fresh air felt delicious and wonderful against his cheeks.

Picknose only nodded thoughtfully.

"Why'd you play such a dirty trick on us, anyway?"

The troll's first response was a shrug, then he seemed to reconsider as he pushed the shutters together again. "Oh, I didn't want to," he sighed. "Not really.

But Greymung was a spiteful old toad. It was death or worse to defy him.''

Cutter grimaced at Picknose's contritely raised eyebrows. "That's a pile of owl pellets.''

Another shrug as the troll paused in tipping more wine into his own mug. "By the way—why *are* you still alive?''

"It's no thanks to you!'' Cutter answered hotly. "It just so happens that we *crossed* the desert and found—'' He was silenced suddenly by a blow to the back of his ribs, and spun around with a snarl for whoever stood behind him.

Skywise returned his chief's glare in furious silence. **Do you have tree bark for brains?**

"Oh . . .'' His cheeks were suddenly hot, and it was all Cutter could do to cross his arms and regain a haughty version of his composure. "Well, it's none of your business what we found,'' he told Picknose with a sniff. "But right now my friend and I are on a quest to locate other tribes of elves.'' He angled a look up at all three trolls. "Can you tell us where to look?''

The fidgety look of discomfort they all slipped one another was nearly answer enough. Maggoty was the first to turn away, trying to take Oddbit with her, and Picknose hurried to push the elves back toward their seats and their abandoned mugs of wine. "We trolls mind our own business,'' he said, unconvincingly. "Always have. Here . . .'' He tipped another dollop into Cutter's mug. "Let me sweeten that for you.''

Oddbit oozed up to Picknose's arm when the troll reclaimed his own chair, rubbing her nose against his in a ridiculous display of trollish intimacy. "You're so clever, my love!''

Whatever she was referring to, Skywise obviously didn't want to pursue it. "Since we're trading tales of escape," he cut in, almost loud enough to rival the trolls. "How did you three survive the invasion of your caverns?"

"Oh, that was all my Picky's doing." Oddbit settled her bulk onto Picknose's lap, lacing her arm behind his meaty neck. "I used to be King Greymung's favorite, you know, but Picknose always loved me. He carried me and Grandmama outside when those awful warriors came." She preened with undisguised pride. "We're the first trolls ever to brave the daylight. The caverns just aren't safe anymore. But *I'm* not afraid," she cooed, molding herself against Picknose's shoulder. "Picky will protect me."

He stroked her hair with unaccustomed tenderness. "I'd face *any* danger to win you, Oddbit my gem."

Skywise sniggered into his hand. "You mean she's your lifemate—'Picky'?"

Picknose shot the elf a vile scowl. "I am not yet worthy of her! First I must be able to give her everything her heart desires."

"*I* desire my sword . . ." Cutter slumped his chin down onto the tabletop, sighing across at New Moon's dismantled pommel. ". . . All in one piece."

"Well, you can't have it!" Oddbit snatched the disassembled weapon off the table and threw it to the floor behind her. "Picky promised me a shower of gold," she nattered waspishly, "and I *won't* be wed to him without it." Picknose's unhappy sigh was an eloquent statement as to the truth of this.

"You know, Picknose . . ." Skywise stood and came to stand behind Cutter, his face alight with a puckish grin Cutter recognized all too well. "If Oddbit Recognized you, she'd be yours whether you had gold or not." He thumped his chief once atop the head. "Right, Cutter?"

Picknose wrinkled his lengthy nose. "What are you chittering about, elf?"

"Recognition!" Seemingly appalled at the troll's lack of knowledge, Skywise clapped his hands on Cutter's shoulders. "My friend here is a perfect example. His lifemate—"

"Leetah," Cutter informed them blearily, tipping back the last of his wine.

"—couldn't stand him when they first met. But now they have two fine cubs!"

"The poor girl!" Oddbit seemed genuinely alarmed. "And she had no say in the matter at all?"

"She had *plenty* to say." The ugly, smelly troll hovel paled behind a veil of bittersweet memory, painted all in the colors of desert, sun, and brilliant emerald eyes. "For the longest time, it seemed she stood looking down at me from a high place, just beyond my reach. But elves are children of the High Ones, and Recognition is the Way. It's worth all the pain." As he'd learned clear through to his bones during those first days and nights that Leetah refused to even speak to him. "Because the pleasure is more than can be told.

"Let me tell you about my Leetah." He climbed unsteadily onto the table, trying to reach that high and distant place where Leetah waited for him in a shimmer of bracelets and wild auburn hair. "She's a lovely flower with sword blades for petals—a wellspring that never runs dry, but always leaves you thirsty for more . . ." He pressed his cheek to the beloved image, and felt her ready warmth even across the days of travel between them. "She had the strength to refuse me *despite* Recognition."

The warmth beneath his face moved, and Oddbit's voice asked, "Why didn't she?"

Disgusted by his very proximity to the troll, Cutter scrambled back to the other side of the table, stuttering some nonsense reply. When he looked to Skywise for help, his friend only threw his arms up in a shrug, pink with laughter.

"Don't look at me!" the stargazer objected. "I've been wondering why she took you in myself."

It occurred to Cutter he could always leave Skywise here when he escaped.

"Bah!" Picknose grabbed a handful of Cutter's tunic and jerked the elf back into his seat. "Siddown!" he commanded testily. "You elves botch everything, even romance. Recognition . . ." He gurgled a thick sound of disgust in his throat. "Revolting! *We* handle things more sensibly. Why, any troll worth his hammer knows a maiden's love is as true as the gold he gives her. And the more gold, the more true her love." He blinked dewy eyes at Oddbit. "Isn't that so, my succulent little mushroom?"

She puckered her moss-green lips in return. "Just so, my big, handsome toadstool."

Cutter clapped a hand over his mouth to hold back his stomach, and Skywise commented dryly, "Picknose may have the hammer, but Oddbit holds the handle."

Maggoty chuckled with approval. "My little darling's always been a practical one."

"I'll bet Picknose is making it all up, anyway," Skywise continued, loud enough to cut off any protest the troll might have made to his first observation. Cutter ducked under the table to try and catch sight of New Moon on the other side of the room. "About the treasure, I mean."

"It's true!" Picknose roared, pounding the table. "True! *True!*" Cutter felt a thump as Picknose yanked Skywise into the chair next to his, and he cracked his head against the tabletop trying to crawl up fast enough to keep from being hauled about himself. "Both of you sit right there," the troll demanded, glaring at them with eyes as hard as mountain gems. "I'm going to tell you all about it!"

CHAPTER NINE

THERE'S A TREASURE, elves," Picknose said with grave certainty, "of *that* much I'm sure. I have Two-Edge's word on it. He's the greatest metalsmith that ever lived—a legend among us trolls." He looked expectantly between Cutter and Skywise, and Cutter thought the horror on his knobby face could only be in response to their own stares of confusion.

"Don't tell me you never heard of him!" Planting both elbows on the table, Picknose leaned forward as though imparting a secret. "No one knows exactly where he came from, but the story goes that he's part elf on his mother's side."

Cutter jerked away from the troll in revulsion. "That's disgusting!"

"It's true!" Oddbit was quick to insist. "But they say she wasn't as ugly as most elves. She may even have had a wart or two."

Cutter made a face at her, unable to reconcile himself to what imagination kept suggesting.

"He comes and goes as he pleases," Picknose went on, either oblivious to their exchange or ignoring them. "Always has. Sometimes he's up in the snow country, sometimes down here with us woodland trolls, and sometimes no one sees him for a generation or more. He's old as the mountains, a drifting shadow who speaks with a voice of stone. He keeps to himself, but he always leaves some trace of his handiwork where trolls can find it and learn. There's no one to equal him as a weapons maker." He swatted Cutter on the shoulder in what the young chief took to be a friendly troll gesture. "He even had the delicate skill it took to make that toy sword of yours."

Cutter didn't like hearing New Moon referred to in such a way, but decided not to draw attention to the sword at the moment.

"But he's crazy—not right in the head." Picknose seemed no more concerned about New Moon than he did about the remnants of their supper. "Must be his mixed blood."

"I guess so," Skywise snorted, then plastered on a false look of innocence when Picknose turned to glare at him. "He'd *have* to be mad to have shown *you* the way to steal all his gold."

"I say he *chose* me to inherit his wealth," Picknose returned stiffly. "In fact, his voice came to me during my journey back through the Tunnel of Golden Light." His voice took on a coarser, more rumbling note, obviously mimicking someone else's words. " 'There he goes, Picky Picknose. There's a treasure for his pleasure, but the key's in the sea, the sandy, sandy sea.' "

He cupped a hand to his ear as though reliving the moment again. "I called out, 'Two-Edge? Have you returned, old wanderer? What're you babbling about?'

" 'Moon-sword, golden hoard,' he sang at me. 'Moon-sword, golden hoard. Find us both, the treasure and me! The sword holds the key—the sword *is* the key!' "

"Interesting," Skywise allowed. "But why did you believe him?"

Picknose nodded sagely. "Because Two-Edge may be crazy, but he's not a liar. The proof's right here." He slapped a hand against the key in his belt, then reached out with the other to cuff Cutter between the shoulders. "You don't know how glad I was to see you today, pup! I've been kicking myself for seven turns of the seasons thinking you and the Moon-sword were gone forever. Now I'll have you both—and Two-Edge's treasure, too, when I find it." He roared a hearty laugh. "Think of it! Picknose the Wealthy, served hand and foot by the son of Bearclaw!"

"Ooooo! Picky, dear! You make me quiver all over!"

Cutter decided that if he had to hear Oddbit gush all over her beloved toadstool one more time, he was going to throw himself in the firepit and be done with it.

Picknose's knees popped like pine knots when he stood. "Who'd have thought it would be Bearclaw to bring me all this?" Tromping across the hovel, he stooped to heft New Moon in one gnarled hand. "We always thought this flimsy little elf blade useless in a troll's hand. Bearclaw won it in a game of stones, and we thought for once *we'd* cheated *him*! What a joke!" He swept his mug high in the air, sloshing purple rain all over the trampled floor. "To Bearclaw!" he cried. "The elf who was almost as smart as a troll!"

Cutter leapt up from his chair. "You take that back!"

He slammed into Picknose before the troll had even turned, and they both tumbled to the floor in a tangle of chains and trollish curses. Cutter twisted for a hold on Picknose's beard, beating at his twisted nose, kicking at his stomach. They rolled up against the table legs, and Picknose grunted with painful surprise. Taking advantage of his distraction, Cutter snatched New Moon out of his grasp and bounced to his feet just as Skywise's sharp mental voice cut through his wine-soaked anger.

Cutter! Out of the way!

He moved without asking why. Chuckling gleefully, Skywise tossed something toward the center of the table, right into the midst of the arguing trolls. Cutter realized it was Maggoty's last pouch of sleeping powder when it *poofed!* a great, foul-smelling cloud into the air and engulfed the trolls. Howling with delight, he danced about the room gathering up their scattered supplies and weapons while Skywise stood near the open window, arms folded, grinning smugly at the coughing, cursing bundle of trolls.

Cutter dashed past his friend to throw his armload out the window. "Come on!"

"Uh . . ." He felt Skywise jerk with surprise, and turned in time to see the trolls emerge from the dusty fog with eyes streaming and scowls set. "It . . . it doesn't work on trolls . . . ?" Skywise stammered.

"Might've known." Cutter hefted himself into the window, nudging his friend with one foot. "I've got our stuff—let's get out of here!" He squirmed through the window without waiting for Skywise's reply.

"Oh, no you don't!"

Picknose's angry bellow was nearly lost in the crash that followed it. Cutter didn't need to look back through the window to figure out why Skywise hadn't followed him.

"Thought you'd make fools of us, eh?" the troll roared. "Thought you'd just up and—*stop your squirming!*"

Casting frantically about for something he could fight with that wouldn't endanger Skywise, Cutter's eyes locked on a slimy pile just below the window. Sweeping up a handful of the discarded troll slop, he hauled himself back into the open window and slung the wad blindly at whatever might be beyond.

Picknose's squeal of fury brought a grin to Cutter's face. Skywise wiggled out from under the troll's arm, lips pursed with concentration, and made a dive for the window even as Cutter dropped to collect another handful of slop.

Cutter!

"I'll get 'im!"

He reached out for Skywise's grasping hand, catching the wrist in as firm a grip as his slimy hands allowed. Picknose growled from between Skywise's feet, and lifted his own hands to display the leg irons he still clenched in his fists. "No!" he shouted over his shoulder at Maggoty. "The day I can't hang on to one miserable, chained elf, I'll sit out in the open sun till I'm crow food!"

Cutter planted both feet against the outside mud-and-stone wall and heaved with all his might. "I hope the crows are hungry!"

Picknose growled something wordless and shifted his grip on Skywise's chains.

Shoulders burning, hands stiff with the strain of holding on, Cutter threw his head back and howled, high and wild, into the sky. It felt good to clear his lungs of the dank air of the troll hovel—better still to hear Oddbit shriek with terror at the wolves' distant reply. They sounded close, their eager minds pricking to his sending touch. Cutter howled to them again. *Hurry! Hurry! Time to flee!*

Skywise grunted, and Picknose's snarling face suddenly appeared too close behind him. "Don't let 'em bring those vicious brutes in here!" Maggoty screamed from somewhere in the darkness of the inner hovel.

Picknose loosed one hand to paw at the tears rolling down his cheeks. "They're not going anywhere!" he roared, squinting away from the sun. "If I have— *Arrrghhh!*"

Skywise tumbled out the window while Picknose collapsed backward out of sight, still clutching the now-empty leg irons. Cutter rolled to all fours, tangling in his own chains even as he snatched up every piece of their equipment he could reach. **He's got to dress!** he sent to Skywise. The wolves swarmed around them, whining and sniffing and trying to understand what had happened. **He can't go out in the sun unless he's covered. Let's *go*!**

Nightrunner bumped him, eager to be running, and Skywise was already atop his own wolf, leaning low to scoop up his bow as Starjumper lunged into motion. Cutter nearly couldn't mount with the great length of chain between his feet, but he finally managed to scramble awkwardly across Nightrunner's back without dropping a single supply. By the time they galloped off after Starjumper and Skywise, Cutter was nearly howling with joy just to be free and on the move again. Even this burned-out forest smelled living and sweet compared to the trolls.

They ran without direction or goal. It didn't matter, really—they only knew where they had come from, not where they needed to go. Just to run made Cutter's soul sing. He found himself wishing they could go on this way forever. But his hands grew tired from gripping his wolf's grizzled mane, and the weight of the iron around his legs seemed to grow with every stride. When they finally reached a copse of blackened stumps surrounded by arrow-slim saplings, Cutter slowed Nightrunner to a walk and sent for Skywise to stop nearby. Skywise did so without protest, rolling straight off Starjumper's back to sprawl in the grass beside his wolf-friend.

Nightrunner slowed less gracefully. The old wolf panted more heavily than Cutter liked to see, and sat with a slow stiffness that hadn't been there only a season before. Cutter hobbled to the closest stump and collapsed onto it with his head in his hands. He'd never had a headache quite like this one—dull and heavy, as if his skull were stuffed with rancid leather. He worked off the first of the leg irons without even opening his eyes.

"My ankles are so swollen," he groaned, groping about for his other foot. "I'm *never* going to get these off." Winding his hand in the toe of his soft leather boot, he pulled it off without really meaning to, but was glad to find that the extra room let him slip the final iron off with little trouble. He let himself fall off the stump with an anguished moan. "A troll could've knocked my head off and it wouldn't hurt this much." He picked up his boot and crawled over to join Skywise. "From now on, I'll take my dreamberries fresh off the bush."

Skywise chuckled softly, but didn't reply.

"At least we got away all right." Cutter meant it to be uplifting, but couldn't help sighing with regret when he pulled New Moon free of its scabbard. "But New Moon is ruined." He wiggled a finger in the hole left by the missing pommel. "How can it ever be fixed?"

A startled little grunt from Skywise drew his attention, and Cutter frowned when his friend reached over to catch his hand and pull it around in front of him. Before Cutter could ask, Skywise spat gently and bounced the key into his palm.

"The pommel!" Cutter jumped to his feet, staring at the key in wonderment. "You filched it when you were wrestling with Picknose, didn't you? Why didn't you tell me?"

Skywise shrugged, still smiling. "I forgot for a moment."

"You forgot." Cutter flopped back down beside him and pressed the key between his hands. "Skywise, thank you!" He dried it quickly on the hem of his shirt, then fit it carefully back into the hilt where it belonged. "Thank you."

Skywise shrugged again, gazing across the countryside as though searching for something along the horizon that looked more familiar than where they sat. Cutter felt him quiet with some private thinking, then Skywise asked, "So where to now?"

Cutter looked up to stare across the land himself. The lowermost edge of the sun was only just smearing to orange at the edge of the world. "Remember what the humans who came to Sorrow's End told us? Somewhere in the direction of Sun-Goes-Down, they said, other groups of humans dwell in deep, green woods that were never touched by the great fire." He glanced over at Skywise, slipping New Moon back into its sheath. "Why don't we search for other elf tribes there? No matter the danger, the souls of our kind have always yearned for the cool, dark beauty of the forest."

"Makes sense," Skywise allowed with a nod. "And it's a sure thing Picknose wouldn't offer us a better suggestion now, even if he could."

"Too true." Climbing to his feet, Cutter leaned back against Starjumper long enough to tug his boot back on beneath his trousers. When he reached to help Skywise stagger up beside him, the stargazer giggled and sat down again on top of his wolf.

"What?" Cutter asked.

"I was just thinking." Skywise stuffed his share of the supplies into his pack, still grinning broadly. "Maybe we'll bump into Two-Edge and give him Picky's greetings."

"And the key?" He was never sure if he should trust Skywise when he giggled.

But it was in all innocence that his friend answered brightly, "What key?"

"To the treasure."

"*What* treasure?"

"Oh . . . yeah." Cutter chuckled and shoved Skywise's supplies into his arms. "Let's get moving. The sun only goes down once every day."

CHAPTER TEN

L EETAH?"

Glancing up from her mending, Leetah looked across her dimly lit hut to find Nightfall crouched, knees to ears, in the open window. The Wolfrider's pale features stood out cleanly in the flickering lantern light, her big gold eyes reflecting the flame like discs of polished metal. Leetah sometimes wondered if these forest folk would ever learn how to use the doors.

"Leetah, come on. It's time."

"Time . . . ?" The healer searched her memory for something that should make this night different from any other since Cutter's leaving. Then she heard a distant elfin voice embroider the night with a thin, ghostly wail, and her heart stuttered against her breast. She wondered how many wolves would be there waiting, and whether or not they'd accept her dark skin among the milk-white features of their tribesfolk. "Ember?"

Smiling, Nightfall only nodded.

"Oh, no! Oh, High Ones! I had no idea it would be so soon!" Needles, thread, and mending frame all tumbled out of her lap as she hurried to her feet and gathered her night skirts up into her hands. When Cutter explained this to her, so long ago now, Leetah had promised herself she would be as calm and competent as a Wolfrider when the time came—not like some pampered village maiden who was still afraid of the night. Faced with the reality of the change rushing up on her daughter, though, she felt silly and confused even though she knew she shouldn't be. "I haven't even talked with Ember! What should I tell her? What should I do?"

"Leetah, relax." Nightfall's gentle laughter eased her a little, but not so much that she questioned when the Wolfrider reached for her hands to guide her out through the window. "You don't have to do anything. Just be there, be happy, and the Way will take care of the rest." Nightfall jumped nimbly to the ground without even looking behind her, then reached up to lift Leetah down after her. "Come on, healer," she said with a smile. "Your daughter's waiting!"

The paths between the painted village huts whispered with wind and the sounds of peaceful slumber. Bright moonslight washed the desert with colors and shadows more gentle than those revealed by the harsh light of the sun. Leetah had grown to love the softer nighttime in these years since the Wolfriders' arrival, learning to pad in respectful silence through this darker world, marveling at the stories hidden in the movements of the stars. Even the spine-thin wail that caromed now off the bare rock above the village filled her with a sense of vivid wonder. A dozen voices joined the first, and they echoed and reechoed through the hills until they sounded like dozens upon dozens upon dozens, weaving a tapestry of song in colors all made for the night. Leetah could suddenly not remember a time when she had willingly slept through until morning.

"Mother?" A child's call, but whispered and quiet, so much like his father's that the fleeting glimpse of Suntop's slim blondness in the dark made Leetah's heart throb with loneliness even as she smiled. She held out her hands, and he ran up to her to prance just ahead of her steps. "We have to hurry, Mother," he informed her, very serious despite his excitement. "Strongbow won't let Ember start until you get there, and Ember's just about ready to bust!"

Strongbow, Cutter's voice said with gruff fondness in her memory. *Always the traditionalist.* She tried to hold onto the sound of those phantom words with her mind. Anymore, memories of her lifemate grew dearer with every day of his absence. She took Suntop's hand, and the wild vitality of his youth made her smile. "All right," she whispered, urging him to run. "Then, by all means, let's hurry!"

Suntop led up between a slope of rocks that seemed too precarious to have lasted the hundreds of years it already had. Nightfall broke away with a last reassuring touch, loping over to join the other elves gathered at the edges of the plateau. Atop a rough boulder so that she stood taller than anyone else there, Ember bounced despite Strongbow's hands on her shoulders, waving to Leetah and Suntop until some invisible signal from the archer got through to her and she fought her jittering down to a more dignified level. Smiling, Leetah waved back anyway, then froze when a rush of movement caught her attention from off to one side.

Briersting, his dusty brown ruff bristled up between his shoulders, surged to his feet with an uneasy snort. He led the pack, Leetah knew—had been its leader since driving Nightrunner out not even a year ago, while Cutter and she hunted for lizards in the desert with the children. That meant the cubs she heard yapping inside some unseen den were his, and that the other dozen wolves gathered with him waited only for his decision as to how they should treat this new outsider.

Leetah stood, very still and silent, as the wolf stalked up to her, ears swiveled forward, tail stiff and high. She hadn't seen so many of the rough predators all together since those first few moons they'd been in Sorrow's End. Cutter had maintained a steady contact with the pack even after Nightrunner was no longer welcome in their numbers. Even Suntop and Ember had spent countless summer nights prowling the rocky dens, stealing peeks at newborn wolf cubs, or watching the stars with their heads propped on this or that wolf's tail. She had thought she was used to Nightrunner now that the wolf stayed close to Cutter during his twilight years—that learning to trust and respect the one great creature would make her immune to the fear inspired by all the others. Feeling the cold, serious nose prod her wrists and belly as Briersting inspected her unfamiliar scent, she knew now that this wasn't true. Nightrunner and Cutter were gone, and Leetah was simply terrified.

Close your eyes. The hard mental voice knifed into her thinking without warning, taking her attention as though between two hands and forcing her to focus on what it told her. **When you stare, he thinks you want to fight him. So close your eyes, and turn your face aside.**

Leetah wanted to shake her head. She couldn't. She couldn't turn her back on a beast strong and fierce enough to crush her child's skull in its huge jaws. But

Suntop's hand in hers was brave and unflinching, and Leetah knew it was only her fear that was dangerous, not these loyal creatures or their elfin kin.

Nodding faintly, she let her eyes slip shut, and turned as though to look back over her shoulder at Strongbow and her little girl.

Briersting's breath was as warm and close as a lover's as he nuzzled her collarbone, the sweep of her ear. Then his hot tongue flicked against the edge of her earring as though to dismiss her and her jewelry, and Leetah heard the casual *click-click*ing of his toenails on stone as he trotted back to join Silvergrace near their den.

Very good, chieftain's mate. The trace of approval in Strongbow's sending was unexpected, and Leetah tried to let him feel her soft smile in reply. She had no idea whether or not her message reached him.

Deep inside the stone hollows, cubling voices yipped and whined, no longer able to maintain their silence. Ember, a cubling so much like them, began to shiver again under Strongbow's hands, her blue-green eyes locked on the den entrance as if in a trance.

"I hear you . . . ," she moaned softly. To whom, Leetah wondered. She didn't think Ember knew anyone else was near. ". . . I hear you . . ."

The faintest trace of a smile crossed Strongbow's lean face. He dropped his hands from Ember's shoulders with a nod. **All right, Ember. He's waiting.**

The young elf bolted forward with a thorough lack of decorum, leaping from the rock with an unskilled, wavering howl. Laughter rippled through the assembled Wolfriders, and Leetah half felt, half heard fond memories of earlier rituals pass among them with

that sound. Not for the first time, the healer felt a
faint stab of jealousy at the deep bonds these folk had
managed to forge in such short, brutal lifetimes. She
squeezed Suntop's hand, not sure whether to wish him
a life like theirs, or a life like her own.

"I hear you!" Ember called in time with the unseen cubs' pitiful howling. "I hear you! It's me—Ember!" She scrambled through the gathered pack, past
Silvergrace and Briersting without even noticing the
sniffs and licks they aimed at her ears and legs, and
into the mouth of the den, until her whole head and
shoulders disappeared into that darkness. Leetah had
to clench her teeth to keep from crying a warning.

"Don't you know me? I'm the one you've been
calling for." Her voice echoed, ridiculously sharp and
small, inside the confining space. "Come out, friend.
It's time to come out. I can't wait to see you!"

Claws scrabbled against unseen rock, and a cascade of complaints rose up from the cubs inside the
den. Leetah watched Silvergrace with some apprehension, unable to believe the she-wolf could stand by so
calmly while her children squabbled and wailed so
nearby. If it had been Leetah's children, she would
have wanted to rush in immediately to dry their tears
and quiet their crying. It had been hard learning to respect the rugged independence allowed by all the
Wolfrider mothers, but her children were more than
merely Sun Folk children, and she had to respect the
wildness in them if they were to grow strong and
healthy. As she had several times in the past, Leetah
longed to ask silly details of cub-rearing from Silvergrace's elf-friend Rainsong. Woodlock and Rainsong were
somewhere down in the village, though, asleep with

their ever-growing family just like everyone else in Sorrow's End. So maybe they weren't the best authority on elf-wolf similarities anymore.

Ember's narrow bottom wriggled as she crawled backward out of the den. A pair of wide yellow eyes followed her, and Ember squealed with delight at the roly-poly cub that waddled out into the moonslight. "Oh, look! Mother, Suntop, look! He's *beautiful*!" Back end quivering from the thrashing of his stubby curl of a tail, he clambered up into Ember's lap as a squirming scramble of energy, all tongue and fur. He was so like Ember, and so unlike the stately adult wolves, as he slathered the elf child's face with wet, wolfish kisses. She giggled in a tinkling like porcelain bells.

"Choplicker!" she declared, eyes squeezed shut against his tongue's assault. "That's *your* name! You're my first wolf-friend, and someday soon I'll ride on your back and we'll be strong and fierce like my father!"

Like her father. Leetah released Suntop's hand so he could run to join Ember in wrestling with the little cub. She didn't want to spoil this night by spilling her emotions all over where they didn't belong.

"Ember is so happy." Nightfall's voice sounded close to her elbow. Leetah turned to give her a smile, grateful as always to have her nearby. "Cutter will be sorry he missed seeing this," the Wolfrider admitted with a wistful sigh.

"Oh, he'll see it." Clearbrook swept her long silver braid into her lap as she settled to the ground next to one of the rocks. "He'll see it through our eyes, just as we see him now through his children." She reached up without appearing to notice and clasped hands with Scouter and Dewshine to either side of her.

Yes, Leetah thought with a throb of heartsickness. *I see Cutter in them every day.* And it tore her apart inside.

Whether she sensed it through the simple bonds of friendship, or Leetah simply broadcast her thoughts too loudly, Nightfall brushed her shoulder against Leetah's in gentle sympathy. "They're your children, too." She nodded at the tangle of children and cub rolling here and there in the dirt. "Their skin is brown, like yours."

"But their eyes are Cutter's," Leetah admitted, not unhappy for the fact. "And their bodies recall his youthful grace and beauty with every movement." She felt the weight of tears swell into her eyes, and turned away from the playing children for fear she'd cry if she watched them any longer.

Nightfall turned with her, slipping her arm across the healer's shoulders. "Leetah . . ."

Leetah sighed and tipped her head to lean it against Nightfall's. "He said he would be gone for only one year," she whispered. "That's little more than a moment in the span of my long life. A year seemed so brief a while. I . . ." She had to laugh a little at herself, then didn't like the brittle thinness of the sound. "I didn't think I would have time to miss Cutter. But now I find myself counting the days until he returns."

"It's your own fault."

Leetah jumped, not having expected someone else to intrude on their discussion. She schooled her face into stillness, though, before turning to face Moonshade. She wouldn't grant the tanner the satisfaction of seeing how deeply her words had cut.

Moonshade pulled away from Strongbow's side as though encouraged to continue by Leetah's attention. "Your place is by your lifemate's side," she said, sliding down the boulder to join them despite Nightfall's warning glower. "You should have joined Cutter on his quest, not waited behind like some fallow doe for his return."

Nightfall thrust out her arm to stop Moonshade from coming any closer. "That's not fair. If you had cubs as young as Suntop and Ember, would *you* abandon them to follow Strongbow on a dangerous journey?"

"I would if Strongbow were chief." She pushed Nightfall aside, that gesture alone making it clear enough that she believed her lifemate to be as good as leader in Cutter's absence. "You know as well as I that a chief's cubs belong to all his tribe. There isn't one of us who wouldn't gladly have helped parent the twins if Leetah had gone with Cutter." She slapped the healer with a dark, searing glare. "As she should have."

She should stay and fight, Leetah knew. Cutter would have wanted that. He wouldn't want her to let anyone say she wasn't fit to be his mate, or the keeper of his cubs. But it was always so easy to find herself outside the paths these elves traveled, and Leetah found that, more and more, she hadn't the strength to argue with Moonshade over something they could no longer change. It took too much of her energy already just to walk through every day without her loved one, not knowing when or if she would ever hold him again.

Turning her back on Moonshade and everyone else in the tribe, she walked away from their distrust and disapproval. It was easier just to be on her own.

"Oh, look what your squirrel chatter's done now." She heard Nightfall hurry after her. "Leetah, wait!"

She didn't. Not really. The young Wolfrider would catch her easily enough, and Leetah didn't want to give Moonshade any reason to think more of her waspish comments were welcome. Crossing her arms against the cool breath of the night, Leetah walked until she came to the edge of the plateau overlooking the sleeping village. It was at this very spot—but much farther below—that she'd first spied on the Wolfriders while they went about the lovely intricacies of their nightly lives. But that was long ago, before she'd taken Nightfall as a friend, or accepted Cutter into her life, or harbored any foolish hopes of being accepted by this strange and wonderfully alien tribe.

"Leetah . . ." Nightfall always announced her arrivals when she came upon Leetah in the darkness. It was as though she knew her Wolfrider footsteps were too soft and subtle for Sun Folk ears to hear, and she wished to save Leetah the embarrassment of being startled by the approach of a friend. The gesture had always endeared her to Leetah, if only because of the thoughtful heart it spoke of, and the loyalty that came with that heart.

Nightfall moved up behind her and slipped an arm around Leetah's waist, pulling her close as though to grant them both some greater warmth. "Moonshade thinks in straight lines," she said, her voice betraying her annoyance with the other Wolfrider. "With her, the Wolfriders' Way is the *only* Way. Pay her no heed. You have the right to raise your cubs in keeping with your own tribe's customs, no matter what Moonshade and Strongbow have to say."

Leetah turned away from the village, swallowing her regret that the reasons for her actions were so easily misconstrued. "Oh, my dear friend," she sighed. "Surely you have seen that I have never been overprotective of Suntop and Ember. I cannot claim motherhood as my excuse for remaining here. Rather . . ." She took a deep breath, summoning more courage than she felt she had to spare right now. "It is pride that holds me in Sorrow's End." She felt the flutter of Nightfall's confusion, but couldn't raise her eyes to look at her friend's face. "Do you remember Rayek?"

Nightfall nodded, still frowning. "Of course. Your . . . mate from before we came here."

"He loved me because he saw in me a reflection of himself. I, too, am proud to possess finely honed magic powers." She lifted her gaze to search for acceptance if not understanding in Nightfall's amber eyes. "No one has died in Sorrow's End since my healing skills matured. It is *pride,* Nightfall. And something or someone as brave as you can forgive even less . . ." She tightened her hands on Nightfall's slim fingers. "Fear."

The Wolfrider shook her head, hurting Leetah more than she could know with the easy dismissal. "Leetah, no—"

"Yes." Leetah pulled away, not wanting pity, but afraid her weakness would drive Nightfall away. "I was *afraid* to go with Cutter—afraid of the unknown lands beyond the desert." Shivering, she looked toward the Bridge of Destiny where it arched across the star-flecked sky, remembering times earlier even than the year of Nightfall's birth. "Twice in my life I have seen the sun turn into a black disc, haloed all around with rainbow streamers of light. Although my father, the Sun-Toucher, patiently explained that it was but the greater moon's shadow passing before the daystar, I was frozen with fear, even when the light finally returned." She turned again, her hands clasped in front of her like a single fist. "The thought of Cutter's world of huge, green growing things and monstrous beasts rouses the same terror in me—terror that would have been a hindrance to him." Unfolding her hands, she splayed them out in front of her, offering them as their own explanation. "I hold the power of life and death in these. Yet I'm afraid of anything I *can't* anticipate or control."

"So was Cutter," Nightfall reminded her. "He was afraid of heights. On the Bridge of Destiny, remember?"

Leetah nodded, the memory of that horrible day making her feel even more ashamed. "But he overcame his fear when Rayek's life depended on him."

Nightfall reached out to hold Leetah's hands within her own. "And if Cutter's life depended on you?"

The thought itself was almost too much to bear. Silent, shivering, Leetah looked away from Nightfall to study the sky above the sleeping village, afraid even to hazard a reply.

CHAPTER ELEVEN

A BRIGHT SUMMER WIND hissed through the grass all around Cutter, carrying with it the smell of dirt, growing things, and the salty sweat of running animals. He hefted the length of trollish chain between his hands, readying himself for the throw even as he crouched deep in the tufted grass to wait. The ground beneath him shuddered, and almost immediately the grunt and thunder of fleeing animals overran him as the wolves chased the herd of grass-eaters over the rise. Cutter didn't see Skywise, but hoped his friend was following the general stampede. Bringing down one of these runners on his own was going to be hard enough—he didn't look forward to combing the plains for Skywise afterward.

The first of the furry runners galloped past him, snorting with alarm. Cutter popped up to his knees to swing the chain above his head. It whistled in the pollen-heavy air, and when he released it to tangle the legs of the nearest beast, Cutter had to squint to keep shredded grass bits out of his eyes as the chain flew through the greenery. It whisked around the beast's rear legs like a length of strangle vine, and the running grass-eater stumbled and went down with an explosive grunt. Cutter dashed from his cover before the beast had a chance to lurch to its feet. He sat his hindquarters on its neck to keep it from standing, the way he'd learned to do after his first couple attempts at a capture.

"There," he told the beast with some satisfaction. "Now that wasn't so bad." It squealed with obvious unhappiness when he leaned across its body to free its legs from the irons.

"Anything broken this time?"

Cutter flicked a quick look over the grass-eater's rump, smiling to see Skywise trying so hard to look composed while he struggled atop his own plunging runner. As far as Cutter could tell, the stargazer had only figured out how to make the beast stagger about in a circle, and they were making their slow way toward him in that manner.

"All in one piece," Cutter announced, throwing aside the ankle chains. "Picknose's irons make pretty handy animal catchers, huh?"

"I dunno." Skywise's grass-eater came to a choppy stop nearby, still churning up the ground with its feet, but not going anywhere. A good distance away, Starjumper and Nightrunner dropped, panting, in the shade of a stand of grass. Cutter had a feeling they thought the high growth hid the fact that they were chewing on the protective leather he'd tied around their feet that morning, but he wasn't fooled. He sent Nightrunner a scolding thought, and got only an impatient sniff in reply.

"Your first try wasn't such a great success," Skywise continued.

"All right, so I broke the little thing's neck. We had to eat anyway." He twisted onto the runner's back to free its head, grabbing at its mane as it surged to its feet and threw its front end into the air. "Besides—" It struck the ground again on stiffened legs, and Cutter grunted at the impact. "I caught yours for you, didn't I?"

Skywise cajoled his own mount to back up a few steps to avoid the new runner's flailing hooves. "Sure. But I only let you do it because it was *your* idea."

Any thoughts of a sharp reply went flying with the runner's first leap. It dropped its head between its knees, twisting and flinging its hind end about as though fighting off a hornet's sting. Cutter felt himself rise up from the beast's sharp spine, only to slam down again so far up its neck that he nearly slid down its skull onto the ground. Growling, he timed his pushes for between each vicious buck, and worked his way back onto the runner's shoulders, where he could at least dig his knees into its rib cage while he fought for a more firm handhold. It reached around to snap at him with square, yellow teeth, and Cutter nearly released his precious grip to thump it on the muzzle. Then he thought about how much damage it might do him to wind up under those hard, stomping feet, and he let the runner tear a hole in his trousers while he clung to its mane and grumbled.

When it finally stumbled to a stop with its legs spread and its sides heaving, Cutter was nearly as spent and sweaty. A sharp smack to the side of the runner's neck was all he could manage, to see if it had enough life left in it to fight him. "You finished?"

"Don't worry." As though impressed by seeing its brother brought low, Skywise's mount bore him forward at a sedate trot, ears flattened. "If it's anything like mine, you'll get plenty of chances to do it all again." He held out a strip of scarlet cloth cut from his traveling cloak, one end of it already tied into a loop. "Would you like to? Or shall I?"

Cutter slid off the grass-eater's back with weary grace, hanging onto one ear just in case it found new energy from somewhere. "You hang onto him, will you? I want to take another look at Nightrunner."

He waited until Skywise had pulled the loop tight over the grass-eater's muzzle, then limped away to join the wolves. When he'd first seen the grass-eaters browsing the open plains, using them to cover the distance had seemed so obvious and simple. He hadn't thought their backs would be so hard, or that their hair would stick like nettle-burrs to his trousers so that even scrubbing with his hands couldn't scrape it off. After catching and breaking only two, the bones in his rump ached as though he'd been thumped with a stick, and the insides of his legs felt weak and watery when he dismounted and tried to stand. He hoped he got used to this grass-eater riding soon, or he'd be too sore to do much else besides waddle when they finally did locate other elves.

"Hey, old friend, how's that eye?"

Nightrunner cocked his head at Cutter's summons, angling his muzzle so that his open right eye could see where his left eye should have. Cutter dropped to his knee beside the old wolf and caught hold of one ear to turn Nightrunner's head. He didn't dare touch the wolf's swollen left eye. The lids were pressed shut in a mat of seep and tears, and Nightrunner's cheekbone no longer traced the same even curve from muzzle to ear. When Cutter slipped his hand beneath the wolf's jaw to convey his concern and sympathy, Nightrunner pulled away with a whine, licking his elf-friend's fingers in silent apology.

"Well, it's your own fault." Knowing that was true didn't make Cutter feel any better about the result. "I'd kick you, too, if you tried to bite my rump." Nightrunner growled, sending images of Skywise's runner with its guts warm and red. Cutter shook his head as he reached to check the lacings on the wolf's protective stockings. "I told you before, these animals aren't for eating—they're for Skywise and me to ride."

"As if that's such a great thing." Skywise stopped his mount far enough from the wolves to discourage further hunting attempts, and held out the lead to Cutter's runner in obvious invitation. The young chieftain stood, touching Nightrunner one last time with his mind and the back of his hand.

"I don't even know what kind of animals these are," Skywise admitted as he positioned his own beast so Cutter's couldn't shy away from the chief's attempts to mount it. "Those humans who came to Sorrow's End had one—at least, I think it was the same animal. It was so skinny, it was hard to tell."

Cutter grunted as the runner shuffled back and forth beneath him. "They look a little like zwoots . . ." He finally dragged himself upright on its bony back, and the runner kicked once at nothing, as if in angry protest. "And they're just about as nasty."

"Yeah, but their backs are flat."

Cutter shrugged. "We can call them nohumps." Nightrunner stood abruptly and stalked away from the milling grass-eaters with his ears flat and tail low, growling. "Hey!" Cutter called after him. "It wasn't that bad!"

Skywise thumped heels to his runner's sides until it started grudgingly forward. "I think he's complaining about the nohumps in general."

Cutter tried to mimic his friend's actions, but only succeeded in startling his nohump into a choppy circle. "Nightrunner . . ." As if arguing with a surly wolf were something he needed right now. "Look at your pads! You've worn them raw with all the traveling we've done—you can hardly walk, let alone bear my weight." He leaned forward to grab the nohump's ear and drag its head in the direction he wanted to go. "Starjumper's in the same fix." And didn't look any happier about it. "So don't be stubborn. You've just got to get used to being old."

His seat was precarious and somewhat undignified, but Cutter couldn't help feeling smug with pride when his nohump finally straightened out its struggles and started off at a jolting trot after Skywise and his mount. "What do you think?" he called as the distance between them closed.

Skywise turned on his nohump's back with annoying ease, and cast a glance first at Cutter, then at the wolves following behind him. "I think it would help if you got used to Nightrunner being old, too," he suggested quietly.

Cutter shot a glare at him, but made no effort either to answer or to slow his mount as they drew abreast of Skywise, then cantered past.

"First the zwoots, now the nohumps. We're starting to make a habit of this."

Cutter finished working the twisted length of fabric free of his nohump's mouth, then rewarded the sturdy animal with a puff of breath into its closest nostril. For whatever reason, it had grown to like that little ritual in

the past four moons of travel, and now threw its ears
forward with interest whenever Cutter breathed on its
face.

"You sure you don't want to kill one this time?"
Skywise asked from where he stood near his own freed
runner. The nohump looked uncomfortable with the
soft, marshy water swilling around its ankles, but had
learned to give up useless fighting scores of days ago.
"Just to make sure?"

Cutter shook his head and walked away from his
own beast. "We haven't had trouble finding food ever
since we left the Troll Caverns." He slapped the nohump's rump to encourage it to move. It twitched, but
relocated by only a step. "They carried us faithfully
enough for more than four changes of the moon. I say
they've earned their freedom." He aimed that last at
Nightrunner, who still glared at the nohumps whenever
an itch or pain reminded him of the remnants of his
healed-over left eye.

Skywise sighed, but pulled Starjumper after him
when the wolf also started looking interested in the doc-
ile runners. "I suppose."

Cutter could tell Skywise thought the extra meat
might have been nice, though. Stepping lightly to try
to keep his feet as free from the muck as possible, Cutter hopped from grass tussock to grass tussock with only
half an eye to their direction. After all, Skywise had the
lodestone with which to correct their course, and it
wasn't as though they had the liberty of choosing a better path through the marshlands just now. Still, he
wished he had some idea how long this sludgy water
went on, and what they might find on the other side of
it. At least the wolves' pads had healed shut. He would

have hated leading Nightrunner into this kind of filth with half-open sores.

Doesn't it bother you that we haven't even seen a *hint* of a forest in all the time we've been traveling? Skywise's sending was unexpected, and underlaid by the bright metallic taste of fear.

Cutter stopped to look back at his friend. **Of course it bothers me.**

So has it occurred to you that maybe the humans who came to Sorrow's End lied? Skywise picked his way between wolves and rushes until he could stand face-to-face with Cutter and let his chief read the doubt creeping in between his thinking. **Maybe there isn't any green woods at land's edge where the sun sets.**

I've thought of that. Cutter picked up the string on Skywise's lodestone and lifted it to spin slowly in the air between them. "Just remember," he said aloud as it slowed to point stolidly at a star the clouds wouldn't let them see, "Savah said she once lived in a forest before she and her family went into the desert. And *that* forest wasn't the holt." He placed the sliver of stone against his friend's chest again, and met Skywise's gaze earnestly. "If there's one thing I've learned on this journey, it's that this land is bigger than we ever dreamed. There are other elves out there somewhere, Skywise—I just *know* there are. We have to keep going until we find them."

And so they went. For a night, and a day, and another long night, and for uncounted days and nights after that. It was like the Troll Caverns all over again for Cutter. The stink of rotten plants stung all the smell from his nostrils, and nothing in the mist or brush gave any hint as to the time of day or the weather. Everything was always wet here, always slimy. They slogged through water that felt thick and gritty to Cutter's touch, and over knobby tree roots beneath curtains of crackling, gray-brown moss. Once, Skywise saw a snake as thick around as a tree trunk, and they spent that day back-to-back in a tree, neither of them able to sleep because of the bitter visions of Madcoil slithering through their memories.

When the morning mist finally cleared, an eternity into their travels, Cutter felt his stomach clench with wonder at the cool green expanse stretching out ahead of them for farther than they could ever hope to see. He stumbled to a stop, struck with the inadequacy of his memories now that he was faced with the reality he'd thought lost to him forever. "Skywise . . ." he breathed in a reverent whisper. "Skywise, look . . . !"

Trees. Not the same as those that had once surrounded the Wolfriders' holt, but tall and straight and lovely just the same. They wove a canopy of thick, knotted limbs above an understory of vines and saplings. The coolness that always hid within a forest's bones sighed out at them with the smell of laurel and greenery. Cutter reached up to wipe a line of wetness from his cheek, knowing it had nothing to do with the fog or the morning dew.

Skywise's eyes looked equally bright and vivid. "I'd almost forgotten how beautiful the trees could be."

Cutter smiled. "Do you want to sleep today?"

Skywise shook his head, grinning, and they started into the woodland together, like cubs bounding into a familiar den.

Cutter's heart ached on the edge of a sob when long, cooling shadows swept over him and his eyes widened to take in more light. Instincts put to sleep by the empty quiet of the desert stirred somewhere deep within him. He felt suddenly the way he had the moment he and Leetah sealed their Recognition—as though he'd been made whole and somehow better by finding his place within a greater pattern. As though, after years of wandering, he'd finally come home.

Tree roots gripped the ground more firmly than they had in the marshlands, and little flowering clumps of skullcap and violet thrived bravely in the few slices of sunlight that reached the cluttered ground. Cutter paused to bury his face between a spray of skullcap and a crush of pine needles, and his heart turned over with joy at the delicate smells. Somewhere nearby, Night-runner exuded waves of laziness and pleasure as he rolled in a crackle of last season's leaves.

A hoarse squeaking drifted through the underbrush, shrill with strain and panic. Cutter lifted his head to listen for the source. Swinging into the branches of the nearest tree just because he could, he picked his way to just above an inlet of brackish water, and crept to the edge of his limb. Below him, an algae-choked squirrel struggled to keep its head above the surface, paused until it sank chin-deep, then shrieked and started struggling again. Cutter pulled his face into a frown, unable just to turn away.

The branch quivered gently as Skywise scurried out to join him. "What did you find?"

"Just a squirrel." Cutter meant to glance back at his friend, but somehow forgot to. "It's drowning."

"Oh." Skywise hopped to the next tree over and swung himself to the ground. "It happens."

"Yeah . . ." Thinking he meant to follow, Cutter stood, then slid under his own branch until he could hang his full length and drop without falling to the marshy patch below. "Hey, Skywise, wait a bit, will you?" He shrugged his bow off his back and slipped the string loose in his hand. "I'm feeling too good to watch anything die today."

He felt the little twinge of Skywise's amusement, but didn't respond to it. It was a friendly emotion, and carried enough fondness that Cutter knew the stargazer understood his motives even if he didn't share them. That almost explained everything there was to know about the two of them, really. Sending back his own fleeting thank-you, Cutter slipped one foot onto a half-submerged log in the hopes it would hold him long enough to reach the dying animal.

"It's okay, little fellow . . . I'm coming . . ." The rotten old limb bobbed and rolled beneath his fragile weight, but Cutter had walked enough live trees to feel out his balance with his toes. He only went as far as the middle of the log, crouching very, very carefully so as not to set it rocking. He reached for the squirrel with the end of his bow. "Grab on," he whispered gently. "We've almost got you home . . ."

When the bow's curving tip touched beneath it, the squirrel exploded into a fit of wild thrashing that sprayed water all around it and into Cutter's eyes. Cutter stopped himself from flinching back, afraid he'd lose the squirrel beneath the surface. Just then, the rodent's little black hands fastened on the smooth, polished wood of the bow and scampered up its length, tail lashing. The fury of its bitter squirrel cursing was enough to make Cutter laugh.

It whistled with sudden terror, alarmed by the sound, and scrabbled back toward the water. "No, no!"

Cutter gasped. He flicked the bow upward. The squirrel slid down onto his hands despite its attempts to writhe away, and Cutter realized what a mistake he'd made even before the squirrel clamped its teeth into the flesh between his thumb and forefinger.

"Why you miserable scummy little—!" He flung his hand aside, and the squirrel went flying. Somehow, it seemed grossly unfair to Cutter that the little demon should go tumbling away onto solid, dry land when the log beneath him was caving in as payment for his kindness. He smacked the stinking water full-length, and barely had time to clamp his mouth closed before going under.

He didn't even open his eyes until he broke the surface again. By then, Skywise's hooting laughter had started half the birds in the forest to screaming. Cutter glared at his friend, swiping a handful of water and weeds out of his hair to throw toward the shoreline. "Shut up!"

The command had no effect on the stargazer. Skywise troubled himself to meet Cutter at the water's edge, though, still laughing as he leaned down to reach for his chief's outstretched hand. "Oh, lovely!" He pinched his nose shut with dramatic flair. "You smell sweet as a blossom!"

Cutter tightened his grip threateningly. "You want me to yank you in here with me?"

"Just commenting," Skywise assured him airily. But he didn't stop giggling even after they'd slogged free of the underbrush and found a weak patch of sunlight in which to strip off Cutter's dripping clothes.

Cutter couldn't help uttering little retching noises while he shook off his boots and stepped out of his slimy buckskin trousers. The only thing he had any hope of wringing dry was the woven shirt Leetah had given him for protection against the desert sun, and even that would carry the fetid smell for days. Yanking the heavy cloth up over his head, he hissed with pain when his hand refused to close, and remembered with a burn of embarrassed anger what had started all this.

"Let me see that hand," Skywise said, frowning.

Cutter shook his head, pulling the hand away from Skywise's reach even as he plucked a spare cloth from the bag over the other elf's shoulder. A cold nose pushed against his palm, and Cutter turned his hand over without looking behind, letting Nightrunner clean the wound while he tore the cloth into strips with his teeth.

Skywise crouched near Nightrunner's face, but made no attempt to take hold of Cutter's hand. "That's a bad bite," he said as he stood again. "And that water was *filthy*."

"Oh, I'll live," Cutter grumbled. He wrapped first one rag, then a second around his throbbing hand, and pulled them tight enough to cut off the worst of the pain. "But I promise you—the first meal we eat in this forest will be squirrel meat!"

CHAPTER TWELVE

CUTTER DIDN'T CON-
sciously plan to rip off his shirt and sling it into the air.
The action just snuck up on him, in a way, masquerading
as irritation at the shirt's gamey odor. He thought he
meant to pull it away from his sweaty chest, but
somehow that became a fierce yank, and the shirt came
off in travel-stained tatters. After that, there was nothing
to do but fling it up over his head and fire an arrow after
it, pinning it to a tree limb high above.

Skywise laughed, looking up after the remnants of
Shenshen's good weaving. "It sure didn't take you long
to become a 'barbarian' again."

Just picturing how the self-exiled Rayek would have
reacted to such a carnal display made Cutter smile. "I
want to feel the breath of the trees all over me!" he
announced, shrugging back into his bear-hide vest. His
sword hand ached with a hard, hot throbbing, refusing
to close into a fist now thanks to that ungrateful squirrel.
But the wind's cool touch felt delicious against his warm
neck and front, and he shivered a little in the false cold.
"By the High Ones! Sand and stone and thorny desert
shrubs can't compare with this!"

He fell back against the nearest tree, sighing with
contentment—

—then jerked upright again when something

crawled beneath his skin, like water beneath a skim of winter ice.

"Cutter?" Skywise came forward a step, halting when his chief turned to stare in thoughtful confusion. "Cutter, what's wrong?"

Come here.

Skywise stepped forward silently, coming to a stop with his shoulder touching Cutter's and his eyes prowling the deep green brush around them.

Do you feel it? Cutter asked, watching his friend's face expectantly.

Skywise shook his head slowly. **What?**

Cutter tried to wrap his mind around an answer, but couldn't. His senses unfolded to their greatest measure, trying to feel about the branches and shadows around him the way his breath might feel through his lover's hair. There was no shape or smell to what he searched for, but when its presence touched him again like the lingering dew from a long-ago rainfall, he knew it. And Skywise knew it, too—Cutter felt the stargazer stiffen and gasp very softly beside him.

They were here! Even Skywise's sending was faint and full of reverence. **Elves! Tree-shaper elves!**

But the traces are so old . . . Cutter worked his fingers into the cracks of the big tree, as though expecting to find something there. ** . . . so faint . . .** Nightrunner stepped up beside him to sniff at where his friend's hand passed.

Cutter, we've got to be careful. If we don't look sharp, we could stumble right into a pocket of the High Ones' magic gone bad, like the one that created Madcoil.

Even such a fleeting thought of the monster made

the wolves draw closer and rumble with low, confused growls. Cutter stepped away from the tree and placed a hand on Nightrunner's muzzle to quiet him. **I know.** Suddenly, the high canopy of the forest seemed safer and more inviting, and he nodded Skywise toward a length of vine snaking down into the darkness behind them.

There are human smells here, too, he sent as he gathered the vine in both hands. The loss of his sword hand weakened his grip, and the muscles in his back and legs felt watery and loose. He kept those thoughts safely separate from Skywise. **And sounds and smells I don't even recognize. But we can't let all this scare us off— not now that we know our kinfolk lived here once.** He jumped up the first length of vine, and nearly fell again before adjusting to the unsteadiness of his own climb.

Skywise, already near the top of the tree, was too far away to notice. **I don't want to be scared off. I just wish I knew what we were looking for.**

So do I. But for now, all he could do was what he'd done on the way to Sorrow's End, what he'd done all his life when there was nothing else to turn to—take each little step with attention and care, and hope in the end that the path he created was leading somewhere.

"Cutter?"

He wanted to be asleep, but his bones only moaned that he hadn't known healthy sleep in days.

They'd stopped for the morning in the bole of a huge length of deadwood, out of the sun and the heat of the day while the wolves prowled away to find their own sleeping hollows until evening. Skywise said this nest was well worn, that it smelled of the musk and pawings of a short-tailed cat. Cutter only knew it was hot, and dark, and hard to sit down in. He hadn't been able to smell anything since sometime beyond remembering, and his eyes could only look in the direction he aimed them; they couldn't truly see.

"Cutter?"

He pulled his knees up to his forehead, hugging himself into a bundle as if to ward off his fever the way he'd ward off a chill. Little snatches of past, present, and make-believe flew in front of his closed eyes, hyperbright and kinetic. His skin hurt like a slow sunburn. Had it really been four moon changes since he'd last put his arms around his Leetah? It felt like only yesterday. It felt like forever.

Hand and mind reached out to prod him back to the present. "Hey, Cutter—?"

Skywise's touch felt somehow hurtful and unwelcome. Cutter jerked his head up with a growl. "What?"

His friend drew silver brows into a worried frown. "Are you okay?"

"Yeah . . ." The momentary flare of anger guttered away, and Cutter felt only empty and tired. He squinted past the entrance to pretend interest in the fading light outside. "Is it time to go on?"

"Not yet." Skywise settled down beside him, unfolding the leather parcel in his lap. "We've got time yet to eat before we head out." He lifted a handful of nuts in offering. "Want some?"

Cutter looked longingly at the food, but couldn't imagine summoning the energy to actually put it in his mouth and chew it. "No," he sighed, sitting back again. "They . . . don't agree with me much, I guess."

Skywise pushed the nuts closer to his nose. "You really should eat something."

"I'm not hungry."

"It's just—"

"Skywise, *no!*" Guilt stabbed weakly through him at the injured surprise on his friend's face, but even that died back too quickly to let him do anything besides add very softly, "Just leave me alone. Okay?"

Silence stretched thinly between them while Skywise dropped the nuts, one by one, back into the square of folded leather. "Cutter," he sighed finally, not looking up. "I'm . . . I'm worried." He rose up on his knees to half-face his chief, retying the food stores to his belt. "I mean, we've been in this forest for days, and we haven't found any sign of other elves since that very first day. I'm afraid we're missing something, that . . . well, that we're wasting our time." Cutter only looked at him, not sure what he was supposed to do about Skywise's concerns when he couldn't even care enough about his own stomach to feed it. After a long moment, the stargazer said, "It's just . . . We don't have that many moons left."

Yes, of course, they were running out of time. Everything was running out. Grabbing for a hold on the edge of the tree's entrance, Cutter stumbled upright and into the damp, dusky open. "Then we should be going—we—" Fever rushed up into his head and overwhelmed him. He felt himself drifting upward and forward, as though he might float away. ". . . Skywise . . . ?"

"*Cutter!*"

He didn't feel himself fall, didn't feel the ground rush up and hit him, or the wolves gallop over to lick his face with whistles and whines of concern. He just knew he hurt, and he felt so tired. If only they'd let him lie here in the cool, quiet forest, he could sleep and breathe in the smell of dead leaves and at least feel peaceful, if not completely well.

"Cutter? What is it? What's wrong?"

Skywise's hands on his face and shoulders were cool and frantic. Cutter opened his eyes without realizing he'd closed them, and reeled a little to find himself standing with his arm around Skywise's neck, stumbling wherever the stargazer led him. "I dunno," he croaked weakly, closing his eyes again. ". . . I . . . Something hurts, Skywise . . . Not sure what . . ."

"Come here."

He moved alongside his friend, unable to care or think, and was more glad than he could have explained when they finally stopped by a noisy brook and Skywise lowered him gently to the ground. Moss, soft and cool, pillowed around him with green fur fingers. Cutter let himself sink into it, listening to the water's crystal song while Skywise felt his arms and legs in search of some kind of damage.

"Your skin's burning hot!" Cool fingers framed his forehead, moved down to touch his cheeks, his throat, his chest. "And you're not sweating." Then a gentle tugging at the knotted rag around Cutter's hand shot a dull spike of pain up his arm, and he winced without speaking as Skywise unwound the days' old bandage. "Oh, Cutter, your hand . . . !"

He didn't have to open his eyes. He knew what it looked like. "Stupid squirrel." Nightrunner had fussed

over the wound before they traveled, every evening licking and sniffing at the swollen skin with lupine disapproval. Cutter had known at least two days ago that the
attention wasn't doing him any good. "I hope I knocked
its brains loose."

"You should have let it drown."

They were back to those cursed "should haves"
again. Cutter sometimes thought they could "should
have" all the way back to Timmain, the ancestress of all
Wolfriders, using future knowledge to second-guess
everything the elders and High Ones had done since
before the very dawn of time. Better to be like a river,
he thought, and just laugh and dance down your path
without worrying about where you were going, or what
you did to the things you passed. Given a choice, he
might have really liked to be water.

"This is a fine time to be smiling."

Cutter looked up, not even aware that he had been.
"Oh, I was just thinking." About water, and rain, and
how cool the moss felt beneath him. "Remember Rain
the Healer? His powers weren't nearly so great as Leetah's, but his hands were always so cool . . ." Like the
rain itself. "He could sing pain away while you slept . . .
so softly . . . so sweet . . ." He sighed, turning to smile
at the carefree little river. "He had such a sweet voice."

"Don't!" Skywise caught his face in both hands and
forced his head around to look at him. It was harder to
focus on the stargazer than Cutter thought it should be,
but he couldn't remember why. His friend's face just
looked worried, and distant. "If you hear him singing,
Cutter, don't listen! They say if you hear or see the dead
in a fever dream, then you're too close to them."

Cutter laughed, and pushed Skywise's hands away. "Oh, I'll be all right."

The stargazer didn't look convinced. "You will if I can find some whistling leaves for you to chew." He stood, not letting go of Cutter's hand until the very last moment. "I know they used to grow in boggy areas near the holt, so I'm hoping I can find some near here. You stay by this stream—it's cool, and Nightrunner will guard you. I'll be back soon, I promise."

Cutter agreed, nodding. ". . . Soon . . ." The song of the river soothed his eyes with misty fingers, pulling him down into its coolness and its sweet, sweet song. ". . . 'Cause we have to find the other elves, Skywise . . . all the other elves . . ."

Darkness drew him off as though he were a leaf upon the water. Behind him, reaching out from the shore, a familiar mind brushed over him with a whisper of gentle fear.

**I'll be back soon, Cutter. Just wait for me . . . please, wait . . . **

Rain and water flooded through Cutter's dreams. It was hot in this black, black river, so hot, and the current was hard to fight and stay afloat in. Cutter wanted just to surrender to the torrent, the pull of the tide that dragged at his spirit to flow down, and under, away and away. But something sharp cut into his stomach, and when he tried to protest, water rushed out of his mouth and left him retching. Without knowing quite how he got there, he found himself stretched out with his face in the mud by the edge of the water.

A wolf's quick, blunt-edged worry pushed past the

fevered veil, and Nightrunner's tongue licked dryly at his face, his eyes, his dripping wet hair. Cutter reached weakly for his old friend, but couldn't lift his hand far enough to touch the wolf.

"Worrywart." Cutter tried for brave fondness, but the words came out as a hoarse, broken whisper. He coughed river-tasting water from the back of his throat and tried again. "I was just thirsty. You shouldn't fuss so much, I'm all—"

Shadow drifted against shadow at the edge of the brush, as flat and chill as a winter breeze.

"—right . . ."

The black wolf drew its shape out of the forest darkness. Amber eyes like glowing half-moons pierced the night while ears larger than Cutter's hands swallowed all the sound in the glade as the huge wolf studied him, silent, waiting. Cutter tensed for Nightrunner to growl a challenge warning, but the old wolf only lifted his head to follow Cutter's looking, and said nothing.

Cutter pushed up on his elbows, squinting at the distant form. "B-Blackfell?" Clenching weak hands in Nightrunner's pelt, he struggled to his knees. "Is it Blackfell?" he asked Nightrunner. The old wolf turned away from the stranger to sniff at Cutter and whine in reply. "It is . . . It *has* to be! It's Bearclaw's wolf! But . . . How can he possibly be here? All this way, after all this time?"

Even reaching out for sending didn't bring the black wolf closer. He dipped his head, slitted eyes still fixed on Cutter, then turned to pace silently into the darkness.

Cutter surged to his feet with a throb of disappointment. "Wait!" He staggered away from Nightrunner, ignoring the old wolf's bark of alarm. "Where are you going? Are you real?" Teeth grabbed at the back of his pants, and he stumbled. "Did my father send you? A spirit to guide me on my quest? *Wait!*"

He pushed Nightrunner's head away from him, feeling the leather of his soft trousers tear as he broke free. "I can't lose him! I can't let him go!"

No branches shivered to mark where the great wolf had passed. Cutter kept his eyes locked on where Blackfell had been, pushing into the underbrush without heeding Nightrunner's calls of alarm. He couldn't wait for the old wolf to catch up, couldn't slow down for fear of losing his way. "Blackfell! Wait! Where are you?"

The phantom wolf waited for him, blurred by time and distance, and another lean, gray form appeared beside him. Elves came then to join them. Cutter fell to his knees as shock punched all the air from his lungs and left him breathless.

"Bearclaw . . . Joyleaf . . ."

His father's image was hard and powerful, just as Cutter would always remember him, his mother's bright and lovely in a way no other elf could match. Joyleaf reached out for him, and the very air around the lifemates seemed to sparkle with the sound of love, and comfort, and distant elfin laughter.

"You want me to come with you?" They didn't speak or nod, but Cutter felt their summons like stranglevine around his heart. "Oh, Mother, Father . . . Must I? It would be such a foolish way for me to die—from a squirrel bite!" He had to use his good hand to lift his arm, unable now to make the limb obey at all. "Why, my Leetah could cure this in the blink of an eye."

A force like many voices crowded all around him, and he shook his head hard to try and drive them away.

"I have a lifemate now! And two strong, beautiful cubs—two!" Tears clogged the back of his throat as he stumbled to his feet. "I—I promised I'd return to them."

So he ran—turned into the darkness and abandoned his parents before they could touch him with too much love to survive. "I'm sorry! Please understand—I can't go with you now! I can't!"

They followed him, calling, singing as he fought his way forward, toward anything but the hopeless inevitability of dying. There was so far to go, so much land to cross, so much sand to swim through before he could wrap himself in the tribe and family he'd given everything to save. Amber blossoms of light smeared the darkness ahead of him—the Tunnel of Golden Light, the signal fire from home.

I can live with the sand, he promised himself as the heat of the fire burned the tears from his face and the light from the fire blinded his eyes. *I can live with the sand, and the heat, and the daytime, just please let me be with my family . . . please . . .*

She was there beside the leaping fire, auburn locks shining, lovely, dark skin aglow in the fierce flame. She turned to him, mouth open, eyes wide, and Cutter reached for her, calling, hurting. "Leetah . . . ! I'm home, Leetah . . ."

An uneven circle of rocks at his feet jerked him forward, and he fell full-length into a circle of warmth, and brightness, and dry, packed-down dirt. Hands reached for him, but he didn't have the strength to try to move. Not when the pungent musk of human sweat fell over him like a mantle, or when a breathless human voice exclaimed, "Oh, my child! What's happened to you? Where did you come from?"

Darkness took hold of him and dragged him down and away before he could remember enough of the human words to answer.

CHAPTER THIRTEEN

CUTTER AWOKE WITH A jolt, choking on the smell of humans and human filth. His arms trembled when he tried to push himself upright, and the hands that pressed down on his shoulders were huge and coarse, the voice chattering over him loud and unlovely. A dry, lined face bent over him, square white teeth bared. He realized with a stab of primitive terror that he was inside a human building, pinned to the floor by human hands.

Nightrunner's wild panic swarmed over him. When the old wolf's voice rose into a roar from somewhere outside, Cutter twisted to thrash against the body leaning over him, desperate to escape. They'd dragged him from his wolf somehow, trapped him in this fever-hot hovel. He could only guess what things humans would do after that. His hand found New Moon at his hip. Wrenching himself over onto all fours, he yanked the sword free and slashed at the grasping human hands. The blade didn't slow enough to tell him he'd connected, but he smelled a bright blossom of human blood-scent just as the woman jerked away from him with a cry.

"Nonna?"

The shout from outside the cottage meant nothing to Cutter. Snarling, he scrambled back against a cold stone wall, using it for leverage so he could climb unsteadily to his feet. The woman stayed where she was, huddled near a pile of blankets with her hand against her lips. She didn't even turn when her mate—a huge, bearded beast with eyes like burned-out coals—burst past the hide that covered the outside door. The flaming brand clutched in the human's hand dashed light all around the tiny hovel and stung at Cutter's eyes. He blinked to try and clear his fading vision.

The man threw the burning stick toward the fire at the center of the hovel, hurrying to his mate's side. He barked sounds in a hard, frightful voice, but Cutter couldn't even guess at the words' meaning until the woman took her hand from her lips and held it out for the man's inspection.

"He cut me," she said. Her lighter voice made the language somehow hearable, the stark emotion in her words somehow real. "He cut me with that strange, bright knife." She looked back at Cutter, and her brow wrinkled into an expression he wasn't sure how to interpret. "Adar, I'm afraid he'll hurt himself."

The man nodded, his lips drawing into a thin line. "Let me get him . . ."

"Don't come any closer!" Cutter jerked New Moon higher between them, having not even realized how far the sword had dropped in his weariness. The man only frowned at the sword's swift movement. Cutter edged toward the outside door, halting again when the human stepped forward with hand greedily outstretched. "*I said no!*"

"Adar, stop . . ." His mate caught his elbow,

pulling him back beside her as she rose very slowly to her feet. "He doesn't want you near him." She looked down at Cutter as he sidled for the door, but didn't try to approach him.

The man stared at his mate in what looked to Cutter like anger. "You understand his language?"

She didn't respond as if frightened, though. Instead, she held his hand while studying Cutter with eyes the color of autumn leaves. "He speaks *our* words, Adar . . . but strangely. I can only barely understand him." Then she shook her head sadly. "The poor child."

The man's hand tightened convulsively on hers. "Look at his eyes, Nonna. This is no child."

The hide door felt soft but firm beneath Cutter's seeking hand. He pushed against it, trying to force it open without turning his back on these monsters. It rattled solidly against its wooden frame. Cutter gasped around a rising spiral of fear as he pounded harder and harder against the door in frustration.

"Oh, Adar, we must stop him! He's mad from sickness!" She abandoned her mate to rush at Cutter. "He'll die in the forest alone!"

Cutter didn't wait to see how she planned to stop him. Spinning, he plunged New Moon through the stretched-hide covering and slit it from top to bottom with a single pull. Night air washed over him, thick and hot, as he fought to part the stiff sides. The outside was so close, freedom so near to his hands. Something snatched at his vest from behind, and he stumbled, shouting in despair. The man was faster than his mate, his hands stronger, his grip more sure. He pinned Cutter's arms together in a single fist and plucked New Moon from his fingers as though taking a twig from a sparrow. Cutter saw the sword flash in the firelight as it was tossed to one side, too far away from him to ever be recovered.

He kicked at the arm that reached out to engulf him, sinking his teeth into the human's wrist and thrashing his head from side to side. The man shouted an angry curse, but never loosed his hold on Cutter as he backed across the room with the elf gripped tightly against him. Cutter tried to fight him, tried to dredge up every wile and strength he'd learned in his short, brutal life. But fever ate his strength just as it ate his senses, and all too soon he lost the ability even to open his mouth, much less clamp it shut on enemy flesh. He collapsed forward across the human's arms, trembling with shock and weakness, and sobbed in silent gasps for the dream he'd lost and the cubs he'd left behind.

"There is such fear in your eyes, Honored One." Her hands as she took him from her mate were strong but gentle. "There is no need for fear. I know who you are."

Then you will kill me, Cutter thought. Humans always killed elves. It was part of the Way. He closed his eyes, shamefully afraid to see what the monsters planned to do to him. The woman settled to the floor with him in her lap, rocking him gently.

Water, clear and clean, cooled his eyelids, his mouth. Cutter cringed away from the touch of her alien fingers, but she shushed him with soft human noises, and brushed fresh water onto his cheeks. The man's heavy footsteps drew near, and brought with them a delicious breeze.

"You must drink something, Honored One."

Cutter let his eyes flutter open as the rim of a smooth container touched his lips. The sweet breath of the fan drove his fear away, and the crisp taste of water in his throat nearly brought tears to his eyes. The woman smiled, setting the gourd aside, and resumed her singing in a gentle, almost loving tone. Above her, the man stroked the air with a broad green leaf. His bearded face looked only puzzled, not full of hatred as Cutter had expected.

Cutter shivered against the confusion that tried to swallow his thinking. "I . . . I didn't know that humans . . . could be kind . . ."

The woman smiled and caressed his face with the back of her hand. "Your folk were always good to my people, Honored One."

". . . My folk . . ." The Wolfriders, who knew nothing but blood and pain and hatred from every round-eared hunter since before the beginning of time. ". . . My elves . . ."

Then he drifted off into silence, and coolness, and impenetrable black.

When Cutter woke again, he was thirsty.

The human woman—Nonna, he remembered— moved beside him as though reading his fever-weakened thoughts, and raised the gourd of water to his lips. He drank more than before, held her wrist so she wouldn't withdraw while he breathed for a moment, then took more. She smiled like a mother who was pleased with her growing offspring's appetite.

"You've fallen so far from your mountain, Bird

Spirit." She spoke in a wistful sigh, and dried his throat and chin with a rag.

From somewhere out of sight across the room, the man's deep voice answered. "If he's one of your flying Bird Spirits, how could he have come to fall in the first place?"

"Adar!" She aimed a reproving scowl at her mate, but now Cutter could recognize the love that moved beneath her expression. "You shouldn't speak of them that way. Look at the long, tapered ears, like wings. And the four-fingered hands." Cutter watched from an abstract distance as she lifted his hand in her palm. The filthy bandage was gone, the wound drained and cleaned until only an angry red hollow remained. "Is he not just as I've always shown you in my symbols? You and I have been greatly honored."

Adar grunted. "I don't know of honor," he said, backing away from the freshly mended door. "I only know that your spirits seem to have no appreciation for a good hide."

As if in answer to his comment, a sharp wind butted against the door and set it thrumming. The scent of wolf and worry spurted in on the air around the edges of the hide: Nightrunner, sweaty and wet, Starjumper, musky with youth, and Skywise's presence closely overlaying them both. Pushing up on his elbows, Cutter strained for the sound of breath and running feet, and registered both a bare instant before Skywise's sword sliced the hide door clean in two and Starjumper plunged through the opening.

Nonna shrieked, crabbing back away from the wolf and its howling rider as they exploded past Adar and arrowed straight for her.

For me, Cutter realized. Skywise's sword whistled downward to strike the killing blow. "No! Skywise, *don't kill!* Don't!"

Obedient to the last, Skywise aborted his swing with the blade bare inches from Nonna's face. Starjumper yelped and slid onto his rump in an effort not to slam into the human. "*What?*" The stargazer shook with fear and fury, his gray eyes locked on Cutter in disbelief. "You're out of your head!"

Am I? Cutter opened himself as widely as he could. He felt weak and nearly hollow, but clearer than he had since they'd entered this alien forest. **Do as I say, and let the humans be.**

He had never known anything to be so hard for Skywise. The stargazer slid stiffly off his wolf's back, still trembling, but didn't seem able to lower his sword. He was thinking of his own mother, Cutter knew, and of the two human boys who had dragged her away to her death seasons and seasons before Cutter was even born. "Did they hurt you?" Skywise asked, sinking to one knee beside his chief without turning his back on the humans. Starjumper slipped out into the darkness. To find Nightrunner, Cutter hoped. To wait. "I swear, I'll cut them down to our size if they did!"

"No." It sounded like an amazing lie. Cutter probably wouldn't have believed it if someone else had told it to him. "I don't understand it, but the woman—she gave me water." He looked past Skywise to where Nonna and Adar huddled together near the back of the hovel. Adar whispered to her, his eyes locked on Skywise, and she only shook her head firmly as though to refute whatever he was telling her.

Cutter forced his gaze back to his friend, then had to put his head into his hands when a wave of dizziness crested over him.

"They didn't hurt me," he said again, plaintively. "But I'm still very hot. I don't know what's wrong."

"Here . . ." Skywise fumbled at his belt and finally tugged loose a thick handful of wilted leaves. "Rain used to say these were the best thing ever for fevers. Chew them up—they'll do the trick."

The whistling leaves felt limp and fuzzy against Cutter's tongue, and the sour, too-old meat taste made him gag. He closed his eyes, bending forward until his head rested on his knees, and forced himself to chew the stringy leaves until the feel of them between his teeth made him want to spit them onto the floor. Then he swallowed painfully, and accepted another small handful from Skywise.

He only managed three doses of the vile plant before his stomach surged up into his throat and refused to accept anymore. Climbing groggily to hands and knees, he stumbled out the door without even stating his intention to leave. If he opened his mouth, he would vomit, and he couldn't bring himself to do that inside any creature's living den—not even a human's. The outside air felt cool and gentle on his face.

Skywise jumped to his feet to block the doorway behind him. "Stay still!" Cutter heard the stargazer growl at the silent humans. "Stay right where you are!"

Cutter didn't wait to see if the humans obeyed. He stumbled to the brush beyond the fire clearing and collapsed across a downed log just as his stomach

gave up every bit of the whistling leaves he'd managed to make himself chew. They'd done their work,
though—he felt shivery cold beneath his sweat as he
tugged down his trousers to empty the rest of his sys-
tem into the same tangle of bushes. The loss of fluid
seemed to take the last of his fever with it. Reaching
out to the presence ghosting up behind him, he
found trust and worry intermingled in Nightrunner's
primitive thoughts. And pain, running like a scarlet
thread underneath it all.

Nightrunner? He sat back on his heels and
let the big wolf come to stand over him. **What is it,
old friend?**

Stiff hair, shortened and sticky with blood, prickled
Cutter's hand as he reached up to fondle the wolf's
head. Nightrunner butted his forehead against Cutter's
chest, whining, and Cutter leaned forward to sniff near
the wolf's right cheek. The smells of burned fur and
burned skin blended together in the wolf's coat. Nightrunner's thoughts moved in response to Cutter's horror.
*Human man hot-light-fire-light, humans take Cutter-
friend, can't see! can't fight!* The old wolf whistled with
distress and dragged his tongue across Cutter's bare
chest.

"Oh, my good friend . . ." Anger at the humans
was all too easy to feel. Hugging the wolf's neck, he
buried his face against Nightrunner's shoulder and
stroked his mind with loving thoughts. Then he stood
slowly and emptied his bladder again before tugging his
trousers back over his hips. **Stay here,** he told his
wolf-friend, fondling one ear. **Keep Starjumper with
you.**

The light in the hut stabbed his eyes after the

soothing darkness of outside. He placed a hand on Skywise's shoulder, casting a reassuring thought in response to the stargazer's worried glance, then stepped around his friend to stalk toward Adar. The human stepped in front of his mate, beard drawn into a scowl. He met Cutter's cold glare with a scowl of his own.

"I've seen Nightrunner," Cutter said—slowly, so the man would understand. "Did you burn him?"

"The wolf?" Adar glanced back at his mate, then down again at Cutter. "I had to. He would have torn Nonna and me to bits. You know that."

The memory of Nightrunner's confusion swept through Cutter's mind. . . . *can't see! can't fight!* . . . For more generations than these humans had known seasons, to be captured by humans meant certain death for an elf. Nightrunner, his loyal bond-friend, would have done anything to save Cutter from such a horror. That these humans had cradled Cutter and cared for him was something the young chief himself could barely understand—he would never be able to explain it to Nightrunner, not even now when the fever had released his brain.

He clenched his teeth around the remnants of his anger, fighting with himself for trust. "I . . . understand," he said at last. "You helped me earlier." He had to swallow twice before the words would leave him. "I want to thank you."

Adar nodded slowly, his scowl fading, and Nonna grinned like a child receiving the blessings of an elder. "I have waited long for your arrival, Honored One," she said, sinking into a squat in front of him. "I feared I would never see your folk again except in my symbols."

"Symbols?" Cutter asked.

"Oh, yes! I have given you a room of symbols, Honored One." She stood upright again, motioning toward another room, too dark to see behind her. "Would you and your brave guardsman like to see it?"

Smiling, Cutter glanced back at Skywise when the stargazer crept forward to join him. **Well, "brave guardsman"?**

Skywise didn't answer; he was too intent on glaring at the humans to respond to his chief. The wordless roil of distrust surrounding him was nearly thick enough to smell.

"Yes, Nonna," Cutter said aloud. "It would please us to see your symbols."

As she turned to gather up a burning stick to light their passage, Cutter pried Skywise's sword out of his fingers and slipped it back into its scabbard. **_These_ humans aren't so bad,** he sent in response to the stargazer's startled glare.

I don't know. Skywise clung close to his hip as they followed Nonna into the darkened room. **I'd still rather hate them.**

The symbol room swelled huge and vivid at the touch of Nonna's firelight. Images drawn in blacks and ochres, blues and scarlets, covered the stone walls in brilliant splashes, dancing like living things in the flickering light. A tingle of sensation rippled through Cutter, and he felt Skywise shiver beside him as they slowed to a stop near the center of the chamber. It wasn't the pictures, he knew, that washed across his soul and set his blood to singing. It was something older, something deeper, something much more real.

It was the unmistakable feel of elfin magic, pouring forth from the smoothly arching walls and ceiling until this den of human living nearly drowned beneath the magic's weight.

CHAPTER FOURTEEN

Y OU LIKE MY ROOM OF symbols, Honored Ones?"

Cutter didn't look at Nonna; he only nodded slowly as he turned to take in the room's great height and length. "Yes, Nonna, we do." The delicate angles and gentle curves reminded Cutter of the shapes Redlance coaxed his plants into as he petted them and sang them into life.

I wish my little Suntop were here. Cutter touched one of the smooth walls. It was cool beneath his hand. **He could tell for sure if this room was shaped by elves long ago.**

Skywise tossed a startled look across the chamber at him. **Elves that shape rock like trees? Is that possible?**

Cutter shrugged. **They did something here. And these rocks didn't pour into these positions on their own.**

I wonder . . . Nonna carefully placed her burning stick on a shelf gracefully extruded from one wall. Cutter didn't miss the interest with which Skywise studied those delicate swirls of rock. **Do you think those old rock-shapers could have been part of a tribe that Savah's family came from?**

**If only there was some way we could ask

her.** Cutter nudged his friend and nodded his attention toward where Nonna awaited them near one of the lavishly decorated walls. **So much we don't know . . . ,** he mused as they moved to join her. ** . . . So many questions . . . ** Could they really expect this quest to answer them all?

"My paintings are very poor," Nonna apologized, passing a hand over the detailed landscape without actually touching it. She smiled down at Cutter, and it made her eyes look soft and kind. "Especially compared to the master symbol-makers of *your* race, Honored Ones. But perhaps you will recognize your high mountain home here, as I have shown it?" Her long finger traced a jagged peak at the center of the drawing. "You see? I have painted a flight of your giant hunting birds soaring above the blue peaks." Her gesture passed like a cloud in front of massive wings and reaching talons. "And between each bird's wings rides a gallant spear-bearer." The sharp points on either side of the riders' heads could only be a human's interpretation of elfin ears.

Cutter's fever-weakened head felt light, pounding with the echoes of Skywise's excitement as well as his own. "Where is this mountain?" He tried to keep his voice light, but the dryness of his throat betrayed him.

Nonna, however, only laughed and clasped her hands together. "You test me? I have not forgotten!" She knelt to his level again, her hands wound together in her lap. "Many, many days' walk it is, beyond the woods, beyond the Valley of Endless Sleep. We must follow the setting sun until the tall blue peaks come into view, and then . . ." She fell silent, searching Cutter's eyes, and for one horrified moment he thought she'd seen through his false calmness and knew him for a land-bound spirit liar.

Then she stood and stepped back to grasp her mate's hand. "You . . . You have not come to take me back there, have you, Bird Spirits?" She pressed close against Adar. His dark arms encircled her in a loving wall of protection. "Please, do not part me from Adar."

"Us? Why . . . no!" Cutter shot a startled look at Skywise, who only looked back at him in unhelpful silence, his face schooled into nonexpression against the humans. "We've been away from the mountain for a long time, too. Haven't we, Skywise?"

The stargazer made a sour face. He glanced up at the humans, not even attempting to hide a throb of irritation from his chieftain. "Oh, yes," he said stoically. "Spirit business. You know—very secret."

"In fact," Cutter continued, "we've been gone so long that we've forgotten what life in the mountain was like."

This is stupid!

Cutter ignored him. "Are we much different from our kinfolk who dwell there now?"

Nonna cocked her head and looked them over, but didn't step away from Adar's supportive arms. "Only in size. You seem smaller than they are."

"Long journeys do that to spirits."

Cutter planted his heel on top of Skywise's toes and pressed down hard in warning. "We plan to go home very soon now," he told Nonna.

She smiled gently. "You must be very happy."

"More happy than you can know." Shoving

backward with one elbow, Cutter steered Skywise toward the outside door. "We must go look after our
companions now. Thank you, Nonna, for your symbols."

"Oh . . . !" She bowed deeply, still gripping
Adar's hand. "It is I who am grateful, Honored
One."

The path to the outside seemed impossibly long.
Cutter knew his breath came quickly, and that his
sending must be almost too rapid and airy to understand. But he could barely contain his eagerness in
front of the humans, and he couldn't withhold it
from Skywise at all. **Think about it, Skywise! It all
makes sense—these humans could be talking about
elves that are allied with birds just as we're allied with
wolves!**

Skywise's sending, while darkened by suspicion,
still tingled with excitement. **If only we could be
sure . . . **

Nothing's sure, my friend, Cutter told him
as they passed out into the sweet-smelling night.
Especially the outcome of this quest we're on.

Nightrunner and Starjumper waited inside the
edges of the surrounding woods. Drained and sleepy
from even so short a walk, Cutter sank to the ground
at the base of a tall, straight tree and let Nightrunner
settle into his lap like a spoiled cubling. It felt so
good to be back outside, surrounded by the sounds
and smells of the living forest. He pillowed his head
on his wolf's narrow back, and they sighed together
in weary communion.

**I don't know, Cutter . . . **

He opened his eyes and looked up at Skywise,

still standing with his face turned pensively back toward the human abode.

Humans are wicked, the stargazer sent with painful effort, **spiteful and cruel. They lie. We'd be fools to trust them.**

Cutter sat up, and made Skywise turn to look at him with a touch from his mind. **That's the past talking,** he told his friend, softening the thought with a taste of his own uncertainty. **The humans who plagued us in the holt were full of hate. These two aren't.**

Maybe they just haven't made up a reason to hate us yet.

He didn't like the bitterness all throughout Skywise—the bitterness that all of them held, hidden somewhere, just waiting for a wound or act of evil to give it life again and set it gnawing. It wasn't just the humans, Cutter knew, who kept the suffering between their peoples alive from season to season.

Reaching up for Skywise's hand, Cutter pulled his friend down next to him on the cool forest ground. **Don't worry, my eyes are open,** he sent as Skywise sat and called Starjumper over to join them. **But the human woman *did* help me, Skywise, and now she's put us on a path that may lead us to other children of the High Ones.**

It's just . . . Skywise's mouth twisted into an expression of frustrated uncertainty. **It's so hard . . .**

He wanted to say more—Cutter could feel it moving all over under his open thinking. But it had already been a hard evening, and Cutter knew better than to try and intrude on Skywise's right to brooding silence.

A thing that's easy is seldom worth much. He clapped a hand on Skywise's shoulder, but didn't require him to lift his gaze. **Keep heart. The trail grows warmer! We'll rest here until my strength comes back. Then we'll follow Nonna's legends, and see where they might lead us.**

"Come on, Choplicker! Smell out the trail!"

Leetah paused in lifting the water bucket clear of the well. Peering gingerly behind her under one arm, she waited until Ember galloped into view before daring to move again. This wouldn't have been the first time Leetah splattered precious water all over the sand because she hadn't paid attention to her daughter's location before emptying her buckets.

"Like this, Choplicker! Smell like this!" Ember struggled gamely ahead of her wolf-friend, nose to the ground, skinny behind jutted shamelessly into the air. "Come on!" Choplicker bumbled along behind, a tumbling weed of cubling enthusiasm.

Ember's bond with the young wolf was proving to be nothing like what Leetah had expected. She poured a thick tongue of water into her waiting jug. Somehow, she'd thought Choplicker's addition to Ember's life would be more like Cutter's relationship with Nightrunner—a friend outside the two-legged family, someone who lived in the hills and welcomed Cutter's wild company whenever the elf crept away at night to run with him. She hadn't expected the cub to move into her home and chew on her pillows and footwear. Nightfall had explained that these first few months of bonding were the most important—that Ember and Choplicker had to strengthen their sense of each other now, so that their minds could never be parted later. But did that have to mean fleas among Leetah's sleeping furs? (It had taken nearly a year to get rid of them after Cutter first moved in.) Or hair in her oils? Paw prints on her rugs?

She dropped the bucket back into the well. Ember had taken to gulping her food with a fierce possessiveness, even when confronted with greens she couldn't stand. She ran about even more tirelessly than before, then slept with careless abandon wherever she happened to fall, sometimes sleeping for half the day. Then, at night, she and Choplicker danced and giggled in the gardens near the hut while Leetah listened with quiet worry and wondered if all this was normal.

As so often anymore, the changes in Ember just gave Leetah one more opportunity to wish Cutter were here. A mere touch of her hand told her the changes in her daughter weren't bad, merely different, and there was certainly nothing wrong or hurtful about the little wolf cub. But these were not changes Leetah had grown up knowing to expect, and their very strangeness left her uncertain what—if anything—she should do to aid her daughter's metamorphosis from Sun child to Wolfrider. For now, all she could do was give Ember and Choplicker every freedom they needed for their growth and exploration, and pet both darling cublings whenever they gamboled into her path.

"Well, there it is!" Shenshen sniffed, sidestepping

the two playmates to slip her own jug onto the well's rim. "Your daughter down on all fours, just as I predicted."

Leetah smiled and emptied another bucket of water into her jug. "When she sprouts fur and a tail, I'll begin to worry."

"None of these Wolfriders are very old," Shenshen pointed out as she reached across the well to catch the bucket's rope handle. "Who knows what happens when they reach father's age?"

Leetah watched her sister drop the bucket down the hollow between them. "I think you're only jealous."

"Jealous?" Shenshen's auburn hair bobbed at her haughty laugh. "Jealous of what? Fleas and raw meat and wild beasts running in and out of my home at all hours of the day and night?"

"Of the howling you hear from my lifemate at all hours of the day and night whenever we're together."

Shenshen *hmphed* again and reached for the well's crank handle. Leetah could tell from both her sister's furious blush and her determined cranking that there was more truth to Leetah's comment than Shenshen wished to acknowledge.

"Why would I be jealous of some noisy lifemate who gives you children such as these?" she countered primly. "You have a daughter who runs around thinking she's a lap pet, and a son so odd I can't tell if he's half-witted or sunstruck."

"Oh, he's okay." Ember waddled by, still on all fours, and inspected the walls of the well along with Choplicker. "He's just got his magic feeling, is all."

"Suntop . . . ?" Turning, Leetah stifled a little

spasm of alarm to see her son standing not so far away, his back stiffly straight, his small hands frozen at his sides. "Suntop, what's troubling you, my son?"

He didn't move or face her as she approached. "It's Savah . . ." His delicate voice seemed to come through him from a very great distance. "I knew she 'went out' again today, but . . . something's wrong." He blinked suddenly, and his eyes filled with fear as he turned to her. "She can't come back."

"*Healer!*"

Leetah jerked upright at the sound of Ahdri's scream. The handmaiden burst from the Mother of Memory's hut, sandals slipping on the stone path as she ran toward Leetah, her young face frantic. "Healer! Come quickly!" She stumbled over Leetah's waiting jug and doused herself in a river of cool water. "Hurry! The Mother of Memory needs you!"

Grasping Suntop by the hand, Leetah pushed Ahdri back toward Savah's hut. "Show me!" It seemed elves were running from everywhere now, closing in on them like zwoots around a watering hole. Redlance and Sun-Toucher held a path for her to the doorway, but even they couldn't keep the press of bodies out of the building itself. Leetah heard the hut fill with a cascade of worried voices as every being in the village pushed into the room behind her.

Savah's circular audience chamber stood dark, and frightfully silent. The Mother of Memory sat still and lifeless in her customary throne, the multicolored glow behind her no longer moving and flickering in response to her inner self. In all the years of her life, Leetah had never seen that rainbow light fade. Releasing Suntop, she climbed carefully up to the base of Savah's dais, reaching out to lay fingers on the Mother of Memory's cold, unmoving hand.

"Bring her back, healer!" Ahdri's words were almost lost in her sobs. "Oh, *please,* bring her back!"

Life fluttered like windblown flower petals beneath Leetah's touch. But weakly, and from very far away.

"Great Sun!" The healer drew back, unsure what she should do. "She's all but completely left her body."

Ahdri swiped ineffectually at her tears. "How? What happened?" She moved around beside Leetah to look fearfully into her matron's lifeless face. "Can't you right what's wrong?"

"This is not an injury, Ahdri," Leetah explained softly. She rested her hands on Suntop's head, taking precarious comfort in the strength of his light and life so close to her own. "I haven't the power to call back a spirit that has taken flight of its own accord."

"But why?" Sun-Toucher's voice sounded crisply above the babble of frightened villagers. "Why would Savah do such a thing?"

Leetah shook her head. She didn't know how to answer.

Beside her, Suntop stirred and moved slowly toward the foot of the dais. He had as much right to touch his mentor as anyone else in the village, and Leetah made no move to stop him when he mounted the bottom step and pulled himself into Savah's lap. So many times he'd sat there, talking with the Mother of Memory, teaching her about childhood, learning from her about his past. He looked so fragile now as he slipped his tiny arms about her venerable shoulders and pressed his forehead to hers. He shivered, then locked into a common stillness with his teacher. Life mingled between the two so faintly that Leetah put her hands to her mouth to keep from calling her son's name. She wanted to run forward and drag him away—shake the life back into him before he drifted into whatever distant place harbored Savah. But her love for Suntop meant nothing if she didn't trust him, if she didn't trust what Savah claimed were his most special powers. Leetah closed her eyes and waited for the silence to break.

"Mother . . . ?"

Leetah lifted her head, not daring to hope. His little voice was so frail and tiny, she didn't know for sure she'd truly heard him.

"Mother!" Suntop scrambled off Savah's lap as if awaking from a bad dream. He ran to her, crying, and Leetah bit her own lip to keep from joining him as he rushed into her arms.

"Oh, my little cubling! What is it?"

"I went to see Savah." His face against her neck was wet and hot with difficult emotions. "It's dark in there, and scary! She's trying to get back, but she can't."

Ember scooted up behind her brother, Choplicker under one arm, and wrapped one finger in her brother's hair.

Suntop turned in his mother's arms to twine hands with his sister. "I tried to help her find her way back," he said, half to Leetah, half to the gathered village. "But it'll take a long time. She's so tired."

Ahdri wound her hands together beneath her

chin and uttered a miserable moan. "I begged her to leave off her search for a while! Ever since Cutter went away, she's been obsessed with guiding him somehow. Just before she 'went out,' she said something evil had touched her—something that Cutter *must not* find!" She turned to the villagers crowding near the doorway, as though seeking some form of absolution. "I couldn't stop her! She *had* to learn what the danger is." Tears burst from her anew, and she dropped her face into her hands. "And now she may be lost to us!"

"Mother, please . . ." Suntop turned pleading blue-green eyes up at his mother. "Take me to Father."

Leetah felt her heart thump painfully against her ribs. "What?"

"*Please!* I've got to tell Father what Savah sees— I-I mean *feels*—I mean—" He shook his head as though to clear out the conflicting images. "I've got to *warn* him!"

"Can't you tell *us*, little cub?" Treestump asked, kneeling beside him.

"No, Treestump—only Father!" The child's voice was adamant, almost frightened. Leetah hugged him closer, afraid to let him go. "It's all in my head," Suntop told her apologetically. "It won't come out until we're with Father."

"But, my darling," she whispered, "we don't know where your father is."

"But Savah knows where he *will* be." Suntop pushed away from her and called across the room at those Wolfriders still waiting just inside the doors. "We still have time to get there. I can show you the way." He gripped Leetah's hands between his own. "Oh, Mother, please!"

Fear battered her like a storm of sand. Unable to answer, Leetah pulled him close, and Ember with him, using them to protect herself against the fierce winds of terror that would blow her apart inside. *I was afraid to go with Cutter—afraid!* When she'd confessed that to Nightfall, she'd never guessed how those words would return to haunt her.

How much more frightened she would feel at this moment, when she was left with no choice but to take her children in search of her lifemate in a land more fearsome than any legend she knew.

CHAPTER FIFTEEN

L EETAH?" FOR ONCE, Nightfall stood in the hut's open doorway, a water flask slung across one shoulder and Redlance at her side. "Are you ready?"

Leetah finished shaking the nonexistent sand from a bed throw and nodded. She'd spent all yesterday sorting through her and Cutter's belongings, putting full bags and jars in storage, giving away anything that wouldn't wait for their return. All afternoon, as she waited for the sun to fall, she'd paced back and forth through the spacious hut with its spacious cellar, looking for something to clean up, or move out, or ready. But there was nothing. Even her little gray-striped sand cat had abandoned the house when Choplicker moved in— it glared at Leetah in baleful betrayal from her neighbor's windows whenever the healer walked by. *Much like the villagers,* Leetah thought with a sad smile. She didn't look forward to facing them with the decision she'd made.

Hands so pale they looked like ghosts against her own brown fingers took gentle hold of hers from one side. She looked up, embarrassed, and Redlance offered a friendly smile as he lifted their joined hands between them. He looked startlingly young in his new white linen, red hair shining like the sunset outside against the green embroidery on his vest and tunic sleeves. It was sometimes hard to remember he'd lived a life even longer than Leetah had known.

"Have you done everything you can for Savah?" he asked. He backed toward Nightfall in the doorway, never releasing his hold on Leetah's hands.

She let him back away until his distance held her arms out straight in front of her, then reluctantly followed in response to his pulling. "Yes," she said, very softly. "I have."

He nodded. "Do you believe your cub when he tells you Savah wants him to carry this message to Cutter?"

"Of course!"

"We—Wolfriders, tribe, kin—must go. Is there any way you can live with yourself if you do less than make this journey with us?"

Leetah slowed just outside the arc of fading sun that curled inside her doorway. "Never."

Redlance stopped as well, as if sensing what it would mean to her if she stepped through that final threshold. "If you believe all those things, why fight what you can't avoid? It's like raging at the weather." He touched his forehead to hers in one of his endearing, fatherly gestures, and Leetah couldn't help but smile. "Often," he said, smiling back at her, "the quickest route to peace is through acceptance."

She laughed a little. "Tell that to the villagers." Then she pushed him back a step against Nightfall before he could say anything to continue their discussion. "Come on," she said brusquely, striding through the doorway. "The rest of the tribe is waiting."

Ember's liquid laughter met them first when they

came out into the cool evening. She was dusty already, rolling on her back with Choplicker suspended, squirming, over top of her. Suntop played quietly nearby with a ball-and-string toy much like one Leetah had owned when she was a child.

"Mother!" Ember popped to her feet and slapped dirt from her rear while Choplicker shook himself. "Is it time to go?"

Leetah nodded and held out her hand. "Yes, dearest. Bring your wolf-friend, and come on."

Ember was on her in an instant, and Leetah had to step lightly to avoid Choplicker until the cub figured out where to walk just a little behind them. Suntop abandoned his own game without having to be told. He played out the string to the end of its length, then handed the toy and ball to his friend Wing with a surprisingly mature touch to the youth's shoulder. Suntop was much calmer than he had been yesterday. As he hurried to take her other hand, Leetah noticed how the slanting light made him look so much like his father—serious, full of important convictions. How could she not have faith in him? she wondered. In them both. She knew with sudden certainty that they were doing the right thing. Even if the her own folk didn't agree.

"Don't leave us, healer!" Adja the Potter scurried around in front of her, his arms thrust out to either side as though to hold back a mountain. "What if your talents are needed? What if someone is injured while you're gone?"

His lifemate nodded seriously from over his shoulder. "Let the Wolfriders take Cutter's son to him."

"No!"

Leetah didn't even recognize that voice, it was so distorted with emotion.

"The Wolfriders can't go—they are our hunters and protectors!"

Nightfall's hand lifted to squeeze her shoulder, but Leetah didn't take her eyes from the ground as they kept walking. So much of this was her own fault. By soothing every little hurt with a touch or a word, she had encouraged her people to be too dependent on her. Now, they were weaker for it, and so was she. She tried so hard to shut out their pleas—she'd heard all of them a hundred times over since announcing her intention to leave. But nothing she said had helped them understand her, and nothing they said was going to change her mind. She raised her head to look up toward the Wolfriders' caves, and concentrated on counting her steps until they got there.

The tribe appeared in a colorful rabble, bounding down the rock face all alive and alert and excited about the upcoming travel. Even their clothing was different— full of ruggedness and wild beauty such as Leetah hadn't seen in them since their arrival seven years before. Scouter and One-Eye stood out boldly in matching green and scarlet, Dewshine was at home again in quail feathers and rabbit-brown, Moonshade blended beautifully beside her lifemate in the soft dove grays that made her eyes so huge and poignant, and Clearbrook's hair made a thick rope of silver all the way past her fawn-colored tunic to the top of her green-trousered knees. It was as though the call to adventure enlivened them, as though they'd waited all these years for any good reason to pick up camp and wander. Leetah wished fervently that she could be as brave and willing as they.

"We're ready!" Dewshine announced, hopping from rock to rock in her path down from the caverns. "And may the High Ones guide us as they never have before!"

"Wait, Leetah, please!" Adja pushed with rude bravery between Strongbow and his son, all but falling to his knees in front of Leetah in his effort to keep her away from the approaching Wolfriders. "What if those human creatures come again? What if mountain lions descend to attack us? Rayek used to guard the village before the Wolfriders took his place. Without them, we'll be defenseless!"

"No, you won't."

Dart's small voice surprised them all. He carefully set his small bag of supplies next to his mother's feet and came to stand near Adja, his arrow whip held between both small hands. "I'm going to stay and teach you to fight for yourselves."

Moonshade's eyes flew even wider. "Dart!"

Leetah felt a sear of wordless anger sweep across the gathered elves, and thought the disapproval came from the Wolfriders in general until Dart turned to bravely face his scowling father.

"I-I *want* to do this," Dart told Strongbow firmly. "I *have* to!" His young voice held steady despite the faintest tremor in his shoulders and hands. "I grew up here in Sorrow's End. I can't just leave it with no one here to take care of things."

"*You*?! You, a spindly, half-grown *youth* will be our chief hunter and protector?" Adja clapped his hands to his eyes with a cry of despair. "Oh, we are lost!"

Disappointment and hurt flashed across Dart's face, but he turned to face the babble of villagers with remarkable control.

"That 'spindly youth' is my son."

Silence swept across the crowd like a wind. Strongbow stepped up behind his son, his narrow face pulled into such a scowl of disdain Leetah felt it in the pit of her stomach. "You scrabble about like a nest of brown-skinned rabbits," he spat. Though harsh with disuse, the archer's voice was hard and far-reaching. "My son is worth the lot of you combined! He can teach you to hunt and fight. It's your own worthless hides if you're too fancy to learn."

The villagers only stared in response, and among the Wolfriders, only Treestump had the temerity to smile. Dart spun to face his father, wide, dark eyes aglow. "Oh, Father, thank you! I was sure you'd disapprove!"

I do.

After his brief excursion into the spoken word, Strongbow's mental voice sounded louder and clearer than usual. Leetah glanced about fearfully for some sign of reaction from the Sun Folk, but they didn't even look up from the huddles into which they'd been shocked. She realized then that Strongbow's sending had been meant for the Wolfriders only, and that she had been inexplicably included in their number.

You're wasting your time on these shivering fawns, the archer sent, his face as unreadable as ever. **But it's *your* decision. Just remember**—He took Dart's chin firmly in one hand and held the boy with both grip and gaze—**you're a Wolfrider. Don't ever forget where you came from.**

Dart nodded once, somberly, and Strongbow released him with no other sign of farewell. Turning away from his son, Strongbow aimed a piercing look across the gathering at Leetah. She tried to send her simple understanding, but couldn't feel if anything happened. Strongbow went to gather up his and Dart's travel packs without giving any sign that he had heard her.

"Then it's decided," Leetah said aloud. The villagers jumped and looked up hopefully at the sound of her voice. "Good luck, Dart."

He tipped his head, respectful, yet eager in his youth. "And good luck to you, too, healer."

"Don't worry about Sorrow's End, Leetah." Rainsong smiled from her place at Woodlock's side, both hands resting on the rainbow-colored dress that draped her swollen belly. Leetah hadn't even seen the lifemates approach, so completely had they taken up the Sun Folk ways. "Even if your journey takes you away for many seasons, the village will have a healer. My father, Rain, had powers similar to yours. In this little one coming, they flow again—I've sensed it."

Leetah reached out to touch the young mother's hand. The truth of her prediction tingled along the healer's nerves. "Rainsong, you are a wonder."

But Rainsong's sweet smile took none of the bitterness from the sound of Shenshen's sobbing behind her. Feeling her hard-won strength dissolve, Leetah went to her sister with her own eyes stinging with tears. "Oh, Shenshen," she sighed, gathering the young girl into her arms.

Her sister's hug was fierce with all the difficult love between them. "I can't believe you're leaving!" Shenshen shuddered as she tried to take a breath around her crying. "Will we ever see you again?"

Leetah closed her eyes to hide her pain. "I hope so, little sister."

"No! Don't even *hint* that something might happen—I couldn't bear it!"

Leetah stroked her sister's hair the way she'd done when they still shared a room as small children, willing her to sleep well and be fearless all the day. "Hush . . . Everything will be all right . . ."

"But what if it isn't?" Shenshen pulled away, her hands to her mouth as if horrified by what she herself had just spoken. Then she turned and fled, and Leetah knew there wasn't time to follow her and try to make things right.

"It's hard for her," Leetah's mother said softly from behind her. She clasped her hands to Leetah's face when the healer turned. "Everything is so different now. First Rayek, now you." She shook her head and slipped her hands down Leetah's arms. "My kitling, this goes against the very purpose of Sorrow's End."

Leetah hugged her mother, wishing she could change so much of what had happened, but knowing it was impossible. "I must go, Mother. I cannot return to the half-awake life I led before Cutter came to me. He *is* life, and this is my awakening."

A high, ringing howl cascaded down the sandstone cliffs, and Leetah drew reluctantly away from her mother. *Time to go,* she thought. But all she could do was squeeze her mother's hands one last time before turning to join the others in the first shreds of gathering darkness.

The wolves materialized as though from nowhere. Slipping down out of the hills, they padded toward their elfin friends, and a strange mingling of voices, thoughts, and touching filled the gentle night. Leetah felt the sudden silence when the Sun Folk retreated to the edges of the village. She couldn't help a little sigh of gratefulness at being released from their control and judgment.

Choplicker frolicked among the feet of the older wolves. If he noticed that his mother, Silvergrace, was not among them, he gave no sign. Leetah didn't know if it was best that Rainsong and Woodlock's wolves would stay behind with their friends at Sorrow's End, or if the young cub would be better off with a parent for familiarity. Then she saw the relish with which Ember and the cubling both rolled beneath Briersting's feet as the big wolf nibbled at them and growled playfully, and Leetah knew such worries were pointless when it came to this tribe.

"Redlance is right, you know." Nightfall handed Leetah the reins to a sleepy zwoot, then stooped to lift Suntop into one of the two riding baskets on either side of the huge mount's saddle. "You're doing the right thing. I told you that when Cutter needed you, you wouldn't fail him."

Such brave words, Leetah thought, sighing. *Such trust.* Smiling at her friend briefly, she let Nightfall make a stirrup for her so she could scrabble aboard her riding beast before turning to the rest of the elves.

"The time has come, my brave new tribe." They looked up at her, excited and happy, and Leetah felt her own heart rise in anticipation. "Your chief—and my life-mate—awaits us."

The howl they sent up to color the night was one of hope for the future, and of simple, wolfen joy.

CHAPTER SIXTEEN

CUTTER FLOATED ON HIS back in the cool forest pond. Water danced and sang down a little staircase of stones, splashing against the surface of the larger pool with a sound like cheerful whispers. His eyes closed, his limbs relaxed, Cutter felt the ghost movement of warm upper water mingling with the cool fluid below, the tickle of his hair as it haloed his head to drift around his neck and his ears. He smiled at the heavy play of light, then shadow, then light across his closed eyelids, and, somewhere on the shore nearby, Nightrunner sighed and rolled over in his sleep.

They weren't that far from Nonna and Adar's tiny hut, but they were far enough. For the first time in an eight of days, Cutter didn't have to smell their sweating bodies, the lingering stink of their feces, the burn of their roasting meat. As kind as they had been to him, Nonna and her mate were still only humans—Cutter hadn't slept untroubled a single day since coming to them. It was good now to simply be out in the wild greenness, with nothing but midges and water-skaters to bother him, and nothing but violets and acorn blossoms to smell.

A great crashing splash shattered the silence in the little glade. Cutter jolted upright as a sharp wave of water slapped over him.

"Look at you!" Skywise snorted with evident disgust, shoving a glossy wall at Cutter with both hands. "If I had been a human, you'd be fish food by now!"

Cutter turned his head aside, trying to deflect the spray with one hand. "If you had been a human," he countered irritably, "Nightrunner would have said something before you got this close." He almost wished the old wolf had, anyway. He didn't appreciate having his quiet interrupted. "Besides, there aren't even any humans around here."

Skywise slipped off his headpiece and tossed it among his clothes above the shoreline. "There's Nonna and Adar."

"They don't count."

The stargazer didn't have to say anything for Cutter to sense his angry disapproval. Dunking himself forcefully under the water, Skywise stayed out of sight as if that might make Cutter forget his arrival. The chief finally had to poke him underwater with one toe to let him know he wasn't getting off so easily. **What happened?**

Embarrassment swelled to the surface in Skywise like a sheen of bubbles, colored darkly by the black of anger. **Nothing.**

Come on, Skywise. Did Adar try to talk to you again? Cutter had spent most of the last few days following Nonna about her chores, asking her questions and listening with wolfen patience to her long and gentle answers. Skywise had spent those same days sulking in the treetops, throwing maple spinners and epithets down at Adar. His behavior obviously hadn't helped the human male understand what about these "spirits" was so worthy of his respect. **Skywise . . .**

Skywise popped to the surface again and combed a fall of silver hair out of his eyes. "He wanted to know what favors we'd grant him if he worshiped us." Bitterness stained his gray eyes. "That's all humans are ever interested in—gain and greed. They're as bad as trolls!"

Cutter decided not to pursue that comparison just now. "Did he want some favor in particular?"

Skywise shrugged. "I didn't really listen," he admitted, leaning back in the water and skimming the surface with his hands. "Some tree rot about taking him and Nonna back to live with their own people."

"Nonna said something about that, too." Cutter let himself bob under the water again so its cool caress could ease the sun on his bare shoulders. "They were driven out of their village because of Nonna's symbol making . . . or something like that. She didn't really say it, but I think she misses being with her own kind."

"Why would she?" Skywise pulled a sour face. "You know something's the matter with humans when they drive away even their own."

"We drove away Rayek," Cutter pointed out.

Skywise flushed, but didn't relent. "That was different."

"Was it? We don't know that." Gathering his hands up beneath him, Cutter stroked to the edge of the pond and pulled his torso onto the shore. "Come here."

At first, he thought Skywise might pretend he hadn't heard. Then Cutter felt the heady movement of water around and beneath him, and Skywise broke the surface beside him. Cutter drew a long squiggle in the sandy bank and pointed to one end of it to illustrate his words. "Nonna told me that her mate found her by following a long river that flows right by his village. Adar walked beside it upstream, through the Valley of Endless Sleep—whatever that is—and right to the foot of the Bird Spirits' mountain." He paused with his finger dimpling the sand at the far end of his squiggle. "Humans always call our kind 'spirits' or 'demons,' don't they? Just think! If Nonna's 'Bird Spirits' *are* elves, that means they've lived in peace with her tribe for moons without number!"

Skywise snorted and pushed away from shore. "Owl pellets!" He disappeared under the water again with a splash. **Humans and elves can't live together!**

Cutter turned with a sigh, this time leaning back against a half-submerged rock rather than follow his friend out into the pond. **If that's true, then how do you explain Nonna?**

Moon madness? Skywise circumnavigated the pool beneath a trail of bubbles. **Bad food? Who knows?**

At this rate, I should have just taken Strongbow on this quest. **You know what I think?** Cutter sent, already suspecting the reception he'd get. **I think we should help those two humans get back into their village.**

Skywise's surprise blasted over him like a storm wind.

After all—the sooner we find that river by Adar's village, the sooner we can follow it to the Bird Spirits.

"*That does it!*" Skywise exploded out of the water directly in front of him. Cutter barely had time to register his presence before the stargazer had gripped the chief's head in both hands and jammed him under halfway to the bottom. "That fever burned up your brains!" Skywise's shout carried blurrily down to him as he struggled to shoot himself back upward. "Help humans?! Walk right into a nest of them?! Why not take New-Moon and cut off your own head? It's the same thing!"

Cutter spat his mouth clear of water, but stayed a safe arm's length away from the stargazer, just in case. "Come on," he said cajolingly frowning. "That's just the way Bearclaw used to talk. Humans *know* things that are important to our quest—just like the trolls did. If we're clever and careful, we can learn even more."

"And if we're not," Skywise shot back glumly, "we can get killed."

The violence of his friend's reaction startled Cutter. Swimming over to find footing beside him, the younger elf took Skywise's shoulder in an effort to reassure him. "We didn't get this far by being timid." When Skywise only scowled more deeply, Cutter sighed and respected his skepticism by releasing him. "Things aren't the way they used to be in the holt," Cutter said, knowing it sounded like an apology, but unable to alter the past. "Sooner or later, we've got to learn to take advantage of the changes—because I have a feeling there are going to be a lot of them from here on in."

Squatting with his elbows on his knees, Cutter watched Nonna hurry from place to place outside the cave-like hovel she'd shared with Adar for so long. She smoothed the dirt where their fire used to burn, swept leaves from the edges of their clearing, carefully cleared away every last rock they'd piled near their door for use or protection. It was as if she wanted to leave the little place clean and attractive for whoever might stumble across it behind them. That simple consideration charmed Cutter and made him smile.

"Come, Nonna!" Adar caught at her skirts from behind, laughing like a much younger man and looking almost handsome despite his coarse features and weathered face. "If we're to make this trip, we should start sometime today."

She flushed and pulled her hands away from their most recent job. "Yes, I know. I'm sorry!" She turned to flash a loving smile at Cutter, then a more subdued nod toward where Skywise hovered near the treeline with the wolves. "Thank you, both. You are most kind."

Skywise snorted too softly for the humans to hear, and Cutter slapped him with a mental chide to keep him silent.

"Everything about this trip will be well," Adar agreed. He handed Nonna a pack to carry over her shoulders, then hefted one for himself from beside the door. "The Bone Woman will *have* to back down and accept us once she sees we're under the protection of good spirits."

Standing, Cutter climbed down from his rocky perch. "Bone Woman?"

Adar nodded. "My tribe's shamanness. She spoke against me when I came before my village chief, Olbar the Mountain-Tall, to present Nonna as my bride. The Bone Woman said Nonna was an outsider from a land of evil demons. It didn't help matters that Nonna was a symbol maker. The shamanness convinced my chief that I had brought bad magic into the village." His dark beard twisted around his sour frown. "I'm sure Olbar still listens to that old hag. She knows how to play on his fears."

"But now she'll see that there is nothing to be afraid of." Nonna tipped her head against her mate's shoulder—a gesture so like any elf maiden's that Cutter couldn't help thinking of his tribe and family far away. "Thank you, Honored One," Nonna told him. "Your gentle folk have always done such good for me and my people."

"And you have returned that goodness." Cutter held out his pink, healed hand for her to see. "All we want now is to see that you are happy, and to return to our home." He tipped his chin back to look at Adar. "Are you ready?"

The question was meant as a formality, but the human male looked around as though uncertain, peering hard at all the trees. "I . . . I'm not sure," Adar admitted slowly. "This wood is always so cursed dark, and the old paths I used to know are changed, overgrown." He sighed and shook his heavy head. "It's been a long time. I don't know if I can find the way."

"I can."

Skywise's light voice cut across the clearing, but he didn't step away from the concealing woods. Slipping the lodestone from around his neck, he held it resting on his palm for a long moment before looking up to meet Cutter's waiting gaze. **This is only because I know the quest matters,** he sent, his face impassive. **It's not for them.**

Cutter nodded his understanding, and the stargazer moved slowly into the open.

Skywise stopped a few strides behind Cutter's shoulder, as though any closer contact with the humans would soil him beyond retrieval. Then he lifted his hand, the lodestone hanging by its braided string, and flicked the shard of rock with one finger so that it spun with languid ease.

When it slowed, the carefully marked eye pointed toward the direction of the Hub star—not even visible in the light of a human day, but always somehow calling to the stone with a powerful, irresistible voice. The left side faced Sun-Goes-Down, and it was this way that Skywise pointed proudly. "Your village is that way."

Adar stared at the stone, dark eyes wide. "It . . . it's *magic*!"

A little tweak of pleasure stirred at the corners of Skywise's mouth. "Yes," he said dramatically. "Magic! A very special kind. The lodestone knows where we want to go, and it will guide us there without fail." Cutter knew that wasn't strictly true, but saw no reason to correct his friend's explanation.

"But . . ." The human male shook his head in slow wonder. "But *how*?"

Nonna elbowed her mate and laughed as if he were a child frightened by a made-up tale. "They are *spirits*, Adar! Magic is in their blood."

He nodded, but didn't look particularly reassured.

Cutter aimed an appreciative smile at his friend while Skywise slipped the lodestone back into place over his neck. **If we're going to have to travel with them,** the stargazer explained, **at least let me have a *little* fun.**

Cutter nodded, but let the humans think the gesture was for them. "All right, humans! We have a long journey ahead of us." He swung into the trees to disappear among the leafy shadows. "The sooner we get started, the sooner we will get it done."

Compared to the moons and moons they spent wading across the endless sea of grass, their days-long trek through these woods seemed barely the beginning of a trip to Cutter. He and Skywise stayed to the trees as much as they were able, with the humans making the best time they could through the dense, unbroken underbrush. Then, a few days into the journey, Adar became excited about recognizing the trees and hills around them. Cutter decided it best to let the human male lead from then on, and Skywise seemed just as happy not to be forced to deal with the humans just because he felt out the way with the lodestone. They traveled like that from then on—humans on the ground in the lead, elves following through the monstrous trees a safe, silent distance behind.

It was all still so weird, Cutter reflected more than once while sitting awake at night to watch the humans in their sleep. In his heart, he knew that elves and humans could never truly become friends—yet here he was, protecting human travelers from every misstep and predator as they joyfully led the way to a crowded human village. Except for a heavy meal of bear meat after a sick old male stumbled into the humans' path, the elves had gained nothing from this queer alliance. Cutter couldn't help but be keenly aware that he'd undertaken this chore only because he hoped to gain something after it was all over. "It's a stupid plan," Skywise had informed him more than once. The young chief was just as glad they hadn't taken the opportunity to discuss it any further.

I say they're not showing up. The sour impatience in Skywise's sending sliced across Cutter's musings now as cleanly as spoken words. **Let's go.**

Cutter tossed his friend a gentle scowl and shifted his seat on Nightrunner. **They'll come.** He and Skywise had come down out of the trees the night before, able to smell the human village even before Nonna and Adar recognized its nearness. On Cutter's suggestion, the elves had killed a young buck in the woods nearby, then crept close to the village border with the stag hung on a branch between their shoulders. Cutter hoped having some sort of peace offering would help when the time came to actually walk among the villagers.

The rumble of excited activity began on the other side of the circle of huts. Humans swarmed to the sound of their own voices like a hive of bothered bees, and Cutter could just glimpse Adar's determined face among the sea of dark heads. Adar let the chattering humans herd him almost to the center of the village before stopping and forcing them to cluster around him.

"I am Adar," his voice rang out, "son of Tolf the Wood Cleaver. My wife Nonna and I have come here seeking an end to our unjust banishment." He raked his eyes across the now quiet crowd, and opened his mouth to go on.

A shrill shriek cut him silent. "Evil! Evil! Evil is here!"

Rattling and clacking like a gourd full of loose stones, a howling, grotesque little monster exploded from one of the human huts. Cutter first thought it must be some sort of demon apparition—bones and beads and polished shells dangled from every fold of its obese frame. Then he recognized the flash of oiled animal hide across its back and realized it was only some natural creature, so decorated with bone and sinew that its original form was now lost.

Skywise jerked as though slapped. **Is-is it a troll?**

Cutter shook his head slowly. **Can't be! Trolls aren't that ugly.** But morbid fascination wouldn't let him take his eyes off the hideous beast as it flounced and screamed around the human couple. Then something in its movements stung Cutter with its familiarity, and he almost gasped. **High Ones, Skywise—I think it's a *human*!**

No!

"Bad magic! Foul magic! Consorters with demons!" The bony monstrosity shook a whitened turtle shell in Nonna's face, and the gentle woman withdrew from the shell's fierce rattle. "Kill them as you should have done long ago! *Kill them!*"

His heart tightening with dread, Cutter reached to lower the stag from his shoulders. If he and Nightrunner could dash through and drive the crowd into a panic, perhaps Nonna and Adar could escape—

The piercing bellow of a hunting horn slapped against Cutter's sensitive ears. He froze, still inside the cover of the forest, and felt Skywise's hand grab at Nightrunner's tail as the agitated humans scattered away from the human couple. The bone creature waddled about, her back to Cutter, but he still heard the wicked triumph in her laugh. "Now, outcasts, you are truly doomed!"

From somewhere out of sight behind the farthest huts stepped the largest human Cutter had ever seen. The man stood a full head taller than his tallest warrior, his chest as broad as that of the flatland bull whose hide he wore. His hair, the same flinty gray as his eyes, hung to his shoulders, and the beard flowing down his chest to mingle with the hair there only served to make him look even more wild and bestial. He stalked past the cackling bone ghoul and snatched away Adar's spear as though taking a toy from a child.

"So, Adar." Even his voice was as deep and crushing as a mountainslide. "It seems exile agrees with you. Or has your woman conjured demons to tend you all this time?"

The villagers around them burbled with tentative laughter, but Adar held his head high to meet the taller man's stare.

"Olbar," he said stiffly, unafraid. "I do not deny that the spirits commune with Nonna."

Olbar grunted. "Then you must know that your return here means your death."

"We gambled on your wisdom, my chief," Adar told him. "It is not wise to destroy those whom the good spirits favor."

The big chief made a face ugly even by human standards. "There *is* no such thing as a good spirit!" And he spat on the ground at Adar's feet to underscore his point. "I know!"

"Please!" Nonna stepped away from her mate's side, her hands clasped beseechingly in front of her. "Listen, great chief! I swear on my life's blood, I mean you and your people no harm. Like the weather, or the mighty river, the spirits I serve can be as terrible as they are beautiful. But they *are* good. We cannot deny them—any of us!"

"Do not be deceived, Olbar!" Clattering with fury, the bone-shrouded creature pushed in front of her chief to shake her rattle at Nonna. "This childless one does not know her place! She dares to make symbols like a man! And *such* symbols—strange and evil. Look!" One clawlike hand snatched out to rip away Nonna's drawing supplies even as the younger woman tried to save them. "The tools of her vile craft are in this pouch!"

Olbar took the little leather sack and frowned into it without lifting it any higher than his waist.

"These two reek of foul magic!" the bone creature continued. "Their tongues are berry-sweet, but their hearts are full of poison thorns!" She stamped thick feet until dust clouds rose. "Kill them!"

Suddenly decisive, Olbar flung the pack of Nonna's supplies to the ground. "No more talk! The Bone Woman speaks true!"

Now, Skywise! Cutter bent for his half of the tree branch and hefted the stag to his shoulder. **Let's get in there!**

"You are outcasts!" Olbar shouted, stabbing a finger at the couple. "You are evil! We cannot have your kind among us. Warriors, slay them! Slay th—"

The huge man's eyes traveled beyond Adar's head in response to the movement near the edge of the village. Feeling the sun touch his cheeks as they moved from shadow into light, Cutter met Olbar's stare with wolfen intensity. Beneath him, Nightrunner drew back his lips into a distrustful snarl.

". . . By the falling Death Water . . . !" Olbar's whisper was as pale and shocked as his face.

When the first villager turned to face them, Cutter's stomach tensed with the age-old fear. They might rush the elves in a mass, throw spears at them, or chase them with fire. Instead, a dark-faced man cried out in painful terror and fell to the ground, sobbing. One by one, the rest of the village followed him, until only Olbar, the couple, and the shrieking Bone Woman were left standing as the wolf-mounted elves padded into their midst. Nonna's ginger eyes practically sparkled with worshipful pride.

Cutter stopped Nightrunner a good spear's throw from the closest human warrior. Even there, he could feel Skywise's discomfort rolling off him like a fever.

"Hear me, humans!" Cutter raised one hand above his head and did his best to sound ancient and all-knowing. "You must allow Nonna and Adar to dwell among you, for they have earned the Bird Spirits' eternal favor. Accept these two exiles into your tribe, and good fortune is yours. Harm them, and the spirits will take terrible revenge on all your people."

Well played. Skywise shifted unhappily. **Can we leave now?**

Be patient, Skywise! We're not through yet. "This meat of the forest we give you in token of our good faith."

How long can you keep spouting this swamp rot?

Annoyed, Cutter pricked his friend into silence with a sharp thought. **As long as it takes to make sure Nonna and Adar are safe.**

The Bone Woman shook herself as though taken with palsy and threw a handful of broken stones at the wolves' eyes. "Begone!" she shrieked, dancing out her own bitter anger. "I *command* you, beast-eared demons! Turn your cursed evil eyes away from us!"

Olbar lunged forward to grab her hair, his eyes wild with fear. "Stop, woman! Have you gone mad? Would you bring the wrath of all the spirit world upon us?"

"Who rules you, humans?" Cutter asked loudly. He

could sniff the human chief's fear from here. "That bag of rattling bones, or Olbar the Mountain-Tall?"

The human chief jerked upright and came one stiff step forward. "I . . . I am Olbar."

"Then tell your people to accept Nonna and Adar, now and forever."

Olbar nodded, his face still deathly pale. "I will."

"No!" The Bone Woman twisted to free herself from Olbar's hold. "Drive the beast-eared ones away!"

The big human threw her to the ground without taking his eyes away from Cutter. "Silence, old one! You forget that I have been to the Forbidden Grove! I have tasted the spirits' vengeance once—that was enough!"

"But these are of more ancient and evil stock than the little winged ones!"

Cutter threw a startled glance across the stag at Skywise. **Forbidden Grove? Little winged ones?**

Cutter, no! The stargazer's thoughts were almost a groan. **Let's just find the river and go!**

Olbar interrupted their exchange in tones as sweet as flower nectar. "Stay, graceful spirits. Honor my humble village with your presence." He motioned timidly toward the stag, his big hands trembling slightly. "Tomorrow we will make a great feast from your gift of sacred meat."

Cutter didn't even have to look at Skywise to know what the stargazer thought of the invitation. "Yes, human," he said aloud, ignoring the grumble of disapproval from his companion. "That will please us."

In retaliation, Skywise dropped his half of the stag and loped back for the forest on Starjumper, not even responding to his chief's anxious mental call.

Sighing deeply to hide his annoyance, Cutter deposited his own side of the branch on the ground beside Nightrunner and nodded once to Olbar before backing away. "Until tomorrow, we will be nearby. Be good to Nonna and Adar."

Then he melted into the woods after Skywise without waiting for the mountainous chief's reply.

CHAPTER SEVENTEEN

WATCH THIS, SUNTOP! ME and Choplicker can't even dig a hole fast enough!"

Sitting in the shade outside their heavy silken tent, Leetah smiled as Ember attacked the sand with wild abandon. A tawny shower sprayed out between her legs in imitation of her cub's cheerful digging, only to slide back into the excavation as quickly as the two could throw it out. This late in the day, the sheer red cliff rising above them cast a thick wedge of shadow around its own feet, and Suntop, Ember, and the cub played about this line of darkness as if it were a feature of the landscape just like any of the other rocks and dunes. The rest of the elves napped fitfully beneath the tent's protection, sipping from bladders of warm, stale water and waiting for the sunset.

They had traveled like this for ten nights before the towering cliffs rose into view. Leetah had let the Wolfriders set the pace, knowing that her tireless zwoot could easily pace the others into exhaustion if she wasn't careful. Even so, the effort of pitching the communal tent at dawn grew more torturous every day, and even Leetah spent much of the blistering daylight hours undressed and half-asleep, dreaming of a breeze.

The Wolfriders had proven brave and loyal travel

companions. Leetah had heard them worry aloud, though, about what it would be like—what it would do to the children—if their supplies failed before Suntop led them out of the desert. She had even caught the fringes of Strongbow's disapproving sends to travelers other than herself, and forced herself not to react to them. Suntop had guided them with certainty and devotion thus far. If they were tracking a different path than the one first taken by the Wolfriders through the desert, then it was only because Savah pointed the child toward some destination other than what they all expected. *It all has to do with faith,* Leetah told herself, shifting to find a cooler position on the warm sand. *I trust Savah, and I trust Suntop. I have to!*

The tent shuddered as if against a nonexistent breeze, and Leetah looked around to see Treestump duck out from under the heavy flap. He smiled at her in greeting, then stepped away into the sunlight to trudge to the end of the cliffs' shadow.

Bored now with her never-growing hole, Ember scrambled away from her brother to shake sand all over Treestump. "Hiya, Treestump!"

He reached down to tousle sand from her hair with a smile. "Hello, cub."

"Whatcha doin'?"

"Oh . . ." He lifted his square face to study the rocks rising up in front of them. "Just looking at the past, I suppose."

Ember turned to frown in the same direction. "You've seen these big rocks before?"

"Aye, Ember." Treestump nodded, not looking

down at her. "Seven turns of the seasons ago. But I saw a different part of 'em, in a different place."

Suntop slipped up to the older elf's other side and took Treestump's huge hand in his own. "These are the rocks the tribe climbed out of when you came to Sorrow's End, aren't they?"

"Aye, Suntop, they are." He gathered Ember up with his other hand and walked them closer to the tall expanse. "We used to live in a place as cool and green as this place is hot and bright. But humans lived there, too, and they hated us for reasons we never did understand."

As Treestump's voice began to soften with distance, Leetah climbed to her feet to follow. She'd heard—and lived through—Treestump's story a hundred times before, but found herself drawn to remember it again now, as if that story's happy ending could grant them the same luck on this new journey.

She drew up alongside the somber trio with Choplicker bumbling along between her feet.

"One night," Treestump told the cubs as they walked along the foot of the rock wall, "humans found Redlance while he was all by himself. They captured him, and took him back to their village."

"They were gonna kill him!" Ember exclaimed.

Treestump nodded, casting a knowing smile at Leetah over her daughter's head. Ember's impatience with exciting stories was a long-accepted fact among the Wolfrider tribe. "Aye, lass, they were. They hurt him something awful before your father and the rest could rescue him. By then, the humans were mad with rage."

"And they set fire to the forest!"

This time, Leetah laid a hand on Ember's head in silent rebuke.

"And it was the fire that drove us to the trolls," Treestump continued easily, still smiling. "Those dirt grubbers promised to help us, but instead they tricked us! They led us down what they called the Tunnel of Golden Light, saying it would take us to a wonderful new land where we could live far from humans and be happy. Instead"—he slapped a hand against the sun-warmed stone—"it led us here, to the foot of these rocks and this place of desperate heat and dryness."

"And they knocked down the tunnel behind you, so you could never follow it back to the forest!"

Suntop reached in front of Treestump to poke his sister. "Ember, hush!"

"But I know how the story goes!" She aimed a petulant glare at her brother as she danced away from his swatting. "Since you couldn't go back, you decided to go forward! Skywise had the lodestone, and it pointed thataway." Spinning, she thrust her whole arm back in the direction they'd come, across the burning waste. "And father said it must be a sort of a sign!"

"That's right!" Laughing, Treestump scooped Ember up against him and clamped a big hand across her mouth. Leetah heard her squeal with delight from underneath Treestump's palm. "So we left the Tunnel of Golden Light and started off across the sands. Mind you, we had no food, no tent, and precious little water among us. We were going on nothing but faith. But your father led us for three days through heat and thirst, and didn't ever give up, even when most of us were ready to."

"And it *did* lead you to a wonderful new place," Suntop pointed out seriously. "One without humans or hurt—it led you to Sorrow's End."

My amazing little child, Leetah thought with a swell of love. *How your father would be proud of you!*

"Aye, lad," Treestump agreed as Ember squirmed out of his arms and dashed away. "It led us to Sorrow's End, and I have never been sorry since."

"Hey!" Ember's voice ricocheted off the rock wall farther ahead of them. "Hey, look at this!" She scrabbled up a fall of jumbled rocks without even waiting for anyone to answer. Leetah realized she had found some sort of cave only when Ember disappeared to the waist inside the rock face.

"Careful, she-cub!" Treestump broke into an easy trot.

Leetah lifted her coat to hurry after him. "Watch out for snakes!"

"There's no snakes in here, Mother." The child's piping voice echoed with youthful certainty. "But I sure smell *something*!" A wiggle and a few awkward kicks carried her completely out of view, and Leetah had to chew her lip to keep from shouting for Ember to come out. Choplicker squirmed his way up the pile of stones and yapped after his elf-friend.

"What's all the shouting?"

Leetah turned as Nightfall and Dewshine waded through the sand to join them. Behind them, Pike and One-Eye were already knocking down the tent's central pole while Scouter and Clearbrook rolled the silk back into its travel wad. Leetah hadn't realized how dark the air was getting, how close it was to leaving time.

"My daughter's gone exploring," she exclaimed with a sigh.

Nightfall smiled and hung an arm over Leetah's shoulders in sympathy. "She's the only one with the energy left to do anything. Maybe we shouldn't let her sleep during the day."

It wasn't the first time this had been suggested.

"*Wow!*" The excited shout reverberated within the tiny cave. "Suntop—wow! Come look what I found!"

Releasing Treestump's hand, Suntop scurried forward and scooped Choplicker out of the way as he crawled up after his sister. By now, most of the tribe had wandered over to join them, and Leetah heard Dewshine quickly recapping the details to each little group as they arrived with their new questions. At the mouth of the cave, Ember popped out like a desert rat, with what looked like a smooth, pale rock tucked underneath one arm.

Leetah had barely focused on the strange object before Ember thrust it out in front of her for everyone to see. "Bones!" the little Wolfrider exclaimed. "This one was the best—it's funny looking."

The Wolfriders all stared as silently as Leetah at Ember's find. One hand to her mouth, the healer moved slowly forward and reached for the graceful globe.

"There's a bunch more in here. Wanna see?"

"No, Ember . . ." Leetah sank to her knees in the sand, pulling off one glove so that she could feel the bone's sweeping contours with her fingers. "This is an elf's skull . . . It's been bare of flesh for only a few years."

"Do you think it was put here by whoever moved these rocks?" Suntop asked.

Leetah glanced up at him. "Darling?"

"These rocks." He pointed to the pile just below the little cave, and to the row of stones lining the mouth of the cavern. "All these rocks were moved by magic. I can feel it."

Moved by magic . . . Leetah looked down at the skull cradled in her lap, and her heart throbbed in her breast with desperate grief. In all her long life, she had only known of one elf who could move objects by the power of his will alone—her darling, prideful Rayek. Rayek, who had left Sorrow's End only a few short years before.

She bowed her head to her knees, embracing the little skull as though anything she did now could protect it. Rayek flooded her mind in a wash of bittersweet memories, the taste of them—the taste of him—so different from the life she shared with Cutter, yet so much a part of making her the elf maid Cutter Recognized on the Wolfriders' first day among them. To forget Rayek would be to forget part of who she was—to lose him, to lose a part of herself forever. She squeezed her eyes shut against the sting of tears.

"Mother . . . ?"

Then Redlance's voice, silencing Ember gently. "Hush, dearest."

But the sound of her daughter's voice called her back to the present. Straightening, Leetah brushed the tears from her lashes, then carefully tugged her glove back over her hand while she stood. She tenderly replaced the pathetic remains in their small tomb.

Farewell, my old love.

The Wolfriders stood around her in respectful silence. She was grateful and surprised by the sympathy she read in those young and honest faces, and thanked them all with a silent nod as she gathered up her children's hands.

"Come, Suntop . . . Ember . . ." She led them toward the waiting zwoots, and toward the gathering sunset. "It's time to go."

CHAPTER EIGHTEEN

C UTTER, I DON'T WANT to do this.**

The young chief looked across the hedge of brambles at Skywise, taking in the stargazer's stiff shoulders and grim eyes as they watched the humans bustle about their village preparing for the welcome feast.

You haven't wanted to do *any* of this, Skywise, he pointed out. **And has anything bad come of it?**

Skywise pressed his lips into a narrow line as baskets and crocks of precious food joined the flowers and idols at the foot of the fur-draped altar. **Not yet,** he admitted.

Then take heart. Olbar's hunting horn blared from the village proper—the signal Cutter had accepted to call them to the feast. He squeezed Skywise's shoulder reassuringly. **If we want Nonna and Adar to take us to the great river, we can at least do what we're able for them first.**

Skywise's snort made it clear he thought they'd done more than enough already, but he said and sent nothing as Cutter led them out of the underbrush and before the gathered villagers.

The humans smelled much less strongly of fear this morning. They stood in an eager arc behind Olbar, dressed and painted in their finest colors, their dark, coarse faces alive with expression. Mounting the cairn of stones that the humans had stacked into their altar, Cutter waited for Skywise to climb up beside him before sitting on the deer hide laid out for their comfort. It was a summer hide, glossy and soft, and Cutter was impressed with this consideration without quite knowing why.

"Welcome, gentle spirits!" Olbar bowed deeply, then came to stand at the foot of the altar. "May your presence bless us and keep our land prosperous for seasons to come." Then he turned to his villagers with an imperious clap of his huge hands, and the celebration began.

Olbar's warriors displayed their strength and agility in a wild, pulsing dance. Drums and rattles provided the driving rhythm, while high-pitched human voices sang in praise of the bountiful forest and the ever-flowing river. Skywise picked listlessly at the deer hide; only glancing up occasionally, but Cutter watched the rite with silent interest. In so many ways, the humans' display was a travesty of the festivities once held by the Sun Folk in honor of the Wolfriders' arrival. The human dancing was heavy-footed and awkward compared to elfin delicacy—the music dissonant and loud to sensitive elfin ears. And yet . . .

For all their age-old and justifiable resentment of humans, Cutter couldn't help but see that, among them, a smile was a smile, a touch was a touch, not unlike the gentle interactions he'd grown up loving among his fellow elves. Perhaps these tall creatures who were so strangely diverse in their appearance, so violently unpredictable in their temperament, were really just like elves after all.

Skywise's disgruntled sending interrupted his chief's troubled thoughts. **Cutter . . . ?**

Hmmmm?

Olbar is staring at me.

Cutter pulled his attention away from the cheerful capers to glance aside at Skywise. Olbar stood off to one side of the altar, studying the stargazer's profile with mists of awe in his hard gray eyes. Cutter smiled and turned back to the village. **I think he's worshiping you.**

Skywise's disgust splashed over him, and Cutter almost laughed. **I *hate* this worshiping stuff!** Skywise complained. He ripped a handful of fur out of the hide beneath him. **Can't we just *leave* here? I've had enough!**

Really? Cutter smiled at the tiny human girl who scampered forward to offer him a basket filled with unshelled nuts. **I think it's a lot better than yesterday,** he sent, taking a handful and waving the girl on her way. **At least that awful Bone Woman creature isn't here.**

I'm serious, Cutter. Skywise reached across to snatch a nut from his friend's hand. **I don't want to stay anymore.**

But there are things the humans might teach us yet.

Nothing we need to know! Your Nonna has told us where to find her Bird Spirits—what can these humans have that could matter more? He scooted around to face Cutter squarely. **There's nothing for us here. Let's go!**

Cutter searched his eyes, and felt a stab of guilt at the depth of tension and fear he could read there. For all his own history with humans and human hatred, Cutter sometimes forgot how many more seasons of suffering Skywise had lived through, how many more friends, lovers, and wolf-friends Skywise had lost to human hate. The stargazer had been good to stay with Cutter this long in the presence of so many strangers. Nonna had given them the chance to find the "spirits" who lived in companion with her own people, after all. If indeed those "spirits" were another tribe of elves, anything they could share with Cutter was certain to matter more than anything these humans would know.

Standing, Cutter touched Skywise's arm in apology and turned to face Olbar eye to eye. "Human! You and your people have done the spirits great honor. We are pleased, but we must leave now."

The big human's face softened with disappointment. "Leave?"

"Yes. Nonna and Adar have a promise to fulfill." He looked across the swarm of human faces until Nonna's gentle smile beamed at him from beneath her husband's arm. "Isn't that so?"

The symbol maker nodded excitedly and waded toward the altar through the dancing villagers. "Yes! And gladly! We will show you the great river and the way to my first home."

"Very well." Cutter raised his hands, feeling a little foolish when he saw the ripple of excitement that passed through the crowd. "Be well, humans!" he told them, trying hard to sound ancient and wise. "Live in peace."

With a great cry of joy and excitement, the humans redoubled their gyrating celebration. Skywise had already jumped down from the fur-covered stones, and Cutter followed him without pausing. The wolves waited in the forest nearby, sleepy with the sunlight and bored without their friends. Mindful of meeting with Nonna at the edge of the village, Cutter woke Nightrunner with a touch from his mind. The old wolf only rebuffed him irritably and went back to his drowsing.

"Spirits?" Olbar's forceful whisper barely sounded above the unsubtle crashing of his footsteps through the brush. "Hear, me, spirits, before you depart. Only you can grant the favor I would ask."

Another favor? Skywise grumbled and kicked at a stick before breaking into an impatient trot. **See, I told you—just like trolls!**

Olbar bulled forward with a frustrated shout. "Wait, I say!"

Cutter felt Nightrunner's explosion of anger just before the old wolf broke cover to snap at the human's hands. Olbar jumped back with a gasp, and Nightrunner stalked close to him with tail abristle, mouth open in a warning display. Even Starjumper, still half-hidden by the understory, snarled in echo of the older wolf's displeasure. Cutter didn't know if it was Olbar's sudden hot emotions that provoked Nightrunner's wild reaction, or simply the loudness of the big human's voice. He reached out to soothe the wolf's troubled mind even as he shouted back at the human chief.

"Beware, human! You must *not* follow us! Only Nonna and her mate have that privilege." He could see Nonna and Adar coming behind Olbar now, Nonna hurrying in response to the wolves' sudden disturbance.

"I . . . I am sorry, spirit . . ." Olbar clasped his hands together, voice now quiet and sincere. But whatever favor he meant to seek was lost in Skywise's sharp cry of alarm.

Cutter spun, New Moon nearly leaping into his

hand as Skywise's own sword hissed like a striking snake through the air. A human voice, hoarse and anguished, pierced the forest in a horrid scream, and a man nearly as tall as Olbar leapt to his feet from the undergrowth not too far from where Skywise crouched.

"My hand!" The human danced about, skin pale with agony as he flailed his thumbless hand above his head. Blood flew in a scarlet spray. "My hand! My hand!"

Skywise's sword shook in his white-knuckled grip. "Next time," he growled, his voice as low as a wolf's, "it'll be something more vital! You humans have too many fingers anyway."

"Thief!" Olbar's hatred and fury told Cutter plainly that this word was the name for this miserable human, and not just an angry curse. "You crazy, scavenger dog! I should kill you with my own hands!" Olbar thundered after the stumbling thief, smashing aside small trees and bushes in his pursuit, with no care for the wolves who chased the villain with him.

Cutter slid New Moon back into its sheath and trotted to Skywise's side. **Are you all right?**

The stargazer nodded, obviously shaken, and tightened his fist around the sliver of stone at his neck. **He . . . he tried to steal the lodestone!** Cutter jerked a handful of leaves from a nearby tree and handed them to Skywise to scrub his blade clean. **Why didn't we scent him coming, Cutter?**

The question gnawed at Cutter with uncertainty. **I don't know.**

"That worm-ridden pick-feast!" Olbar tromped back to them, his breathing hard and his great hands clenched. "I should have killed him long ago!"

"But . . ." Adar backed out of the way when Olbar pushed past him. "Wasn't that your brother, my chief?"

"No more! He has no name—I took it away from him! He is only Thief now." Halting a respectful distance from Cutter, the big chief fell to one knee and bowed his head in meek contrition. "Forgive this insult, gentle spirits. Do not take revenge upon my people for the acts of one evil man."

Knowing how much he loved his own people, Cutter appreciated the duty that led Olbar to humble himself so. "We are angry, but we will forgive." Cutter motioned above Olbar's head to the couple who waited behind him. "*If* you keep your promise to treat Nonna and Adar well."

Olbar nodded gravely. "They will be honored members of my tribe."

"Good." Then, remembering the only other human, from this tribe who had tried to hurt them: "And beware of your own Bone Woman, human. She is a crooked old weasel, out for her own good. Don't think that we didn't realize she was missing from our feast just before Thief attacked us. You might find she thinks for him as much as she thinks for herself."

Olbar raised his head to meet Cutter's steady gaze. "If ever that filthy hag sets foot in my village again," he promised grimly, "I will kill her and leave her for the ants to pick her bones. You have my word on that, spirits."

The great river, wide and wild, thrashed its rocky bed full of foam as it rushed through the forest to throw itself roaring over the edge of a towering cliff. Cutter didn't approach the drop-off close enough to see the water crash far below, but the sound of it shattering against the jagged rocks at the bottom was so loud that Adar had to shout just be be heard above it.

"The Valley of Endless Sleep lies that way," the human bellowed, pointing out beyond the edge of the cliff, where the river could be seen weaving its way among the distant trees like a twist of silver string. "Far beyond the valley is the Blue Mountain where I found Nonna. The quickest way to get to the valley is by climbing down these cliffs where the Death Water falls. It is very dangerous, but *I* did it, and I'm not even a spirit."

Climb? Apprehension grew thick in Cutter's throat as he tried to imagine the height of the climb. Silently, Skywise's mind nudged against his, offering what support he could.

Adar slipped a thick coil of vines off his shoulder and held them out toward Cutter. "Vines like these helped me make my descent long ago. If they held me, it's certain they'll hold you."

Cutter accepted them with hands now cold with reawakened fears.

"What a pity that you do not have your great bond-birds to ride." Nonna helped him settle the vines across his arm, the way a mother might help a precious child. "But no matter—you will walk safely in the valley. It holds dangers only for foolhardy men, not for Bird Spirits."

Cutter accepted her help without looking up to meet her eyes. He'd grown to hate himself for that first impulsive deception. He wanted to tell her everything—that he was just a being as real as herself, with no special powers, and no wants in this world but to live a life without heartache or fear. But there was too much false-hood between them, and Cutter couldn't see how trying to change things now would do anything but hurt her.

"You have served us well, Nonna," he said at last. The words sounded harsh and aloof, and he tried his best to soften them. "Thank you for saving my life. And for leading us here."

"I should be the one thanking you, Honored One. Adar's tribe has accepted me as you commanded, and we never need be alone again. I am happy."

"But . . ." Cutter studied her human face, wonder-ing if his reading of it could be trusted. "You look sad."

To his surprise, her warm smile flickered and a bleak shadow fell over her eyes. "Oh, it's just . . ." She knelt before him, reaching up to wrap her finger in his hair, to trace the delicate curve of his cheekbone with the back of her hand. "You are both so fair," she breathed wist-fully. "Like the dawn. Beside you, we are no better than coarse and clumsy toads."

Only a short while ago, Cutter would have agreed. But now what moved inside him was neither hatred or disgust. He found his heart suddenly swept up in want-ing not to see her hurt herself like this.

"No . . ." Cutter took her hand in his and pushed it back to her side. "You are the first humans to touch us with love instead of hate. We are different, you and I, but I see no ugliness in you." He released her, and stepped away one final time. "Go now. Be with your people."

Adar put his hands to his mate's shoulders and urged her to stand. They smiled, as fitted to each other as Cutter was to his own mate, and the young chieftain felt a sting of loneliness as he watched them drift obediently into the forest, leaving him and Skywise behind. *Oh, Leetah, I wish so that I were home with you!*

He turned to search for Skywise and the wolves. Nightrunner sprawled, sighing, on the warm rocks just above the water's edge, while Starjumper and his elf-friend hovered at the lip of the sheer precipice, peering down toward the raging water below. Just the thought of creeping that close to the drop-off made Cutter's insides go limp and chilly.

"Death Water!" Skywise's words barely coalesced above the drowning roar. "I can see why the humans chose that name!"

Cutter forced himself to pick up his feet, one heavy leg at a time, and move at least a few steps closer to the terrible edge. Skywise came back to join him, lifting the coil of vine out of his chief's hands.

It's quite a climb, the stargazer admitted, carrying the bundle to a tree overhanging the edge. **You'd better not look down while we're doing it.**

Cutter nearly laughed aloud. **You think I'd planned to?** He wondered if it wouldn't be easier to have Skywise knock him unconscious and simply lower his lifeless body down. **What about Nightrunner and Starjumper? They can't follow us this way.**

Skywise paused in playing out a length of vine. **Maybe they could take a longer way around,** he suggested, rising to look across the valley. **They could circle back the way we came, then meet us in the valley later.**

**Maybe . . . **

Grateful for an excuse to leave the staggering drop-off, Cutter trotted back to where Nightrunner waited near the edge of the cool forest, above the worst of the foam, where the water was not so loud. The old wolf stood with his eyes locked on something farther back in the green, his grizzled tail low, his broad back facing Cutter. He didn't turn when his elf-friend approached him. When Cutter reached out with mind and hand, the old wolf only jerked irritably and snapped at the young chief's fingers. Cutter drew his hand back slowly, staring at his old friend in hurt and surprise. **Nightrunner . . . Why?**

Sighing, the wolf only turned to the forest again as though considering.

Cutter sank to his knees beside his old friend, stroking his mind with gentle respect and sifting through the primitive thoughts and feelings he found there. The great wolf's mind was full of weariness, tattered with the need to rest for a time, to be alone. The hollow longing in the simple flow of Nightrunner's thoughts was unmistakable. Cutter risked touching the old wolf's mane as tears pushed into his eyes.

**Oh, Skywise . . . ** Cutter felt the other elf approach quietly from behind him, asking Cutter what was wrong in silent concern. **He's all worn out. He . . . Nightrunner won't be traveling with us anymore . . . **

Dropping down to all fours, Cutter moved up along the big wolf's side and rubbed his cheek against Nightrunner's muzzle. The old wolf looked away from the forest as though distracted by a playful cub, and responded to his elf-friend's caress by dropping his head and mouthing Cutter's ear.

**My first wolf . . . ** The tender blossom of memory between them drew a sigh from Nightrunner, and he rested his head wearily on Cutter's shoulder. **These old bones ache, don't they? Your coat is dry and dull, eyes are bad . . . **

His thoughts spiraled down away from words after that, until only the touch of loyal feelings remained. Cutter dug his fingers into the wolf's wiry fur, feeling out all Nightrunner's favorite scratching spots, and attending to each one with devotion and care. The old wolf answered by rolling side to side, legs in the air and tongue exposed. Crawling on top of him, growling playfully, Cutter bit at the old wolf's muzzle, and accepted a fond nip on the nose in return.

The Now of Wolf thought granted the old male a kindness Cutter couldn't share. He knew that Nightrunner didn't know that they might never see each other again. The old wolf only knew that he hurt, that he was tired, that the nearby forest beckoned him to rest in its cool and shadowy depths. Big feet once strong enough to knock an elk off its stride now pushed Cutter gently onto his own back. Then Nightrunner rolled stiffly to his feet and delivered a single sloppy lick across his elf-friend's face. Only the faintest and simplest of farewells brushed across Cutter's thoughts before the wolf shook himself and walked slowly into the forest.

Cutter rose to his knees, scrubbing tears from his eyes. He glanced aside once as a flicker of gray movement whispered past him, then shot a startled look at Skywise while Starjumper trotted off in Nightrunner's footsteps, disappearing just behind the old male.

The stargazer met Cutter's questioning gaze with a shrug. **He'll miss Nightrunner,** Skywise explained, coming to join Cutter as the chief climbed to his feet. **As much as I'd miss you if you were going away. And

Starjumper's still strong. He can look after Nightrunner . . . hunt for him until . . . **

Cutter nodded, stopping the direction of Skywise's thinking before the sad truth could pass between them. **Yes . . . ** he sent, bidding the old wolf a last silent farewell. ** . . . Until.** Then he turned back toward the raging falls, and the rest of the journey still waiting before them.

CHAPTER NINETEEN

C UTTER TUGGED THE LAST heavy knot in the vines around the tree's thick trunk, then planted both feet on the tree and pulled with all his might. **There!** he announced proudly, hopping down. **This ought to hold eight of us easily.**

Good, since it only needs to hold two. Skywise scooped up Cutter's bow and tossed it to his chief. **Let's get going, huh? We're still too near the humans to sit well with me.**

Cutter caught the weapon out of the air, then tucked it under one arm so he could grab for the pack Skywise threw after it. **Don't be so skittish! We survived it, didn't we?**

Skywise looked decidedly unconvinced. **For now.**

Cutter busied himself with strapping his pack to his belt, leaving his friend to his brooding. Excited as he was by the prospect of finding new and different elves, he felt almost brave enough to walk right up to the drop-off's edge—but only almost. He stopped a good two strides away to gaze across the forested valley below.

I can see the Blue Mountain, he told Skywise, pointing. **It looks so clear, I could almost touch it! Something tells me our quest will be—**

A shot of shock slapped into his open mind, and

Cutter twisted about in time to see Skywise topple, face-down, to the stone. He stared at his friend's body in dumb surprise, unable for that moment to understand what was laid out before him. Then the bright well of blood in Skywise's silver hair impacted on his thinking, and his sensitive ears suddenly heard a rhythmic *whit!-whit!-whit!* slicing through the air at the edge of the forest. He whirled to face the sound, drawing New Moon even before his eyes recognized Thief as the spinner of the long leather strap. The tall human released one end of his whirling thong, and Cutter ducked reflexively from the dark projectile that hurtled at his head. A rock cracked against the wrist he drew up to guard himself, and New Moon clattered from suddenly numb and useless fingers. Snarling like an angry wolf, Cutter lunged for the weapon as Thief roared toward him with club upraised.

"Away, demon!" the filthy human shouted. "The magic stone is mine!"

The human swung his club with clumsy force. Cutter leapt nimbly into the air, avoiding the blow even as he delivered a sweeping slash of his own. Then his heart stuttered with shock when Thief twisted just as agilely aside. The human's brutal laugh rumbled like rolling stones.

"The Bone Woman's magic oils give me speed to match *yours*, demon! And take away my scent so that your demon-mounts can't find me!" He tore the club between them again, missing again and giving Cutter the opening he needed to straddle his friend's fallen body. "Soon," the Thief crowed, "I will have the magic stone that gives you *all* your powers, and you will lie as still as your companion!"

Cutter snarled up at the human, a growl boiling in his throat. "You like to kill, human?" He tightened his grip on New Moon's hilt. "So do I, when I must. Your blood will fall on bare rock and nourish nothing!"

"You?!" The Thief straightened from his fighting crouch. "*You* would stick *me* with your single spine, little quill-pig?" Beady human eyes squinted shut on vicious laughter, and Thief let his club fall to his side in honest amazement. "I could wear you in place of my lost thumb!" he scoffed. "Are *you* the mighty spirits I was taught in my youth to fear? Bone Woman is right— the legends lie! Your powers are nothing but a magic stone for men to steal and use. You *can* die!" He gestured brusquely at Skywise's still form. "You have blood, and it flows as red as any beast's! Before this day is done, I shall be the greatest chieftain of them all! And I will have a *new* name! No more will they call me Thief—they will call me Master! Spirit-Slayer!"

Cutter dashed forward, burning with fury, and drove New Moon under the tall man's breastbone, past his place of breathing and into his evil human heart. Thief blinked in surprise, but not until Cutter had wrenched the blade loose and backed away did the dying human look down at the gush of bitter scarlet spilling over his hands.

"You . . . You've *killed* me!"

Cutter lowered his arm to let the foul human blood run off his blade onto the stone. "You made it easy for me, human."

Thief's club dropped with a heavy thump, then rolled out of sight over the lip of the precipice. Stumbling, the human turned to look after his fallen weapon, only to lose his footing and plummet over the cliff's edge after it.

Cutter thought it was over—that the man would disappear like last year's winter, and there would be only his broken body to spit upon as the Wolfriders hiked past it on their way to the Blue Mountain. But some unexpected well of strength leant the human desperate speed. He caught himself on the edge of the cliff face with hand and elbow. In front of him, Skywise stirred weakly, groaning. Cutter glared impassively at the incredulous, bug-eyed human face staring up at him as if for help. *It's fair,* he thought with savage simplicity. *I bought his life with yours—you're not even worth what he means to me.*

Then Skywise pushed up to all fours, and the black of Thief's eyes suddenly constricted to manic pinpoints as he focused on the dangling lodestone.

". . . The stone . . . ," he gasped, reaching out with one hand. ". . . M-Must have . . . magic stone . . . !"

Thief's fingers closed on the stone too quickly for Cutter to stop him. "Skywise!"

The stargazer jerked, only to be held down by the length of string binding the lodestone to him. "No!" He grabbed at Thief's wrist. "Let go!" His final shout echoed against the valley walls as Thief's falling body yanked taut against the lodestone necklace and pulled the tiny elf over the cliff's edge with him.

Cutter dove for his friend, skidding across the stone until he dangled half-over the precipice, desperate hands closing on empty air. Even the cry of horror tearing about inside him seemed unable to find the surface. He stared, immobile, at the two bodies bouncing off the long rock face below him, then buried his face in his arms when he realized what he was watching. A hard, convulsive shudder gripped him at the sound of a heavy splash far below.

Then silence. Silence, and a creeping coldness that sucked all the strength from Cutter, until he feared he'd never climb to his feet again.

** . . . Cutter . . . ?**

He jerked his head up with a knife-sharp gasp. **Skywise?!** Leaning far over the edge, he searched first the bottom of the drop, then realized the insanity of that and looked instead for his friend partway up the ragged cliff.

Skywise hung one-handed from a tree root only halfway down the long drop. His other arm hung by his side. Cutter couldn't see his friend's face clearly enough to discern any real expression, but Skywise's sending was blurred, and thick with waves of pain. Stumbling to his feet, Cutter hauled the coil of vines to the edge and flung it over.

Here! The bundle played out down the cliff face like a green snake. **The vine—grab it!**

Skywise watched the line slither down beside him, but didn't move to take it. **I-I can't! My arm won't work!**

For only a moment, Cutter held his breath. **All right . . . ** He looked down with new eyes then, knowing suddenly that he intended to climb, and sickness crashed over him until he staggered. **Hang on!** he sent, turning his back on the precipice in the hopes that this would help him. He gripped the vine as tightly as he could in both sweating hands. **High Ones help me, I'm coming for you!**

Hurry!

The first step over the edge was the worst. For an instant, Cutter felt strengthless and without breath. Then he forced his eyes to lock on the gray and solid stone before him as his hands felt their way down the vine one painful grip at a time. *If I don't look down, it will be all right. If I don't look down, it will be all right—*

As it was, he had to glance down between his feet twice to make sure he was coming down on top of Skywise. Both times his blood fled his heart in such a dizzying rush that he nearly fainted. He bit his lip to bleeding every time his vision faded, knowing that his failure would mean the death of both of them, with no one to tell his mate and cublings what had ever become of them.

He crawled down beside Skywise with the tiny, careful steps of a child. Skywise still gripped his tree root tightly, but his face was white and sweaty with pain. Looping his arm around the stargazer's waist, Cutter braced himself against the wall as best he could, putting all the strength and trust he could muster into his mental voice. **Come on—I've got you!**

He pulled Skywise against him, balancing him on one knee. The injured elf finally made a convulsive grab for Cutter's neck with his good arm, and they fell against each other in limp relief.

Skywise . . . ?

He sagged against Cutter's shoulder, the last bird-like flutter of his thoughts fading off to dreamless darkness.

"Skywise!" Biting back his panic, Cutter shook him desperately, feeling his own stomach roil with terror when the frantic movement loosened the contact of his feet against the wall. "Skywise, wake up! You've got to stay awake!" The stargazer stirred weakly against him, but no awareness responded when Cutter probed into his thoughts. "Skywise, you've got to hold onto me! I can't pull us up without both hands!"

He hugged his friend's limp body against him, his arms beginning to tremble with fatigue. If he dropped Skywise, he could go on—climb down to the valley, go search for other elves. But what would be the point? How joyful could be the discovery of other elves without his lifetime friend beside him?

Tears of rage and frustration pushing into his throat, Cutter threw back his head and howled with anger. "*Curse you, humans! Curse every last one of your murdering souls! And a curse on me, too—for ever trusting* any *of you!*"

Then the vine beneath his hand shuddered, and Cutter's breath jerked out of him in a gasp. As it reeled steadily upward, Cutter realized with a spasm of fear that only a human had the strength to draw them up so quickly. He prayed their savior was Adar—they were in no condition to survive another thief.

"Well, now! Is Olbar included in your curse, little spirit?" The human chief leaned over the edge of the drop-off to smile at them, the vine held easily in his powerful grip. "If so, what a pity. After all; it is my 'cursed' hand that aids you now."

Cutter could only stare at him, too frightened and confused to know what to say.

"How lucky you are that I found the courage to follow you against your command. But wait!" Olbar sat back on his heels as though pondering some question that had only just occurred to him. "I think I'll just let you dangle there for a bit."

I knew it! Cutter bowed his head against his friend's in tired despair. *Skywise was right—they're all of them evil! We have no hope against them!*

"Why don't you fly to save yourselves, Bird Spirits? Can it be that you have no *real* powers? That, perhaps, you are not even spirits at all? If I cut this vine, I think perhaps you will fall and drown." Olbar switched the vine from one hand to the other, and now no smile split his weathered face. "But then you could not answer my questions, could you?" He hauled the vine upward with a single mighty pull.

When the elves were nearly even with the lip of the cliff, the great chief simply stood and raised them up above ground level. He swung them gently over the solid stone, then lowered them to safety with a patience and care that surprised Cutter. Still trembling, his heart still racing in his chest, Cutter eased Skywise flat a far distance from the drop-off's edge, then knelt to inspect him while Olbar waited silently a respectful distance away.

Skywise blinked up at him, chill and pale, and Cutter returned his frank gaze with a sigh. No words needed to pass between them for both to know that the awkward angle of the stargazer's arm meant the bones inside it were broken.

This isn't too convenient, Cutter commented for lack of anything better to say.

Skywise grinned wanly in appreciation of the sentiment. **So sorry, my chief.**

Standing, Cutter rounded Olbar with stoic care to retrieve New Moon from where he'd dropped it after killing the shiftless Thief. Already it seemed a long time ago, but the blood on the blade was still warm. He wiped it quickly on the knotted vines around the lonely tree, then swung up into its crown in search of narrow branches with which to fashion a splint.

"What are you?"

Cutter looked down through the leaves at Olbar, surprised that the human had asked such a thing.

"You are not immortal," the man pointed out. "You feel pain—you fear death just as we do. Yet you look so strange." He stepped aside to give Cutter room to jump down, but followed the elfin chief as Cutter crossed back to where they'd left their supplies. "There are ancient tales of beings like you who once ruled the forest. I've always feared the spirits, but . . ."

He fell silent as Cutter emptied one of their travel bags and tore it into strips. When Cutter caught at Skywise's wrist to pull and straighten the twisted bones, Olbar turned his face away in deference to the other elf's shout of pain. The unexpected consideration touched Cutter. He didn't interrupt when Olbar moved to speak again.

"You are not spirits. And yet you are not men, children, or beasts. Answer me truly—what *are* you?"

Cutter looked up from tying the strong, straight sticks into place, and shook his head slowly. "No human has ever bothered to ask. We have no answer for you." He quickly folded a sling from the remaining fabric and looped it around Skywise's arm. "What you call us doesn't matter, though. It only matters that humans never needed to fear or hate us."

Olbar nodded solemnly, flinty eyes grave. "I will remember." Then he sighed, a sound like the rush of the great river, and looked across the valley below. "If only you *were* spirits. Then you could grant me the favor I tried to ask earlier. My daughter, Selah . . ." He looked somewhat timidly back to Cutter. "She ran away to the Forbidden Grove with a youth I despised. When my hunters and I gave chase, we were driven from the grove by an angry swarm of tiny, winged spirits who dwell there. To this day, I have not seen my girl-child again. I had hoped that you could enter the Winged Ones' domain safely, and discover what became of her."

Cutter thought about how much he had wanted to learn of Olbar's "Winged Ones" earlier, and about what the chief had done for them today. "Maybe we can. Where is this Forbidden Grove?"

The big chief stood and pointed to a thick clump of trees rising above the patchy, wooded areas of the valley. "There." Cutter came to stand beside him and follow his gaze. "No one goes there, for it is a cursed place, as deadly as a spider's web is to a fly."

And until only a few days ago, no elf would set foot in a human village for much the same reasons. "We will see what we can find for you," Cutter promised. "If your daughter's there, we'll send her to you."

The genuine longing on the human chief's coarse features moved Cutter's heart with sympathy. "Thank you."

Olbar lingered long enough to watch Cutter finish securing Skywise's arm against his body, then picked up all the elves' belongings in one of his huge hands and passed them across with steadfast reverence. "Nonna's right," he said, motioning toward Skywise. "With bones as slim and fragile as those, you *must* be related to birds." Then, without warning, he stretched his hand between them and stroked his fingers against Skywise's chin with the same tenderness a father would use on his cub. "Farewell, then, little bird bones. Perhaps you can give me a daughter again soon."

Cutter nodded a wordless good-bye, and Olbar backed away to leave them to their journey. Skywise, his good hand pressed to his face as though amazed to find it still there, only stared after the retreating chieftain in silent shock.

Clapping a hand on his friend's shoulder, Cutter asked, **Ready to leave?**

Skywise nodded numbly. **More than ever!**

But there was one last farewell before they began their long, dangerous climb. Taking a deep breath, Cutter aimed a soulful howl at the woods, mingling his voice with Skywise's beside him. From somewhere distant and out of elfin sight, two eerie voices sang back at them— Starjumper, still high and lyric, and Nightrunner, now deep and rusty with age. Unable to ignore the knowledge that this was the last time he would hear the old wolf's call, Cutter turned away from the forest to face the future. The Way existed in the Now—and only Now could truly be lived in and changed.

When Skywise's own howl fell silent, Cutter motioned him over to point his attention across the valley at the distant, misty peaks. **There it is, Skywise. The Blue Mountain.**

Just being able to see it is closer than I thought we'd ever come. Skywise draped his good arm over Cutter's shoulder and smiled with a trust Cutter feared would prove misplaced. **Congratulations, my chief! From here on in, our journey ought to be as soft as Moonshade's finest leather.**

CHAPTER TWENTY

"Hey, Cutter—look."

The young chief pulled his attention away from the endless stretch of alien landscape and looked obediently where Skywise pointed. They were two nights' walk into the Valley of Endless Sleep, but Cutter felt no closer to their goal than when they'd started.

"There are the two stars I gave you and Leetah on your joining night. Right overhead."

The forced brightness in the stargazer's tone told Cutter that Skywise had noticed his heavy mood. He tipped his head back to look above the scrappy trees, squinting at the distant pricks of light. "They seem far apart," he remarked. He'd meant it to masquerade as idle conversation, but knew the comment sounded withdrawn and sullen the moment he'd uttered it. "At least, I remember them closer."

"But they're always together."

"Yes . . . I suppose . . ." Hardly encouraged by the sight, Cutter pulled his eyes away from the heartless stars and continued hiking through the tangled growth. After a frustrated moment, Skywise followed.

"You know," Cutter told him, watching the ground, "it's good to know that Leetah and the cubs are safe in Sorrow's End. She was wise not to come with me on this quest."

Skywise raised a testy eyebrow. "And I suppose that makes me a fool."

Cutter shook his head, too bothered by troubling memories to give in to his friend's teasing. "If you hadn't grabbed that root when you fell . . . if you'd drowned in the Death Water . . . I-I don't know what I—"

"*You,*" Skywise cut in with bold assurance, "would have marched right up to the Bird Spirits and announced yourself with your sword, just like always. Luckily, *I'm* still here to make apologies for my chief." He bumped one shoulder against Cutter, ensuring the other elf's attention. "A chief who *still* has a foul disposition and the manners of a troll."

Startled, Cutter scowled at his companion, then softened when he remembered Skywise describing him with just those words years ago during his courtship of Leetah. He grinned maliciously and snatched at his friend's travel bag. "Trolls get even," he warned in a mocking growl.

Skywise bolted with a squeak that left his bag still dangling from Cutter's hand.

They raced through the trees, shattering the valley's ageless silence with shouts and breathless laughter. Cutter darted, ducked, and dodged with every skill at his disposal, and still Skywise pulled steadily ahead of him. He couldn't believe how fast and nimbly the stargazer could run, even with his right arm confined to a sling. Trying to anticipate Skywise's next shift in direction, Cutter swung himself around a hollow tree trunk with a triumphant howl, and nearly ran Skywise over when the stargazer slammed to a stop just ahead of him.

"What are—?" Cutter blinked into the darkness where Skywise pointed, and fell silent. Glossy falls of spider silk draped the arms of twisted trees, knotted into thick cocoons on branches, stumps, and vines. Within the grove, not even leaves bobbed gently in the starlight, and no owls or night peepers broke the stillness with their songs.

Skywise glanced back over his shoulder at Cutter. **This is the place the giant human chief told us about, isn't it?"**

Cutter nodded. Sending in lieu of speaking seemed particularly appropriate, given the unnatural silence. **The Forbidden Grove. Olbar claimed his daughter went in there and never came out.** He wondered what really happened in these woods to make Olbar so afraid to come back here. **Well,** he sighed, **we owe him a favor. Want to go in and look for the human girl?**

Might as well . . . ** Skywise didn't seem particularly interested in the prospect, though. **But it's probably a waste of time.

Cutter led the way into the gummy mess. The thick webbing stuck to everything—their boots, their hands, their hair. Cutter tried scraping the worst of it off the soles of his feet as he walked, but finally gave up when not paying attention to his head caught him faceful after faceful of the sticky stuff. He did his best to spit a mouthful of it off his tongue, then stopped to peel the rest from his eyes while grumbling about whoever had spun such a mess in the first place.

Now I know why the humans call this the Valley of Endless Sleep. Skywise had somehow managed to pick his way through the webbing without tangling himself quite so much as his chief. **It's so still, you can't even feel the night breeze.**

But you *can* feel these sticky spider nets. They're all over! Streamers of gossamer silk hung from every tree Cutter could see, shimmering in the starlight.

Hey! Look! Skywise darted beneath a sweep of gossamer-covered branches. **Cocoons! Too many of them to count!** Cutter swept his arm back and forth through a curtain of webbing, trying to catch up to his friend. **What kind of insect spins thread like this?**

No spider or caterpillar *I* ever heard of. Climbing through the last tangle of foliage, Cutter found his friend crouched beside a dead log all matted over with gummy white nodules. There was no mistaking the eager glimmer in Skywise's eyes. **Let me guess—you're curious, aren't you?**

Skywise grinned up at him disarmingly, and Cutter relented with a put-upon sigh. **All right,** he agreed with dramatic fatigue. **Let's cut one open and see what it holds.** In many ways, exploring with Skywise wasn't unlike peeking into new places with his daughter, Ember.

New Moon's tip slipped into the nearest cocoon with ease, but drawing it through to make a slit proved somewhat harder. The gluey threads bound against the silver blade, stopping it, then refusing to tear loose when Cutter tried to wiggle his sword's point free. He finally resorted to snipping out short, awkward slices of thread until the bundle of darkness inside showed through.

Feathers and peeping exploded out of the torn

sack. Cutter jumped back, gasping, and Skywise started so suddenly he had to grab at his arm with a hiss of pain. The wren they'd freed from its sticky prison arrowed into the trees overhead, scolding them roundly.

Well, Skywise commented, rubbing at his arm, **whatever they are, they're meat eaters. They must trap live creatures in cocoons to keep the blood fresh.**

Looks like. Cutter glanced around as he gingerly peeled the sticky threads away from New Moon's blade. The glade in all directions was filled with lumpy cocoons, some of them piled on top of others, some of them covered with seasons' worth of leaves. **But why is there so *much* meat here, and none of it eaten? All these cocoons are perfect, unbroken. It's weird.**

Skywise turned to follow his chief's gaze. **More than weird,** he agreed. **Where are the web weavers themselves? *What* are the web weavers?** He lowered himself to the ground beside the cocooned log, cradling his arm with a frown of pain. **Assuming, of course, that we want to meet them.**

Cutter touched hesitant fingers to another cocoon, then pulled them away again, filmy with netting. **Skywise, remember what Olbar said? He was chased away from here by "winged spirits." Do you think he meant whatever spins out these webs?** He scrubbed his fingers clean on the leg of his trousers. **Skywise?**

His friend sat stiffly against the fallen log, biting his lip as he tried to settle his arm more comfortably across his lap. Cutter squatted beside him, stung with his own guilt, and bent to set their gear on the ground beside him.

Hurts? Cutter asked, nodding to the broken arm. Skywise nodded, but didn't complain. It occurred to Cutter that they'd traveled two hard days into this valley, and he hadn't stopped to consider whether Skywise needed extra sleep or resting. It seemed he was running roughshod over everyone these days in his hurry to come to the end of this quest.

Why don't you sit here and rest for a while? Cutter suggested, standing. **I'll do a little more exploring, see if I can't find something for us to eat.**

Skywise nodded. **That sounds good. It's peaceful enough around here—you shouldn't get into too much trouble without me.** He closed his eyes and tipped his head back against the web-laced wood behind him. **And I am . . . tired . . . .**

Cutter waited until he felt his friend drift off into weary dreaming, then crept away into the darkness to explore without disturbing him.

Much to his surprise, Cutter found that Skywise's curiosity was catching.

He seemed to find the cocoon bundles everywhere as he moved deeper into the Forbidden Grove. In trees, under them, attached to grass stalks, attached to stones. He experimented with sacs of different sizes and shapes, snipping them open just enough to let their occupants wriggle loose, then jumping back to watch whatever finally emerged. He freed a sleepy, irritable badger, a chipmunk, and some shimmering green creature that seemed to be part-bug and part-bird. It buzzed out of its confinement with wings an angry blur, hovered in the darkness to chitter like a field mouse, then zoomed off into the underbrush too fast for Cutter to follow. He smiled after it, wishing he'd had a chance to see it in the sun.

His foot nudged against something behind him, and his heel stuck to the soft surface the way he'd stuck to everything since coming into this grove. Turning, he hopped on one foot and scowled down at the irregular sac. It huddled up close beneath the arms of a scraggly bush, roughly oval with its broad, rounded end and awkward point. It was the largest cocoon he'd found so far.

Well, let's see what's hiding here . . . Cutter knelt and pushed the drooping branches aside to reach the nodule with New Moon.

Like all the rest, the webs clung to themselves and to the sword's point like strings of year-old honey. Cutter ended up leaning close over the bundle so he could hold the foliage out of the way with his head and pick the muck off New Moon's blade with his free hand. Webs tickled his eyes and clogged his nose long before the first bristly tufts of gray fur poked through the tattered webbing.

"Oh!" Taking a handful of webbing in each fist, Cutter tore the cocoon open with a soft, purring rip. "Where did *you* come from, little brother?" The sleepy wolf cub inside the netting blinked up at him and yawned.

Cutter petted streamers of web away from the cub's whiskered cheeks. It licked at his hands, swallowing half the goo, then bounded into the elf chief's arms, all energy and wagging tail. Cutter laughed and let the little cub knock him over to gnaw at his hair and ears.

"You're a friendly little one, aren't you?" He grabbed the cub's tail and started it into a frenzied circle. "You're well fed, too. Your pack can't have abandoned you too long ago." Abruptly, the cub exploded into excited yapping, and tumbled all over itself trying to escape from its own tail. Cutter hadn't realized just how much he missed Nightrunner's company in his life and mind until right now. He scrubbed the cub's ruff between both hands and sat up to nuzzle the soft fur between its ears. "Nightrunner wasn't much bigger than you when he and I first bonded."

As if lifted to the surface by thoughts of Nightrunner, family, and home, a tender mental image of his laughing, red-haired daughter bloomed in Cutter's mind. Even her scent, dry and spicy, filled his nostrils. He pushed the cub off his lap, wistful, and the scent and image faded.

Startled, Cutter grabbed up the cubling again and held it close to his face. Ember's scent again, as strong as though she stood right there beside him. He scrabbled to his feet with the cub tucked under one arm. Loneliness and melancholy might fool his own senses about the world, but he knew one elf who wouldn't invent familiar smells just to ease an aching heart.

He ran a more direct route back to Skywise. No more straying to investigate curious blobs and bundles, no forays into thickets and trees in search of movement or life. He hopped logs and ducked under branches with no concern for the wolf cub's grunts and wiggles, and burst into the clearing where he'd left Skywise without even thinking to check first if the stargazer was alone.

Flutters of color, like shreds of spring blossom,

darted all over the moonlit clearing. What Cutter took at first to be the peeping of hatchling sparrows re-solved suddenly into laughter and peevish complaints. Tiny, mothlike creatures darted in and out among the branches, thread sparkling like ice from dozens of little mouths. In the midst of them all, cocooned in web from his toes to his knees, Skywise slept with a grin on his face, snoring peacefully.

"What are you doing to him?!"

A shriek like the squeal of poorly tuned pipes went up through the cloud of flying spinners. They scattered when Cutter leapt among them, trailing fluid streams of glittering web and dashing away from his sword slashes as though he were nothing more than a branch waving in the breeze. Skywise jolted awake with a grunt, and the wolf cub squirmed under Cut-ter's arm to yap and growl at every colorful sprite that passed him.

Skywise stumbled to his knees. **Cutter . . . ?**

"No!" A flash of scarlet and amber whirred in front of Cutter's face. "Noisybad Highthing!" He had barely a chance to recognize a four-limbed, sticklike body with eyes as huge and glossy as a mantis's before the creature loosed a spray of webbing right for his eyes.

Soft and sticky, it blinded him as surely as a fist-ful of mud. Growling with frustration, Cutter dropped the wolf cub and snatched out at the sound of fragile wings. His fingers brushed against something at the level of his eyes, and he clenched his fist with light-ning speed. He knew from the resultant screech that he'd made contact. "Caught you!"

The bug-thing squirmed and chittered, little bird-like feet kicking angrily beneath Cutter's fist while its pastel wings trailed over his fingers in a graceful curve.

"You spit those webs on me again," Cutter warned it, "and I'll crack you like a snail's shell!"

The creature tittered off an annoying trill of high-pitched glee. Skywise crawled to his feet to stare at it in amazement. "What in Timmorn's name is *that*?"

"Highthing can't squash Petalwing!" it sang. Its giggles pierced Cutter's ears like rose thorns. "Try! Try!"

Cutter squeezed it first one-handed, then double-fisted, and made no effort to hide his annoyance when a satisfying squirt of bug guts didn't dirty his hands. "Your skin's as tough as thick leather!"

That seemed to amuse it even more, and Cutter found himself wondering if it would hold up so well to tromping, or the smacking of its little head against a tree.

More of the multicolored pests reappeared in a shrieking swarm. Cutter ducked as a dozen sharp claws tore at his hair and uncounted tiny teeth sank into his neck and ears. "We scratch!" they squealed. "We sting! We chase away bad Highthing!"

"Stop it!" He twisted, cursing, and slapped at the cloud of flapping wings and limbs. "Stop it, or—" At a loss for how else to threaten the little monsters, he seized his captive's wings with his free hand and displayed it like a weapon. "Or I'll pull this one's wings off!"

The cloud of little creatures shrieked and beat on him, but the ruby and amber sprite in his fist only cooed with distress and blinked limpidly at him. "Poor Petalwing!" it moaned in its high, silver voice. "Don't pull! Don't pull! Beesweets and juiceberries we fetch for you!" It stroked its head against his thumb, big green eyes locked with his. "*Nice* Highthing!"

Cutter couldn't decide which was more disgusting—this thing when it was being a pest, or now when it was trying to curry favor. "You tell your friends to leave us alone and—*maybe*—you can keep your wings."

Petalwing nodded enthusiastically, then whistled a piercing tune to its embattled companions. "Go way! Go way! Petalwing say so!" Then it smiled up at Cutter with the utmost adoration in its emerald eyes.

Tittering with uncertainty, the flock of colorful creatures scattered. Cutter watched them disappear into the trees' leafy canopy, then keeping a grip on the creature's body with one hand he carefully released his captive's wings long enough to peel the worst of the sticky webbing from his eyes with the other. "Well," he grumbled down at Skywise, "now you know who mucked up the woods with all this goo."

His friend grinned up at him and grabbed playfully at the wolf cub's tail. "But it looks like you've brought me another mystery." He yapped back at the cub when it barked at him. "Where'd you find this one?"

"That doesn't matter." Cutter nodded at the cub with his chin. "Take a whiff of his fur and tell me if I'm crazy."

Frowning, Skywise gathered the wolf cub up with his good hand and tucked it against his nose. Almost instantly, Cutter saw his eyes fly wide with surprise, and he jerked a startled look up at the chief. "Ember?"

Cutter's heart throbbed with an almost desperate belief. "Then it's true!" He brought his hand up in front of his face to scowl at his tiny captive. "You! Petalwing! Tell what you know about this cub—and no tricks!"

"No tricks! No tricks!" It craned its slender neck to blink down at the frolicking cub. "Fursoft yapthing come two darks ago. Come with *other* Highthings—two little, one big."

"Others? Like me?" Cutter tried so hard not to let himself hope, but he couldn't keep from shaking the little pest in frustration. "Where are they? *Where?*"

Petalwing pinched its face into a waspish pout. "Won't tell!" And it loosed a great gob of webbing at his eyes before Cutter could throw a hand up to protect himself.

He felt the hard little body wriggle out of his grip, and flailed about trying to catch it again even as he scraped the gummy webbing from his eyes. Blindness and anger slowed his strike, and the sprite disappeared into the shadows with a trill of maddening laughter.

Beside Cutter, Skywise turned to follow Petalwing's escape. "Little bug talks a lot, but doesn't say much, eh?"

Cutter pushed away from him and ran for the edge of the surrounding trees.

"Cutter?"

Casting his mind out into the darkness, the young chief tested his surroundings with every sense at his command. No sounds drifted back to him through the deathly still forest, but he sent out into that silence as loudly as any shout, pleading for an answer—demanding one with every fiber of his being.

Then, faintly from the tangled darkness, came a faltering, unskilled response.

Cutter's heart soared into his throat, and he plunged into the trees. Fanning that feeble response with his desperation the way his breath might fan a flame, he cut and squirmed and climbed his way through the underbrush until that flicker of elfin thought led him to a huge web construction at the base of a long-dead tree. Cutter dropped to hands and knees and crawled up to the bundle with his breath quick in his chest.

"No no no!" Petalwing flashed down to batter his head with tiny fists. "Don't cut wrapstuff!"

He pulled New Moon without even taking his eyes away from the bundle. "Go away, bug."

It landed on his hand and tried to drag the blade away. "Bad Highthing!"

"Go away!"

Petalwing avoided his slash easily enough, then retreated into a nearby tree to scold him and rant about its pretty weavings. Cutter ignored it as he slipped the sword under the first layer of gummy webbing.

With the most delicate care, he sliced through the glossy threads strand by sticky strand. When the moonlight caught the first glimmer of gold, the first gloss of dark skin, the first shine of auburn hair, he felt hot tears flood his disbelieving eyes. Sweeping away the last silky filaments of webbing, he stared in wordless wonder at the three lovely faces he'd just exposed to the night.

Leetah stirred under his hand, and blinked sleepily. ". . . T-Tam . . . ?" Then, seeming to come suddenly awake, she launched herself into his arms with Ember and Suntop cradled joyously between them. "Oh, Tam!"

Cutter took them all into a hug no less strong and fierce than his missing of them since the night he left them all behind.

CHAPTER TWENTY-ONE

LEETAH CLOSED HER EYES
and crushed Cutter to her, loving the smell of his tangled hair, the warmth of his pale skin, the strength of his young embrace. He felt so hard and real against her when she'd feared she'd never touch him again, and she found herself whispering his soul name over and over again, like a magic spell to keep him there.

Then Ember, engulfed in the same marvelous clasp, stirred against Leetah's hip and piped, "Hiya, Skywise!" Then, with even greater enthusiasm, "Choplicker!"

Leetah's eyes flew wide in an agony of regret. Skywise crouched a short distance beyond Cutter's shoulder, watching their ardent reunion with impatient interest.

"Oh, beloved . . . !" She pushed back from Cutter's arms, both hands covering her offending mouth. "Beloved, forgive me!"

Her lifemate frowned at her, then twisted around to follow her horrified gaze. Skywise only met his chief's questioning look with a shrug, and Cutter turned back to her, laughing, before Leetah could find the courage to remind him of what she'd done.

"It's all right," he said gently, cupping her face with his hand. "Skywise knows my soul name, Leetah. He has *always* known it."

Relief flooded her like the heady rush of spring rain.

She called Skywise to her and hugged him with the same devotion as Cutter did their shivering cubs. "Of course! Brothers in all but blood—I should have guessed!" Then she felt Skywise's flash of pain even before his gasp, and she pulled away to let her eyes find what her healer's senses already had. "Your arm!" she cried, reaching for Skywise's tattered sling. "What happened?"

The stargazer gaped at her, hugging his arm to him and away from her touch. "Troll warts and lizard skins, Leetah! My arm can wait!" He waved wildly at her and the cubs. "What are you doing here?!"

The concept of explaining everything was over-whelming. Leetah opened her mouth, not even sure what was about to come out, but Ember chattered past her with all sorts of information about Choplicker and how poorly he got along with the cat, while Suntop tried excitedly to recount Savah's ill-fated journey and their own long trek across the desert. Leetah herself struggled to squeeze in a few words about their loss of the Wolfriders, and the tragic flight that brought them to this strange and frightening grove.

Cutter, his gaze darting from one frantic face to another in silent confusion, finally gathered the cubs against him and fell over on his back, howling with laughter as though none of the stressful months between them had happened.

Leetah slapped at his foot the way she had seen Ember slap at Choplicker's tail. "Oh, beloved, it isn't funny!"

"I know . . ." Cutter rolled up into a sit again, bundling the giggling children across his lap and breathing deeply of their hair. "I'm sorry," he said to Leetah, still smiling, "it isn't funny, I know. I have just missed the chatter of these lovely voices so much."

Thinking of all the other voices she feared were lost forever, Leetah's eyes stung with tears. She crawled closer to Cutter, to hug him and the children together.

He rubbed his cheek against the top of her hair, and she felt the strong, wild touch of his mind against her own. "I know sending is still hard for you," he whispered. "But if you and the cubs will trust us, we can help you show us what happened."

She felt Skywise move up close behind her, and nodded faintly. *It's the past,* she told herself. *It can't hurt you now.* But the memories themselves were still so painful. She opened herself to communion with another mind, and spread herself as best she could across the access to her children. They had thoughts and knowledge that mattered to what their chief-father meant to learn, but she could at least protect them from the ravages of adult terror and guilt.

Cutter's presence slipped gently inside her thinking and coaxed her wider, more open to his guidance. His inner self was so like his soul name—free and powerful in a way Sun Folk had not been bred to be. Beside him, just as fierce and bright, Skywise flashed by as quick and playful as a breeze, with a still, deep undercurrent that only age gave an elf's agile mind. Her little cublings, as hot and lively as their Wolfrider names, were spirits familiar to her from the moment their seeds first quickened in her womb. Leetah accepted the combined light of all their strengths and passions and let herself spiral into the otherworld of memory, where the tale of what had happened was still spinning, waiting for someone to rise up and make sense of it all.

In the tangle of Leetah's conscious thoughts, the path to this forest began with her first sight of growing green things. The Wolfriders were finally free of the desert, weary from their long nights of traveling, and had stopped for their day's rest by a narrow river that sliced through a long, lustrous valley. Leetah was surprised now to sense how aware she had been of their happiness at leaving the flowing sand. The crossing had lasted days and days longer than any of them had expected, and even the extra food, water, and shelter carried by the hearty zwoots only made the ordeal almost bearable.

Now, after following a steep cut in the sandstone wall for more than a hand of days, they had come out into a sweet, grassy plain filled with tufts of downy seed plants and long-necked flowers that smiled up at the passing travelers like patches of nodding sun. Leetah sat with her children on the cool ground, relieved to see that Cutter's world was not so unlike her familiar desert—still flat, still gentle, and not at all the frightening place of beasts and shadows she'd always feared it would be.

Suntop's memories butted into hers. Overlaid with anxiety, cluttered with deep imperatives that even now Leetah could only sense but not find. He'd been fussy from the moment they stopped that morning. "It isn't the right place," he kept complaining, pacing in circles around Leetah and his sister. "We can't stay here—it's dangerous!"

Moonshade, the same soft yet unapproachable she-wolf in all their minds, petted Suntop's hand as he stalked past her. "It isn't dangerous, little cub. We have all the hunters here to protect us, and we'll be on our way again soon."

"*No!*" He jerked away from her, and Leetah remembered her shock at the hard edge of tantrum in his young voice. "I want to go *now!*"

"Gently, Suntop! Be calm." Leetah reached for him, and was glad when he let her gather his little body into her lap so she could try to soothe him with gentle strokes of healing power. "We are all tired—we need to rest."

"And Choplicker's hungry." Ember's memories pushed through, as forthright as her words. "He needs meat!"

Tears and confusion unraveled Suntop's resolve like spider's silk. As he melted against her, sobbing bitterly, Leetah looked across at where Moonshade settled into the tall grass nearby. She remembered feeling envious that someone could blend so effortlessly with the sigh and sway of the natural world; Ember remembered crossing her legs in mimic of the tanner, trying to sit among the tall stalks with the same stillness and ease.

"I've never seen him act this way." Moonshade tucked a strand of hair behind Suntop's ear with a maternal care that startled Leetah. "Is he all right?"

Leetah looked down at her son and shook her head. "He's exhausted, Moonshade. Savah's warning is a terrible burden for one so young."

"Look at the size of that bird!"

Treestump's shout distracted everyone. Ember remembered hopping to her feet and craning a look upward as Strongbow rose in more leisurely silence to join Treestump. They both stood on the edge of the collection of elves, Treestump shading his eyes with both hands as he peered off in the direction of Sun-Goes-Down. In the distance, a long, graceful shape rode the air currents as lightly as a leaf. "There's enough meat on him to feed us all! Think you can get 'im, Strongbow?"

"Think you can get him?" Hmph! The memory of the thought came from Suntop, but the words and gruff disgust were clearly Strongbow's.

"Look, Suntop!" Moonshade shook his foot fondly,

clearly proud of her mate's lean profile with his bow. "Strongbow will get us our evening meal, then we can continue to search for your father."

"No!" The force of Suntop's terror, which echoed now in Ember against her will, shattered through their mutual sending like a bolt of lightning. "He mustn't kill that bird!"

But it was too late—the archer's bowstring sang, and the shot was fired. Ember remembered waiting with her stomach crawling with hunger, and Leetah remembered trying to coax Suntop into telling her why this bird had frightened him so. Suntop remembered nothing except drowning in painful desperation.

Moments later, Strongbow's target came crashing out of the sky. Elves and wolves swarmed over it with delight. Its feathers were a glossy, smoky amber, its wings a magnificent expanse as long as six wolves set nose to tail. Deafened now by fears and future knowledge that none of them could know of then, Leetah barely knew when she picked up Suntop and carried him to join the rest of the tribe in their feasting. After that, memories that had been abbreviated by panic and confusion tumbled past almost too quickly to relate.

The tribe had barely finished the first rack of warm, pale meat when Scouter suddenly jumped up and pointed toward Sun-Goes-Down. From behind a curtain of flame-colored cloud, a flight of seven majestic birds—each of them much larger than the slain one—came gliding toward the makeshift camp. It was an awesome sight, beautiful and surreal, but not one to inspire fear. Until too late.

The first of the birds peeled away from its companions and swooped down among the Wolfriders, claws extended for the attack. Elves lunged for weapons, wolves poured into snarling whirlpools and snapped at the tails of the birds that followed the first one. In moments, Strongbow had fired his last arrow. The slender shafts that had killed the smaller bird could not pierce the thick hides of these soaring monsters, just as Pike's forcefully thrown spear rebounded and clattered uselessly to the ground. Leetah remembered hearing screams, but Suntop's memories boiled to the forefront before her dream-self could turn to see who cried out for her.

His understanding of what was happening did not pierce as deeply as his mother's. Suntop pulled away from her, his young attention fixed only on the snarl of images and pressures in his own head as he ran for their frantic zwoot.

Leetah's fear for her cub splashed across the confused scene. "Suntop!"

"Brother!" Ember's shout was one of simple irritation.

Suntop leapt for the edge of the zwoot's side basket, for the darkness inside, for the chance to run. "I have to find Father!" It ran deeper than that, as powerful and needful as his body's own breathing, but those were the only words his young mind could find to say. "I have to find Father! I have to!"

"Wait for me!"

And then Ember, Choplicker clutched tight against her, was running after her brother, and Leetah was calling to them, the terrible knowledge of their fragility deafening her to the sounds of fighting around her. She stumbled through grass now whipped into a frenzy by the force of giant wings, and tried to catch Ember before the girl-cub scrambled into the basket after her brother.

"Suntop! Ember! Come down! It isn't safe for you up

there!" It wasn't safe anywhere—not Sorrow's End, not the Wolfriders' holt, not here—!

Cutter's gentle caress soothed the turmoil in her mind. *Over, it's over,* the powerful wolf-voice in him purred. *Nothing here can hurt you, my love . . . It is over . . .*

Yes . . . over . . . A great black shadow swept over them like a cloak. Leetah ducked beneath the zwoot's belly, and she heard her precious babies shriek in fear of the sudden darkness. "Hide, my little ones! Hide deep in the basket!"

The bird's talons snapped open like polished daggers, big enough to straddle the zwoot's tall back. Then they jerked suddenly skyward again when a compact flash of green and scarlet jumped at the bird's outspread tail.

"Run!" One-Eye tumbled to the ground with a monstrously sized tail feather hugged to his chest, while the bird surged upward, screaming. "*Run,* Leetah!"

The terrified zwoot gave her no choice.

Bawling coarsely, the huge brute plunged away from the turmoil. "No!" Leetah grabbed for its harness, not even thinking that the panicked beast might drag her, caring only that her children were on board its sloping back and she *would not* lose them! Her hands closed around the zwoot's sweat-slicked breast strap, and in the next moment she was jerked off her feet, hanging beneath its chest as it left birds, wolves, and fighting far behind.

They crashed through water—Leetah again felt the sear of frigid wetness; Ember, high in her basket, recognized it as the stretch of friendly river near their chosen camp. Then grass, and rocks, and the endless thunder of the zwoot's pounding hooves as it ran on and on with the mindless stamina that only a zwoot could have. Leetah

clung to its harness, afraid her strength would give out before the zwoot's did. Then, after what still seemed in memory like a torturous eternity, the zwoot finally stumbled to
a ragged, panting stop. Exhausted, bruised and beaten by
the rough terrain, Leetah made herself uncurl her fingers
from around the animal's harness. She sank painfully to the
ground.

Ember's and Suntop's child-simple view of the past
took over here. Immersed in the contact, Leetah sup-
pressed a jolt of surprise as she recognized now how weak
and unaware she'd truly been of their surroundings. The
cubs climbed down from the zwoot's battered basket, one
of them a swirl of worry over Leetah, the other peering
about at the twilight gloom of the dense forest that surrounded them. As they helped her sit up, Leetah's own
memories painted in the details of the stillness, the blackness, the endless clutter of cocoons. She'd realized then
that this was the true green growing place of Sun Folk legend. It was even more mysterious and frightening than she
had ever imagined.

"It's going to be all right now, Mother." Suntop
stood and looked around them, his blue-green eyes sparkling brightly in the moonlight. "This is the place Savah
told me to look for. I know we'll find Father soon."

So she and Ember followed him, just as they had since
leaving Sorrow's End, and "soon" receded farther and farther from their reach as they wandered the alien forest.
Night grew heavy and deep, and at last Suntop admitted
that he had reached the limit of the guidance imparted to
him by Savah. They were lost.

They were also desperately tired. Leetah sank wearily
against the base of a huge, hollow tree, and drew her cubs
into her lap as if she could protect them. Now, in passing

these memories on to Skywise and Cutter, she felt the moment when the children fell asleep without her—their dropping out of the mutual contact left her feeling vulnerable, and horribly alone, just as she had when the events first transpired. When Choplicker finally wandered away to chase some lovely, winged flutter, Leetah remembered Cutter's descriptions of butterflies, and smiled. She drifted off to join her cubs in sleep, dreaming dreams of butterfly song and dance as the string of painful images finally unwound to a close.

CHAPTER TWENTY-TWO

L EETAH OPENED HER eyes and felt a dizzying sense of disorientation to find herself in the same darkened grove, but in a different lighting, and at a different perspective. Cutter, his hands still warm against her arms, shook his head in confusion. "But *why* did you come here?" he asked. "Why did you risk so much to find me?"

"It's Suntop!" Ember exclaimed. As usual, she was pleased to know the answer, and bounced up to slap at Cutter's shoulder as she explained. "Savah put a message for you inside his head. Didn't she, Suntop?"

"What?" Cutter frowned at his silent son, then lifted the cub's chin with one finger when Suntop wouldn't look up at him. "I don't understand . . ."

The young cub met his father's gaze with solemn composure. "Savah 'went out' of her body to help you, Father. She found something bad—something you mustn't go near. I 'went out' to see her, and she told me to warn you. Only . . ." Very real, cubling tears filled his eyes, and he lowered his face away from Cutter's hand. ". . . We came all this way, and now . . . I-I don't know how to do what she told me." His voice was the saddest of whispers. ". . . I don't know *how* . . . !"

A tenderness such as Leetah had learned to love about wolves and their riders moved through Cutter's eyes. Standing, he took Suntop by the hand and urged him to his feet. "You are my son," he said with certainty. "I trust you." Then he locked huge, nighttime eyes with Leetah, and said softly, "Let us be alone for a while."

She nodded. Cutter slipped into the darkness so silently that he and Suntop seemed almost to have misted away, like sunlight on the morning fog.

"Well . . ." She made herself turn away from wherever they had gone. After all the days of travel and trusting and waiting, she could certainly wait a short time more—or so she told herself. Letting Ember prance off to roll with Choplicker in the grass, Leetah thrust an imperious hand toward Skywise and ignored his questioning tilt of an eyebrow. "As long as they're gone, we can at least do something constructive. Let me see your arm."

"Gladly."

She helped him slip out of the soiled, threadbare sling. His arm, although adequately splinted, still throbbed with pain when she touched it. Leetah could feel the clenching of tired muscles under her hand, the fevered swelling of tissues all filled up with blood. She let her eyes drift half-closed, relaxing, and reached out beyond the physical touch of her body.

Smoothing away the knotted muscles was easy; coaxing a path for clean blood hardly took a thought. It felt good to have a purpose again, to be of some use to someone on this journey, and not just an extra piece of baggage who slowed up the likes of quick Scouter, and irritated the likes of solemn Strongbow. She stitched the bone together as effortlessly as, she imagined, clouds blowing apart and reforming. Skywise's relief and appreciation flowed across her senses like cool water.

Happy and at peace, she sat back and nodded at his arm. "How's that?"

He flexed his fingers gingerly, then quickly tugged loose the straps binding his splint together and rotated the arm through its full length, shoulder to wrist. "It feels great! Good as new!" He winked at Ember, clapping his hands. "Watch this!"

Ember shrieked with delight when the Wolfrider leapt over the top of her and jumped for a tree branch above her head. Before she had even scrabbled to Leetah's side to watch him, Skywise swung himself in a graceful arc up and over the branch, then followed through again in the same smooth circle. "Just like a long tailed tree-wee!"

Ember bounced like a jumping bean, eyes shining. "That looks like *fun*! I *like* the woods!" she declared to Leetah, and ran to stand under Skywise with her hands straining upward toward his feet. "Teach me to be a tree-wee, Skywise! I want to do it, too!"

"You will, Ember." Cutter's voice, although quiet, combined with Suntop's somber eyes to remind Leetah of the seriousness of the problems still before them. "There's much for you to learn here."

The little she-cub bolted across the clearing, Choplicker yapping at her heels, and flung herself into Cutter's arms. "What did Suntop tell you?"

"It . . . can't be explained in words." Cutter returned her gently to the ground beside her brother, but kept his eyes on Leetah and Skywise as he spoke. "Savah was right. There is a danger—and it has to do with the Blue Mountain," he said pointedly to Skywise. "But the pictures and feelings in her warnings are not very clear. Suntop and I have to try again later to make sense of it all." He rested a hand on his son's bowed head without appearing to think about it. "Right now, we've got to find out what happened to the Wolfriders. The quest means nothing if they've come to harm."

A whistle like the shrill of the highest silver flute pierced the silence. "Petalwing remembers!" a bell-tiny voice declared. "Petalwing remembers!" Then something thumped firmly but softly against the back of Leetah's head and proceeded to bury itself in the falls of her hair.

Startled, she reached back to feel the flutter of fragile wings against her palm. "Is it a butterfly?"

"Softpretty Highthings!" Something hard and smooth, like a polished stick, rubbed against the sweep of her thumb. "Petalwing go with you!"

Cutter scowled at whatever it was, lower lip out-thrust. "Think so?"

"It *speaks*?" When Cutter's only response was to grab her shoulders and spin her until her back faced him, Leetah raised her eyebrows at Skywise. The stargazer only shrugged, looking more than just slightly annoyed.

"Nooooooo!"

Leetah winced at both the high-pitched scream and the four stubborn handfuls of hair the creature held onto when Cutter tried to pull it free.

"No no no no no! Petalwing want to staaaaay!"

"Let go, bug!" Leetah felt Cutter shake the little thing warningly. "You're not welcome!"

"Ooo!" Ember tried to push past Leetah, then jumped up and down when her mother held her clear of whatever her father was doing. "What *is* it? Can *I* see?"

"Later, darling," Leetah whispered. She rather hoped to get a glimpse of whatever it was herself.

Abruptly, the hold on her hair vanished, but the thing's pitiful squealing did not. Leetah turned, still gripping Ember with both hands, and gasped to see what Cutter held at arm's length between two fingers. Its wings, pinned together by the young chieftain's merciless grip, were wide and delicate—they looked like they would blow apart in the first stiff breeze. Color blended throughout them from the palest yellow to the most vivid red, and Leetah was reminded of a stormy sunset against the sandstone cliffs of home as the creature flailed its stick-thin body and scolded Cutter in a voice high enough to scratch glass.

"What makes you think we'd want you around us, pest?" Cutter asked it. Leetah assumed her lifemate and this ethereal creature had met before. "You and your winged friends trapped my family in your webs! And you'd do it again if you had the chance."

"No! No!"

"There!" Cutter flung it away from him with a flick of his wrist. "*That's* where you belong!"

Its little scream sounded more angry than frightened, and Leetah heard it crash into the bushes with a muffled "Bad Highthing!"

Skywise laughed. "So much for the evil spirits of the Forbidden Grove."

Cutter only snorted and gathered Leetah's hand into his own. "When we come out of this wood, can you guide us to the place where you were attacked?"

"I think so. I will try." She took Suntop's hand in turn, and followed along beside Cutter as he led them away from the thicket where he'd found them, back into the huge, scary inner workings of the forest itself. "It is sadly ironic, beloved," she sighed, leaning her head against his shoulder. "The Wolfriders came along to protect the twins and me during our search for you. Now our family is reunited, but . . ." The thought of what might have befallen them made her shiver. "Nightfall! Redlance! Pike! And all the others! Where are they?"

"We'll find them." He rubbed her hand against his cheek. "We'll track them until we find them."

He made it sound so simple, so sure, even though Leetah knew he must be as frightened for their safety as she was. They walked in a silence almost as smothering as not knowing the tribe's fate, and Leetah felt Suntop begin to tremble against her, too brave to say anything, too young not to be afraid. When Choplicker galloped between their feet in pursuit of a dizzy moth, Cutter released Leetah's hand to jump after the cub and sweep him up into the air.

"So!" He made the exclamation light, his examination of the cub suspended above him manfully critical. "This is your wolf-friend, eh, Ember?"

She nodded and ran up to walk beside her father. "His name's Choplicker!"

"Hello there, Choplicker." Cutter turned the cub left and right, then rotated to walk backward so he could display it for Skywise behind him. "Look at the size of his paws! He's going to be huge! Bigger even than Nightrunner was . . ." Leetah was startled by the words, startled even more by her lifemate's sudden sobering as he bent to hand the young cub back to Ember. "I mean is."

Ember took Choplicker in her arms, but frowned at

her father's pensive expression. "Where is Nightrunner, Father?"

"He's with Starjumper, Ember. They . . . went away for a while." He tried to sound casual and untroubled, but Leetah heard the wistful distance in his tone. "Nightrunner's an old wolf, you know. All this travel was hard for him."

Ember nodded seriously. "We'll see Nightrunner and Starjumper again, won't we?"

"Maybe." Leetah could tell he didn't believe it even as he said it. "But anything can happen in the woods. You have to be ready for it." It was perhaps the kindest way of preparing the child, and Leetah said nothing to interfere.

"I'm ready now!" Ember declared. She darted for her father, and he neatly avoided her grab by leaping for a tree branch and pulling his legs up above the ground. As though the change only made the game better, Ember shrieked with delight and jumped up to wrap herself around his feet. Even Cutter laughed, swinging there, and within a moment Skywise had joined him and they were passing Ember back and forth between one limb and the next.

Smiling, Leetah folded her hands atop Suntop's head and watched her daughter and her lifemate play. Suntop interlaced his own hands on top of hers, and Leetah felt a little sting of uncertainty as the boy-cub leaned back against her with a contented sigh. He could watch his sister, Leetah realized, but he felt no interest in joining her in such rough and wild play. Ember was a Wolfrider, through and through, suited to Cutter's world of trees and humans and plant life almost from the moment she was conceived. But what of Leetah and

Suntop? Could they ever feel so at home in Cutter's world? The healer was almost afraid to find out—mostly because she was afraid the answer was no.

As though her unease had reached him across the soul-deep bond between them, Cutter brushed cool eyes across Leetah's, then jostled Ember where she hung from his feet. "Get down now, cub," he told her gently. She obeyed without question, and he dropped lightly beside her to paddle his hands on her bottom with the same rough fondness the wolves used on their own cubs. "Think you and your brother can find some food with Skywise while I talk with your mother?"

"Sure!"

Cutter flashed a grin and a wink at Skywise. "Good."

The stargazer winked back and bounded to his feet. "Come on, cubs! I know just the place to look." He lifted Suntop clear of Leetah's skirts, balancing him comfortably against one hip as Ember clambered over to join them. "Have you ever cut open one of these cocoons?" he asked as they walked off out of the clearing.

Cutter slipped up to wrap Leetah in his arms. She clenched her hands in the fur of his vest, breathing in his wild scent. "I'm sorry about all you've been through," he whispered warmly against her ear. "But I'm glad you're here."

I'm glad, too, she thought, afraid to tell him *I never should have let you go!* Instead, she turned to fit herself beneath his shoulder and linked her fingers with his. "You have to tell me everything. What is this Blue Mountain you and Skywise speak of? Where have you been since leaving the cubs and me?"

As naturally as a bird flies to its roost, he began

walking between the trees. Leetah followed because she loved the feel of his step at her side, and because she never wanted to let him out of her sight again.

He talked of trolls, and fires, and moons and moons of walking through places so frightening and strange that Leetah almost couldn't listen. The strong calmness of his voice shamed her. *What is past, is past,* it seemed to tell her. *You claim to live with this wolf, but you never learn from him. Live in the present, and stop fearing a future you cannot see.* She tightened her grip on his waist and tried to imagine a life within the eternal nowness of a wolf's mind.

Water giggled and pattered from somewhere a short distance ahead of them. Cutter pricked his ears toward the sound, then tugged at her in silence as he crept in that direction. Parting the webby brush, he led her onto a soft carpet of green that smelled of crushed plants and moist wood. A small stream glittered past at the foot of the wide bank, and a thousand million dancing lights kissed the night around it like weightless clouds.

Leetah watched the cool gold sparks weave slow patterns on the night air. "Tam . . . ?" The beauty of their movements stole her voice away. "Have the stars come down from the sky to dance above the water?"

"Those are fireflies," he told her. The normal softness of his Wolfrider tone fit this world just like everything else about him. "Skywise likes to call them 'little star cousins.' This is their dance of joining."

"I . . ." She blinked as a firefly bloomed into silent beauty right in front of her. "I have never seen *anything* so . . ." No word she knew could even touch on this reality.

"You see, Leetah?" He lifted a hand beneath the

smear of light, and for one magic instant, the firefly glowed against his palm before its wings became a quiet blur and floated it away. "The wood isn't the deadly place your tribe's legends have made it out to be. But you have to move and breath and *think* with the forest in order to live in it. You have to become a Wolfrider."

"How? I'm a Sun Villager." When she reached tentatively for one of the lights herself, it vanished before it even touched against her skin. "How can I change?"

"Well, first . . ." Cutter stepped around in front of her and slid his hands down her arms to her wrists. "You'll have to get rid of all this jingling jewelry." He held his face very close to hers as he gently slipped her bracclets from her hands. "A wolfrider's steps are always silent . . . secret . . ."

". . . Yes . . ." She shivered at the brush of his lips against her fingers. "But if my jewelry must go because it is too noisy, then it seems to me, beloved, that this coat of mine, which rustles so loudly, must go, too . . ." She freed one hand from his to unlimber the belt at her waist, then let the coat fall from her shoulders without even stepping away from him. The night was chill, but she knew his hands could warm her, and she had longed for them to do so since the night they left Sorrow's End.

**Tam . . . I have missed you . . . **

And they moved with the starlight and the forest in a joining dance of their own.

CHAPTER TWENTY-THREE

CUTTER DRIFTED AWAKE to the soft touch of female skin close beside him, the warm, desert scent of auburn hair beneath his nose. He opened his eyes, hardly daring to hope, and felt a sharp throb of joy to see the slim brown body curled up on the moss beside him. It hadn't been a dream, then. After all these moons of loneliness and fear, Leetah was with him, Leetah and their cubs. He raised up on one elbow to move gently on top of her—

—and fell in a twisted knot when it turned out his feet had been webbed to the ground.

"*Petalwing!!*"

Leetah bolted awake with a gasp, and the cloud of chittering web-spinners around them scattered into the woods. Cutter fumbled over onto his stomach and groped for New Moon among his discarded clothes while Leetah, laughing, pulled her coat out from under them and shook it free of moss and leaves.

"What *are* these tiny, talking creatures?" she asked, carefully pulling her own feet free while Cutter slashed at the webbing with his sword. He wished a particular one of those talking creatures was within sword range right now. "They seem to spin their webs for no reason."

As if in answer to his wish, Petalwing landed with

an exuberant rustle in Leetah's hair. "Petalwing got reason!" it shrilled, peeking beneath an auburn curl. "Wrapstuff keep softpretty Highthings safe and sound! Petalwing go with! Take *gooood* care of Highthings!"

Cutter snorted. The thought alone made his stomach burn with irritation. "That's some joke! What are you good for, anyway?" Free of the sticky webbing, he snatched up his scattered clothing and Leetah's piled jewelry. "All you do is spit goo on everything! Look what you've done to this wood! It isn't even fit to live in!"

"Is fine!" The sprite jounced with a squeak in Leetah's hair as the healer hurried to keep up with her lifemate. "Petalwing say so!"

"Petalwing say so!" Cutter mimicked. "You think anything that falls asleep here is fair game for y—" Then he stopped, his eye caught on something huge and white and glossy peeking out of the vine-covered clearing ahead of them. He felt the tickle of Petalwing's passage as the sprite fluttered past him and into the clearing.

"See? See?"

Handing his clothes to Leetah, he followed Petalwing with New Moon still balanced in one hand. The little bug danced and capered all over the silent construction, petting it and smiling in admiration of its own handiwork.

"This biggest wrapstuff we ever do!" Petalwing declared proudly. "Bigthings been stillquiet here long time! Is pretty? Is pretty?"

Cutter wasn't sure how to answer.

"It's enormous!" Leetah breathed from behind him. "What could it be?"

"Considering how I found you and our cubs, I have

a guess." He motioned behind him for Leetah to stay among the bushes. "Wait here."

If I have to cut open one more of these things, Cutter thought with a sigh, *I'll never get New Moon clean again.* He climbed carefully up the rounded hump, and fitted the sword's point neatly into the first layer of thread. Above him, Petalwing squealed in indignation and darted down in front of him as he drew a long slit down the length of the cocoon.

"Bad Highthing! No cut wrapstuff!" It sprayed a glittering shower of webbing over the new cut, and Cutter swatted it with the flat of his blade.

"Quit sealing up every cut I make! I know what I'm doing."

They had only one more altercation after that, then Cutter pinned Petalwing beneath one hand and finished his hasty snipping. Only when he'd exposed the contents in a dozen different places and the forms inside the tattered cocoon began to move did he release Petalwing and dive back for the brush cover where he'd left Leetah.

Clapping a hand over her mouth to forestall the questions he saw forming in her green eyes, he pulled her to her knees along with him and pointed back toward the grove. "Now be a Wolfrider," he whispered. "Watch and listen and *be silent*!"

Crawling free of the last remnants of the torn cocoon, the two dark-skinned creatures within yawned and sat up. "Malak?" The female's voice was deeper than Cutter expected, firm and forthright. "We have slept but a little, I think. It is not yet dawn."

Abruptly, Leetah's sending reached him in a flash of horrified scarlet. **Humans?**

Cutter nodded, but didn't look away from the lovers as they stood and stretched in the cool moonslight. They were not without grace, these tall, healthy creatures, and they moved around each other with such tenderness and care. For just an instant, he imagined how Olbar must love his daughter, and how beautiful she must have looked in his eyes.

"I . . ." Leetah drew very close to him, her words almost unhearable in the night. "I always believed that humans were monsters!"

"So did I."

"But they are made much like we."

He smiled at Leetah, touched by the quickness of her understanding. "You begin to see as I do," he whispered, gripping her hand. "The old beliefs are not always true."

"Bigthings remember Petalwing?"

The tall human girl twisted left and right, trying to track Petalwing's looping flight about their heads. "Oh!" She raised a gentle hand, and Petalwing grabbed gleefully onto her large fingers. "It is one of the good spirits! Thank you again for saving us from my father."

"Yes," the man said, smiling. "We thank you!"

Whatever Petalwing said in response was lost beneath a thin chorus of wolfen howling. Cutter's heart soared up into his throat, and Leetah grabbed at his arm with a gasp of joy. "Oh, Tam!"

"I know! I hear them!" He backed away from the humans in the clearing, eager to reunite the pieces of his scattered tribe. "Let's go find them!"

The humans had already fled, crashing into the nighttime trees. Still gripping Leetah's hand, Cutter loped in the direction of Skywise's and Ember's answering calls, adding his own voice to the growing song. He didn't even realize where the humans had gone until he heard Skywise shout ahead of him, "Ember! Suntop! Stay back!"

Then the hiss of a familiar, knife-sharp voice fitting itself around the hard edge of human words: "Go away, tall ones! Our calls were not meant for you!"

The humans suddenly appeared, tall and frightened, between the trees ahead of him. Cutter skidded to a stop before he and Leetah could stumble into the clearing. Skywise crouched, pale and grim, on the other side of the human couple, with his sword drawn. Cutter didn't see his cubs, but he smelled them nearby, and could just make out the mingled scent of Redlance and Nightfall on the damp air. A bow, clearly of Redlance's shaping, barely showed in the bushes to Cutter's right, and two wolves—Firecoat and Woodshaver—snarled from either side. Faced with the wolves, the bow, and Skywise, Olbar's daughter did what Cutter himself would have done in the same situation—she grabbed her lover's hand and ran back the way they'd come, nearly running Cutter and Leetah down in their haste.

Wrapping his arms around his lifemate, Cutter rolled aside to let them past. "Don't shoot!" he shouted when he saw Nightfall's bow sweep to track the retreating figures. "Nightfall, let them go!"

Ever faithful, Nightfall relaxed her pull on the bowstring and withdrew into the bushes. Cutter lay on his back, Leetah clasped on top of him, and watched the humans disappear into the darkness. *Well, Olbar, we're even.* He wondered if the girl and her lover would head back to their home. He almost hoped they would—they had an anxious village waiting for them.

My chief-friend?

He sat up at the touch of Nightfall's mind, and lifted Leetah to her feet. **We're here.** Skywise had already called the cubs forth from their hiding place, and Choplicker frolicked forward to leap at Woodshaver's tail, yapping excitedly. As Cutter and Leetah joined them, Nightfall crawled free from her concealing bushes with Redlance close behind.

"Cutter! We've found you!" She ran to him, flushed with relief and pleasure. "My eyes see with joy!"

Cutter clasped her hand and pulled her into a fierce hug. "My hand touches with joy!" He grabbed Redlance as well and held the older elf tight to him. "If I've ever been happier to see you two, I can't remember when!"

"Oh, Leetah!" Nightfall threw her arms around the healer's neck. "When your mount ran away with you, I feared for your life! Thank the High Ones you're sa—" Cutter knew what she had seen the moment her voice went dead and her eyes flew wide with surprise. "Uh . . . What's this in your hair?"

I'm going to kill that thing, Cutter promised himself. He only had to figure out how.

The multicolored web-spinner rocked back and forth deliriously, giggling in shrill bliss. "Petalwing *sooooo* happy! Got *many* Highthings take care of now!"

Cutter flicked at the useless thing in frustration. "Never mind about that," he grumbled as Nightfall released Leetah and sat back on her heels. "What about the Wolfriders? And the giant birds? What happened?"

Redlance settled to the ground beside his mate and shook his head sadly. "I wish the tale were easier to tell, Cutter. But I'm afraid Nightfall and I were the only ones to escape the great birds' attack." He plucked a sleeping dandelion and coaxed it to blossom and seed while in his fingers.

"There was no way to fight them," he said at last. "It happened too fast! Out in the open, we were as helpless as fish trapped in shallow water. One by one they plucked us up from the ground like worms off a log. The birds went after Strongbow first. When Moonshade saw him carried into the sky, she just stood there and let herself be taken, too.

"The rest of us took what cover we could. Most of us dove into the river, just to get out of sight. The water wasn't deep, but we hoped it was deep enough that the birds couldn't dive down and spear us with their claws. Nightfall and I stayed under and hugged the riverbed until we almost drowned. We were safe, but others weren't so lucky. We saw Pike scooped out of the water not a wolf's length away from us.

"Leetah's zwoot nearly trampled us when we came up for air. Its hooves knocked us back beneath the water. We recovered and dragged ourselves to the riverbank, but by then the monsters were already flying away with their catch. Seven birds, seven out of ten Wolfriders captured, we don't know which ones. We couldn't find whoever was missing."

He looked up, and tears clouded his green eyes despite the calmness of his tone. "It took us a while to decide what to do. All we had left were the wolves, and the knowledge that Leetah had escaped with Suntop and Ember. We decided to track them, because we knew that Suntop could lead us to you. It was just luck that you were near enough to hear us when we howled for you."

Nightfall wound her hand with her mate's, and Cutter took hold of their combined grip, wanting to soothe them, but not knowing what he could do. "Scouter said he thought he glimpsed riders on the birds' backs," Nightfall said, wiping at her eyes. "That may be so. I only know that our tribefolk are gone."

"Gone . . ." The word burned through Cutter like the hottest desert sun. "To the lair of the Bird Spirits. We wanted to go to Blue Mountain," he told Skywise bitterly. "Now we *have* to go."

"*No!*" Breaking away from Skywise, Suntop ran to press small hands against his father's shoulders. "Didn't you believe me?" he wailed. "Don't you even believe Savah? I tried to give you her warning!" The honesty of the young cub's desperation ate at Cutter's soul. "*Please,* Father! You mustn't go near that mountain!"

Cutter pulled Suntop against him and rocked him with the greatest care. He hated everything that stood before them now, and wished somehow he could shield the child from it. "You did well, my cub. Savah can be proud of you, as I am. But a Wolfrider *faces* danger—he doesn't run away. Especially when his tribe needs help." Cutter lifted his head to match earnest gazes with his enigmatic little son. "That's all that matters, Suntop— the tribe. And we're going to find out what happened to them if it's the last thing I do."

CHAPTER TWENTY-FOUR

The FIRST BLUSH OF morning sunlight crept into the grove from behind Cutter, smudging away the last nighttime shadows and stroking the webs and treetops around him with liquid gold. Cutter felt the trunk at his back warm slowly as its leaves reached fingerlike for the breeze, and tasted the dance and curl of waking smells that drifted upward from the forest floor far below. Rotten leaves and wet spider's silk predominated the tapestry of aroma.

Suntop and Ember had twirled into a puppy-huddle of exhaustion only a short while ago, Chop-licker sprawled across Ember's tummy, with his tail under Suntop's chin and all four paws in the air. Apparently, the sleep of Petalwing's timeless cocoons was not a restful slumber. By the time Redlance had slung together a hammock of moss and vines for the cub-lings, Leetah was curled beneath Cutter's shoulder with arms and legs wrapped protectively around him as though she were afraid he'd drift away again while she slept. Without waking her, Cutter spirited her up to the limb he'd picked out for their bed place and Sky-wise and Nightfall each gathered up a twin to join Redlance in the treetop. It probably wouldn't take three of them to make sure the cubs didn't tumble out on their first time sleeping in a tree, but Cutter appreciated his tribefolk's vigilance. He felt warm for their caring, and free of loneliness for the first time in far too long.

Now Leetah groaned a little noise of discomfort and burrowed her face against his neck as the sun's rays finally crept across her cheek to bat at her eyes. Cutter smiled and turned his chin to shadow her, bringing his hand up to cover her fluttering lashes. Her skin felt warm and soft beneath his fingers.

Tam? Leetah's unskilled sending brushed across his thoughts like a whisper. **Sleep, beloved.** He felt her belief that he would need his strength in the days to come, but she seemed unable to form the words without using her breath for the sounds.

I will, he promised. The slow, flower-bright pulse of many movements drew his attention, and Cutter watched in silence as Petalwing's cousins settled sleepily on the sunward face of countless leaves all throughout the grove. Pastel wings spread and folded, spread and folded in the silent breathing of animate flowers too numerous and beautiful to believe. **I'm just thinking about the tribe, and how I wish they knew we were coming for them.**

Leetah scooted to sit more upright beside him. "They know." Her eyes still looked shadowed and bleary, but they glowed with such trust that Cutter's heart throbbed when she reached up to stroke his hair. "They know that nothing short of death could keep you from them, and that belief will keep them strong until you get there. You mustn't doubt that—not even for a moment."

**I don't doubt it. I only fear . . . **

The distance, and the darkness, and the stark forgetfulness of the ancient shadows. A chill, stuttering menace had flirted with Savah like the brushing of a moth's wings, only to alight in Suntop's uncertain mind and burrow into hiding there so surely that even Cutter's forthright probing hadn't been able to slice it away. He'd only been able to smother a fraction of his son's anxiety with wolfen bravado and adult half-lies. What fears still remained lived now in Cutter's mind as well, licked and tended by a patina of lifeless nighteyes, broken feathers, and the cool, bloodless stare of pale maidens with no heartbeats, no thoughts, and no names. Even dipping into the black waters of those senseless images stabbed him with a panic that he knew could only grow worse with increased knowledge. He shook his head against the terrible power of Savah's message, and switched to speaking so that Leetah wouldn't share in the horror of this morass.

"I'm afraid the Wolfriders have already been taken beyond where I can save them. I'm afraid that all the things I've seen, and learned, and been told of since leaving you and the cubs at Sorrow's End haven't been enough to prepare me for the Blue Mountain and what waits for us inside." He turned to tangle his hands in her hair, his fingers too cold and shaking to feel the silken curls of its fall.

She touched his mind fleetingly, a glimpse-and-gone like that of the fireflies above the water as she dipped unconsciously beyond her thinking and into his own. It was enough, though, to let Cutter taste her warm devotion, and the raw edge of her bravery. "You Wolfriders are unlike anything else in this world," she whispered, her lips very close to his ear. "You are parts of the same creature, so tied to your wolves and each other that nothing can tear you apart." She sat back and reached out to hook his chin with her fingers. Love mingled with the forest shadows in her eyes. "You once survived the loss of half your tribe, and all of you survived the loss of your home." She nodded toward the elf-made hammock below them. "You even gained two beautiful cubs."

"And that isn't a thing to be taken lightly." Cutter smiled and tipped his forehead against hers. "I love you too much, you know. All of you."

"Then have faith in us," she breathed, catching his topknot in one hand. "Have faith in yourself. Don't let early morning fears set your directions for you."

Early morning fears. He'd almost forgotten how tired all the travel and loneliness had made him—how much the creeping brightness of dawn could erode his convictions and sorrow his heart. He'd forgotten how much of his bravery was now grounded in this dark desert healer.

Wrapping Leetah into his arms, he sat back against the warm bark and let her snuggle herself full-length against him. "We should sleep now," he said. "The sun will make things hot here soon enough." She nodded against his chest with a contented sigh.

Cutter touched her hair with his lips and watched the iron-gray outline of the Blue Mountain harden beyond the tops of the distant trees. Mist clung to its summit, tattered like the grove's ancient webbing, and the coppery reflections of sunlight on stone picked out minimalist details down the length of its naked flanks. Three days' walk, Cutter estimated as the glare of the day finally forced his eyes closed. A sharp mind-image of the distant mountain lingered on the inside of his lids. Three days, and then they would be with the Wolfriders again. Three days, and they would know if the "spirits" living inside the Blue Mountain represented an end to their long quest, or the beginning of a new one.

I'm coming, he sent, as far and free as his wolf-born mind could reach. **In three days, no more, we'll all be with you.**

Hopeful whispers stirred at the edges of his thinking, but sleep washed over them with gentle force before Cutter could decide if they were really only his imagination.